W9-CQV-626

PAC HEIGHTS

SURVIVING THE DOT.COM BUST
WITH A DOWNSTAIRS CAREER

A NOVEL

TONY PEREZ-GIESE

PAC HEIGHTS

TONY PEREZ-GIESE was born in Texas. He graduated from the University of California at San Diego and currently resides in San Francisco. This is his first novel.

PAC HEIGHTS

TONY PEREZ-GIESE

ARCHWAY
PUBLISHING

Archway Publishing books may be ordered through booksellers or by contacting:

Archway Publishing
1663 Liberty Drive
Bloomington, IN 47403
www.archwaypublishing.com
1-(888)-242-5904

ISBN: 978-1-4808-0117-2 (sc)
ISBN: 978-1-4808-0118-9 (e)
Library of Congress Control Number: 2013910096

Printed in the United States of America

Archway Publishing rev. date: 6/13/2013

Author's Note

The characters and events depicted in this book are fictional. Any resemblance to persons living or dead is purely coincidental.

ONE: THE PERFECT FIT

1999 WAS THE WRONG YEAR to be out of work in San Francisco. The economy was blasting into orbit on the twin rockets of Internet technology and optimism; every idiot who could turn on a computer and print a business plan was becoming a millionaire. If these tech-astronauts hadn't already cashed out and parked the private jet in the hangar, they had millions worth of stock options that made them feel just as secure and smug. I went to booze-soaked website launch parties and listened to college drop-outs brag about how much money they had *lost* that day as they chased pharmaceutical grade ecstasy with Grey Goose vodka. The city had become similar to Washington, D.C. in that you couldn't talk to anyone for more than five seconds before they asked what you did for a living; more specifically, they wanted to know if a business plan handed to you had any chance of finding its way to venture capital. When I told people I was unemployed, you could see the lights go out. Standing alone at the bar with a bottle of Budweiser, I felt like the prospector digging for emeralds during the gold rush.

While I had fled to San Francisco to escape the fall-out from a particularly nasty break-up in Denver, my little brother Stevie and our roommate Chase had come for their share of the tech-action. San Francisco had been built by guys like them: 49'ers with picks and pans, hippies in the Haight during the 60's, wannabe tech millionaires in the late 90's. They showed up with the idea that success was as much a matter of osmosis as hard work.

The three of us couldn't even find a place to live.

After two months of fruitless searching for a rental amid the swarms of other new hopefuls, we came to the conclusion that the only way we were going to secure an apartment was if we made up jobs for ourselves—occupations that would set us apart from all the other prospective tenants willing to pay thousands of bucks a month for the privilege of residing in the tech boomtown. We decided that we'd all be employees of my brother's nascent company, Sharkattack.com. Stevie was president, I was VP and Chase was the CFO. Stevie, being the only guy with any actual interest in Sharkattack.com, had thin business cards printed up at Kinko's. We started wearing our interview suits to open houses we found on Craigslist, our ties loosened as if we'd just come from long negotiating sessions instead of four-dollar buffet-line turkey sandwiches. Chase would call Stevie's mobile on the sly, and when it began to ring my brother would hold up one finger and pretend to take a business call. I didn't have a cell, so I couldn't play along. The landlords saw right through our charade. I mean, who wore a *suit* to work anymore?

We finally found a place in the Richmond. The Richmond District was the last resort for renters. Closer to the Pacific Ocean than to the Transamerica Pyramid building, this forty-by-forty block of neighborhood on the foggy side of Golden Gate Park was inhabited mostly by non-English speaking Russians and Chinese. Every building was a drab-colored three-story affair with sun-faded newspapers and take-out fliers littering the stoops. The area was strictly residential, and nobody was having launch parties out that far. But after several weeks of searching and wearing out our welcomes on friends' couches, a landlord finally called to say he'd rent to us. Even after he cashed our $5,000 deposit check, we still thought it was a joke. In our anxiousness to have an apartment, we hardly noticed that, despite the monthly rent of $3,000, to get to the third bedroom, we had to walk through all the others. It was a "railroad flat", which nearly all the apartments out there were, with the kitchen, bathroom, and living areas all laid out in a straight line. On our first night as official S.F. residents we moved the backseat of Stevie's SUV into the living room to serve as our temporary couch, and divvied up the rooms. Stevie needed the big one because he was going to be working his start-up from home and required space for his command center. Chase and I Rock-Paper-Scissor'd for the room with a closet, and I lost. But I graciously accepted defeat, thinking my brother was positioned to strike-it dot.com rich, and we'd soon be cooling our heels in a glassy downtown condo. I moved into the tiny cubicle in the back. At twenty-six years old, I didn't even have a door to my bedroom.

———

Stevie took the first week after we moved in to set up his office. He had a Bezos desk (named after Amazon.com's Jeff Bezos, whose first office was, according to start-up legend, an old door resting on two sawhorses in his garage) laden with his computer, Lee Iacocca's autobiography, a telephone, and maps of the country thumb tacked to the wall. Thusly organized, he sat down and waited for the money to roll in. As far as I could tell, his days consisted of talking on the phone with his girlfriend, re-writing his business plan, and playing Atomic Cannon on his computer. According to Stevie's numbers, Sharkattack. com had something like a $430 million market cap. His idea was to sell interactive advertising space on the side of big rig trucks. While cruising on the interstate, a driver would spot the Sharkattack.com advert on the side of an 18-wheeler, call the 800-number listed, answer a quiz question, and somehow Stevie would get paid. I never really did understand how it was all supposed to work, or even why he had to have ".com" on the end of the company name. Apparently all the investors Stevie had pitched didn't get it either, and four months into the game Sharkattack.com hadn't earned a dime.

A couple weeks in town had infected me with the same get-rich-quick fever that had everyone else in the Bay Area running a temperature. I could see the dot.com era flashing past me like a stolen Porsche with hundred dollar bills floating out of the sunroof. Before arriving in S.F., I'd been under the impression that the whole thing was a giant nerd revolution, and that in order to get in you had to have a computer science degree and pants three inches too short in the legs. The reality was that the great bubble was taking all comers—frat boys, farmers, and phrenologists alike. Put ".com" at the end of anything and you were on the road to riches. I had never thought of myself as particularly greedy, but I knew that if I didn't make a jump for the loot while the money was still stupid, I might not get another easy chance to become a tycoon for a long time. I had complete faith in Stevie's company, but I felt we ought to spread the family talent around. Besides, I was starting to go stir-crazy in that apartment of ours. I figured that if I could just get in on the ground floor of any of the thousands of Internet enterprises springing up around town, I would be financially set for life.

So I called a temp agency.

I dressed in what I thought passed for business casual and caught the bus downtown with my brother's briefcase in hand. There was nothing in the attaché besides my three paragraph résumé and the *Cannonball Run* videotape I'd forgotten to return to Blockbuster before my appointment. I realized my outfit wasn't right the moment I got off the bus at Market Street. I was wearing tan slacks and a tweed sport jacket that might have passed muster in Denver, but in downtown San Fran it made me look like a door-to-door magazine salesman.

Guys my age in $2,000 Armani suits pushed through thick glass doors while chatting with lovely women in tight skirts. E-commerce millionaires in blue button-down shirts, chinos and black leather jackets made plans for lunch on their cell phones. Advertising hipsters in Fred Siegel jeans and artfully messy haircuts slipped into the backseats of sleek black Town Cars. Big Ideas seems to float in captions above their heads. I may as well have been squeezing an accordion with a dancing monkey.

The Perfect Fit's waiting room was decorated with fake plants, reproductions of classic paintings, and inspirational posters. Several bulletin boards displayed minimum-wage increase memos and company picnic snapshots. The chairs looked as though they'd been borrowed from a cheap shrink's waiting room. One other sorry unemployed person hunkered down in the far corner. This prospective temp was a woman about my age wearing a pantsuit almost as outré as my sport jacket. She balanced a clipboard on her lap while chewing the end of a pen. I stepped up to the reception desk. The last time

I'd felt like such a loser in a waiting room was back in college when I'd gone to Student Health thinking I had the clap. But this was worse, because at least copping to VD indicated you were getting laid. Another big problem with being unemployed in 1999 was that all the women who weren't Internet millionaires themselves had become accustomed to $300 champagne dinners at Le Colonial and riding in BMW M3s. Anything less and they weren't going to put out, so my offers of Applebee's and bus fare certainly weren't cutting it.

"Good morning!" the receptionist called out in a startlingly chipper voice. I guess you've got to be upbeat when faced with a bunch of depressed, out-of-work fucko-s like me coming through the door. Just like at Student Health, there was a bowl of lollipops on the front desk.

The receptionist handed me a sheaf of forms and advised me to take a seat. I brushed aside a partially-deflated bouquet of helium balloons, and picked a chair as far away from the other applicant as possible—desperation needs its space. By the time I'd completed the packet I had taken off my jacket and rolled up my sleeves. I handed the clipboard back to the receptionist and flipped through a *Red Herring* magazine with a cover story about an eighteen-year-old tech wizard. In the accompanying photo the punk was behind the wheel of his orange Ferrari, grinning like he'd just figured out how to jerk off. His contribution to humanity was an online method of (illegally) "sharing" episodes of *Air Wolf* and *Dr. Who*.

I was halfway through the article when a cherubic woman of about thirty-five stepped into the waiting room and mispronounced my name. This was Clarissa. She led me back to her office. Clarissa scanned my documents, occasionally marking something in the margin with a pencil bearing a Smurf eraser.

"What kind of work are you looking for?" she asked finally.

"I want to do something interesting," I explained.

"Interesting?"

"You know, like do you have any jobs chasing hookers out of yacht clubs or blowing up garbage cans? Maybe something that calls for riding a scooter around an office all day and getting a lot of stock options?" Clarissa cocked her head and stared at me for two seconds before she figured out I had made a funny and laughed. I was sweating and hoped like hell that my deodorant would last through the interview.

"I'll be straight with you," she said. "I've got plenty of temp jobs, but I don't think any of them qualify as 'interesting.'" She used her chubby fingers to make quote marks in the air.

"Perhaps I misstated my position," I said. "I want—need to have—a job. Seriously, I just need to get my foot in the door somewhere. I figure I can work my way up from there."

Clarissa said she understood, but the bottom line was that she didn't want to put me in an opening where I was going to get bored after one day and quit.

"I get new postings in every morning," she assured me. "I'm going to keep my eyes peeled for something—how shall we say?—*unusual*. Like I said, I could start you filing at a law firm tomorrow but you'd hate it. So trust me here. I'm sure I'll have something for you by EOW."

I raised my hand. "Eee-oh-double-u?"

Clarissa raised an eyebrow, "End of week. Trust me here, I'll find something for you. It may not involve hookers or yacht clubs or being a batboy for the Giants, but it won't be filing or data entry. I promise you that. So go home and enjoy the afternoon. Okay?"

I reached across the desk to shake Clarissa's hand.

"Honestly," she said, "I wish we had more open-minded candidates like you. It's so much more fun!"

I walked out of her cubicle and grabbed a lollipop off the receptionist's desk. I was no longer unemployed. I was a candidate.

———

Clarissa called the next afternoon. I got the message after returning to the house from Sam the Sandwich Man's, where I'd picked up hot pastramis for Stevie and myself. The sandwiches cost $2.50 apiece. Top Ramen with a can of cooked chicken was on the menu for dinner. Stevie had taken three bites out of his sandwich before he remembered to give me Clarissa's message. I put down my pastrami and dialed The Perfect Fit.

"Oh," Clarissa said, her voice heavy with regret, "I just gave it to somebody else."

"Gave what?" I asked.

"The job. I just got off the phone with the other candidate."

I asked for clarification. She told me that she had found a prime gig at a leather goods warehouse, no filing or data entry involved. Apparently in the ten minutes it had taken for me to hit the sandwich shop and come home, some other go-getter had snagged what I envisioned to be a cushy, teamster-type job. I glared at Stevie. If not for him I'd be getting ready to drive a forklift and get discounts on motorcycle jackets. Clarissa assured me she'd come up with something else, but I was feeling crushed about the leather gig. It wasn't a start-up and there was no mention of stock options, but it sounded pretty sweet for starters. I contemplated having Stevie hold all my calls for the rest of the afternoon so I could walk to the Blarney Stone and drink Irish Car Bombs until I passed out.

Clarissa called back when I was almost out the front door.

"Okay," she said, "this definitely counts as unique." The job required running a few errands for a wealthy matron, who was holed up in a mansion in Pacific Heights. There was a 10 a.m. reporting time with a 6 p.m. quitting time.

"And they'll provide lunch." I could tell she was reading the posting off a sheet on her desk. "Mrs. Phelan specified that she wanted someone intelligent that she could have a conversation with and that they be..." Clarissa trailed off. "Hmm..."

"Mrs. Felon?" I asked.

"Mrs. *Feel-an*," Clarissa said, getting back on track.

"Do I have to screw her?" I asked.

"What?"

"It sounds like a gigolo thing."

Clarissa laughed. "Thirteen bucks an hour and it'll be a one or two day assignment. By the time you're finished with that I'm sure I'll have something good for you. What do you think? Sounds great, right?"

I was in no position to argue.

Two: The Temp Gig

PACIFIC HEIGHTS IS SAN FRANCISCO'S premier neighborhood, a ridge of red brick mansions commanding an unobstructed view of Golden Gate Bridge and the bay. The lawns were perfectly groomed squares that looked as though they had been vacuumed instead of mowed. But as I walked the clean sidewalk looking for the address, I realized that the true value of this exclusive neighborhood was the abundance of parking spots. Only after a few months in San Francisco could I make that connection; every other neighborhood had you circling in three-block radiuses five or six times before you found a place for your car. If you scored a spot near your apartment, you came up with lots of reasons to leave it parked. Even the posted parking signs in the Pac Heights were snooty, boasting a three hour limit as opposed to the lowly two hours every other neighborhood in the city was granted.

I checked street numbers until I found myself standing in front of the house. Unlike its imposing neighbors, which were tall and columned, it was an elegant Cape Cod, complete with white-washed window shutters, and was covered with ivy. The house had an eight-foot wall in front, which separated the entrance and lawn from the street. It looked as if it really belonged along the beach in Malibu, not parked up high in the San Francisco fog. It certainly didn't appear grandiose enough to warrant a house manager, whose name I had on my scrap of paper. I reached to ring the doorbell when I saw a small brass plaque with the inscription *Please Take All Deliveries to Side Door*. I went ahead and punched the bell. A voice came over the intercom a couple of seconds later.

"Hello?"

"This is Tony." I paused before adding, "From the temp agency."

"Okay."

A buzzer sounded and the door clicked open. I walked through to a small courtyard and took a neatly manicured walkway up to the front door. It was wide open. Standing in the foyer with her back to me was a young woman in pink stretch pants, a short black leather jacket, and expensive-looking pink mules. Blonde hair fell to just below her shoulders, and a violet g-string peeked over the waist of her pants. The woman was talking to herself as two movers in white coveralls tried to keep their balance and grip on a walnut chest of drawers.

"We could put it right over there," the woman mused. "Pictures, a couple vases. Flowers. That's not a problem."

The movers were popping sweat as the woman tapped her toe on a dark Persian carpet and continued to scout potential locations for the heavy chest. Beyond the front door, I could see a wide, curving staircase led upstairs. Off to my right was an elegant dining room table set for ten. The antiqued living room to my left was filled with several chairs that didn't look as if they'd ever been sat in. Downtempo samba music wafted out of unseen speakers. One of the movers noticed me standing in the open doorway and the woman pirouetted. Her bright smile faded ten watts. She'd obviously been expecting someone else.

"I'm from the temp agency," I explained. "Are you…" I looked down at the piece of paper in my hand, "… Linda?"

"She's downstairs," the woman said. "Go through the kitchen."

I wiped my feet on the doormat. The movers shuffled to the side to let me pass. I walked down a short hallway and came upon half a dozen people standing around the kitchen's marble-topped cooking island, eating. Forks paused halfway to mouths at my sudden appearance.

"I'm looking for Linda," I said.

A forty-ish woman wearing a velvety tracksuit and a blue blazer asked if I was from the Perfect Fit.

I confirmed that I was.

"Right," she said. "Come with me." She picked up her plate, which was heaped with cucumber salad, and went through a doorway off the kitchen. I followed.

We descended a flight of stairs to a gleaming laundry room and pantry, which was about the same size as my entire apartment. We turned off the pantry and into a spacious office. The white shag carpet was so deep that I could feel it dragging on my shoes. Without further conversation, the woman, who I assumed must have been Linda, handed me a typed list that took up two pages. She retrieved an envelope from a heavy blonde wood desk drawer that slid out on silent castors. I looked inside the envelope. There were three hundred-dollar bills.

I gave her a questioning look.

"I need you to take care of this list by the end of the day," Linda said, glancing back at her plate. "You know the city pretty well?"

I lied and said that I did. She walked me back through the laundry room, down a corridor lined with cabinets which

ADVICE TO INTERNATIONAL PASSENGERS ON LIMITATION OF LIABILITY

Passengers embarking upon a journey involving an ultimate destination or a stop in a country other than the country of departure are advised that the provisions of a treaty known as the Warsaw Convention may be applicable to their entire journey, including the portion entirely within the countries of departure and destination. The Convention governs and, in most cases, limits the liability of carriers to passengers for death or personal injury not to exceed $75,000. Additional protection can usually be obtained by purchasing insurance from a private company. Such insurance is not affected by any limitation of the carrier's liability under the Warsaw Convention. For further information please consult your airline or insurance company representative.

For most international travel, including domestic portions of international journeys, the airline's liability for loss, delay, or damage to baggage is limited to approximately $9.07(USD) per pound / $20.00(USD) per kg for checked baggage, and $400(USD) per passenger for unchecked baggage, unless a higher value is declared and an extra charge is paid. Where the Montreal Convention applies, the airline's liability for the loss, delay, or damage to baggage is limited to 1,131 Special Drawing Rights per passenger.

NOTICE OF BAGGAGE LIABILITY LIMITATIONS

For travel wholly between points in the U.S., the airline's liability for loss, delay, or damage to baggage (except for disability devices) is limited to $3,400 per passenger, unless you purchase excess valuation coverage. Special rules and exclusions may apply to certain fragile, valuable, irreplaceable, or perishable articles. Excess valuation may be declared on certain types of valuable articles. Carriers assume no liability for fragile, valuable or perishable articles. Further information may be obtained from the carrier.

CARRIER RESERVES THE RIGHT TO REFUSE CARRIAGE TO ANY PERSON FOR ANY REASON, INCLUDING ACQUIRING A TICKET IN VIOLATION OF APPLICABLE LAW OR CARRIER'S TARIFFS, RULES OR REGULATIONS AND FOR UNRULY OR DISRUPTIVE BEHAVIOR.

matched the blonde desk, and out to a separate entrance. She opened the door for me. I paused for a moment to see if she was going to give me any further clue as to what was expected of me.

All she said was, "Hurry."

Three: Kitty Grass

Five minutes, three hundred bucks. Not bad, I thought as I stood at the top of the Phelan's driveway reviewing my orders. I considered taking the money back to my apartment and calling it a career. Suddenly a BMW 850 coupe pulled to the curb in front of me. The driver, an older guy with round frameless eyeglasses, scowled at me through the windshield. After a couple seconds, he blew his horn. Realizing that I was still standing in the driveway, I stepped aside onto the sidewalk. The old man shot me another sour look before he drove into the garage. I had just reached my Nissan down the block when another BMW—this one a green 750 sedan— came from behind me, and screeched to a halt in the middle of the street. The tinted window slid down and I saw it was the blonde woman with the peek-a-boo G-string from inside the house.

"Hey," she said, pushing her Prada sunglasses up onto her forehead. I could tell they were Prada because it said so on the side in big, block letters.

"Hey," I replied.

"What are you doing?" the woman asked. A Federal Express truck stopped behind her.

"I think I'm working," I said.

"Great!" she said. "Everything look okay?"

I checked the list Linda had given me. "Do you know what kitty grass is?"

The FedEx driver tapped his horn, but the woman didn't seem to notice. "It's for cats," she explained.

I nodded my head. "Okay. But what is it?"

"I think it makes them throw up." The blonde thought about it for a moment. "That's pretty gross."

The truck driver gave the woman a more assertive horn.

"Gotta run!" she said and sped off.

The only other information about kitty grass was an address in the Marina. I found a parking place three blocks away from the shop and ran into a Deli to buy a Snickers to get change for the meter. The store turned out to be a "Pet Boutique" and I discovered that kitty grass comes in 5-inch plastic pots, each of which sprouts bright green shoots that look like something you'd add to your protein shake. $4 apiece. I bought two with one of the C-notes, which caused the turtle-necked clerk to grimace as he stowed the little pots in a brown paper sack with cord handles.

The next item on my to-do list was pick up ground coffee, and again it specified a store. This shop ended up being in North Beach, which was only about three miles from the kitty grass spot, but took me half an hour to find as I was using a United States road atlas on which San Francisco only got a quarter of a page. I then headed for the Federal Building. My instructions said I was to retrieve two passports, and as I circled the block looking for parking, I wondered how I was supposed to waltz inside and grab these with no documentation.

The answer was I wasn't. After I'd waited forty-five minutes in a plastic chair next to a group of anxious Chinese, the agent behind the bulletproof glass told me I had to get a release signature from Mr. or Mrs. Phelan before he could give me the passports. I got back to my car just as the red "expired" flag flipped up on the meter. On the way back to the house I double-parking in front of a dry cleaner and rushed inside to grab several packages wrapped in blue paper and tied with string. I pulled away from the curb just as a meter maid started to approach my car, ticket book in hand. Once I'd managed to find yet another parking spot by the Phelan's, I walked around to the service entrance and somehow buzzed the intercom without dropping anything.

I peeked into the house manager's office and saw that Linda was talking on the phone. It didn't sound like business.

"The *nerve!* I mean, who do these people think they are? Just because I work for the Phelan's doesn't mean I know where they are every second of the day," she drew out the last word of every sentence like a high school cheerleader would. There was another plate of food on her desk, this time a variety of poached fish. I stood outside her office waiting for her to notice me.

"Sheets?" someone behind me asked.

I turned to see a stocky Asian woman wearing an apron and thick, tinted eyeglasses. Her hair was done up in a sort of afro and her flesh colored socks bunched above her red slip-on tennis shoes.

"What?" I asked.

She pointed at the blue dry cleaning packages. "Sheets?" she repeated in her thick accent.

"I guess so."

"You put here, please." She gestured to the washer and dryer. I carried the packages into the laundry room.

"What else?" she asked.

I handed over the other bags and she peered inside both approvingly.

"Good." She started up the stairs with the kitty grass and coffee, but stopped and turned back to me. She was standing on the third step so we were at the same eye level. "What your name?" she asked.

I told her.

"My name is Junko," she replied. "You errand person from temp agency?"

"I didn't know I was called an errand person."

"In a way, you run all the errands."

"Just for today," I clarified.

"Ah, yes. Errand person one, two days then gone."

"There've been a lot of them here?"

Junko continued up the stairs. "In a way, yes. Last one here three days, then get fired."

I walked back to the door of Linda's office. She was still gabbing on the phone. The other line buzzed and she put her friend on hold to pick it up, answering, "Phelan residence." She told the caller that Bailey was at the studio for the afternoon, took a message and then clicked back over, picking up the conversation right where she'd left off.

I looked around the outer office while Linda gabbed. There was a long desk against one wall with two PCs on it. The desk fit in the corner with a gentle curve and it was stacked with Sotheby's antique catalogues, unopened correspondence, and pictures of the young blonde woman in the green Beemer with a pair of babies. A stack of CD cases, a cell phone cradle and a china coffee cup and saucer had been left under the desk on the floor. There was also a wine glass half full of Chardonnay, the rim smeared with pink lipstick. A multi-line phone sat next to the computer and there was another one at the end of the desk next to the other PC. And there was one more phone on top of the filing cabinet outside the door to Linda's office. Counting the phone that Linda was on, that made four phones in a ten-foot radius.

The walls of the basement were painted light green, which combined with the sunlight coming through the windows, made the office very bright. Surprisingly, there was a view of the Bay. Judging by the front entrance, I'd thought that the ground floor was subterranean. Instead, the house had been built into the side of the hill so there was still a view from the bottom floor. I looked around one more time and came to the conclusion that I would have been happy to live in that basement for the rest of my life. Or at least until the next big earthquake hit and the whole house slid down the slope onto the Marina District.

Linda hung up the phone and I coughed a few times to let her know I was there.

She rolled her Herman Miller chair into the doorway that separated the two offices and frowned at her wristwatch. "That took an awful long time."

I explained about the passports. I also told her I'd successfully knocked off the cat grass and java, as if that was something to be proud of.

"You should have been back an hour ago," she said. "Julie came home unexpectedly and needed some light bulbs changed."

"Is Julie the blonde lady?" I asked.

"Julie is Julie," Linda said. "I'll write up that letter." She took out stationery and loaded it in the printer.

"Do you still need me to change the light bulbs?" I asked.

"No. Because you were God-knows-where, I called the handyman and he came over. Next time you really need to call if you get hung up like that. Don't you have a cell phone?"

"Those things are expensive," I said.

"Well, if you're going to keep working here, you might think about investing in one. Have you had lunch?"

I told her I had not.

"Go on upstairs and Frank will feed you."

I started out of the office, but Linda called me back. "Clarissa sent you, right?'

"Sure. From the Perfect Fit."

"Did she show you the listing?" Linda looked me up and down. I thought maybe my fly was undone.

"You mean the job description?" I asked, subtly checking the zipper of my chinos. "She read it to me over the phone. Am I dressed wrong?" Although I'm 6'2" with brown hair and blue eyes and I played enough rec-league basketball back in the day to think that I still had an athletic build, the way Linda was checking me out made me feel like I'd failed to meet an important appearance qualification.

"Forget it," Linda said and rolled her chair back to her computer to start typing.

Upstairs, a deeply tanned middle-aged guy stood over the kitchen range working an array of steaming pots. Under his apron he wore a tight yellow Polo shirt that showed off his huge biceps. He was talking to another gentlemen who was leaned against the marble cooking island. The other man looked to be in his late fifties and was dressed in slacks and a button down shirt. He had a big gut, gray hair and a trimmed beard; at first glance I thought it might've been the jerk who'd honked at me for standing in the driveway.

Two older women, one big and black, the other tiny and blonde, sat at a breakfast nook eating lunch and watching TV. A baby monitor had been set on the table between them.

I closed the door to the basement stairs and all four of them looked over to stare at me. I said I was looking for Frank and lunch.

"Well, hello," the older guy with the beard lisped as he blatantly checked me out. I decided that he wasn't the guy in the BMW.

"Are you the new errand boy?" the man stirring pots asked.

"I guess so," I replied.

"I'm Liam." The bearded fellow extended his clammy hand like he expected me to kiss it.

The chef wiped his hands on his apron and reached over the counter to give me a vice grip. "I'm Frank," he pointed his spatula at the two women. "Over there is Astrid and Patty." The women waved their forks as they chewed.

"What do you want for lunch?" Frank asked.

"What is there?"

Liam giggled.

Frank opened the door of the stainless steel Viking refrigerator like it was bank vault. It was crammed with Tupperware containers. He started pulling them out and reading the masking tape labels on the lids. Poached salmon, roast chicken, Maryland crab cakes, prime rib, garlic-roasted potatoes, cucumber salad. The chef was obviously enjoying the demonstration.

"Frank," the little blonde woman called from the nook, "just fix the boy some sandwich and stop showing off." She had a Spanish accent that didn't match her Nordic looks.

"*Grand puta! Tetes grandes!*" Frank shot back. He winked at me.

"*Aye!*" The little blonde exclaimed, "*Tienes una boca muy sucia.* And we have new company!"

"*Culo grande*," Frank said. The black lady shook her head and kept eating.

"Don't let Frankie e-scare you," the blond said. "He learn words like the—*come se dice?*—like the little bird that talks? *Un pajaro.*"

"A parrot," the black lady said.

"*Si,* a little nasty parrot. Have the parrot make you a sandwich."

Frank said a sandwich was too easy. He could fix me up a nice prime rib with horseradish and *au jus*. I told him I'd make myself a plate from the food in the Tupperware containers. The phone rang but nobody made a move for it. A moment later the intercom on the phone buzzed.

"Astrid?" Linda called over the intercom. "Patty?"

The two women glanced at each other.

"Astrid or Patty pick up line one. It's Bailey." Both of them immediately started to get up, but little blond was much faster and had dashed to the phone before Patty had managed her feet.

"Hello? Bailey? Is Astrid." She listened for a few seconds, said okay and cradled the phone.

"She want us to wake up the little monsters and meet her at the studio," Astrid reported. "Can you believe it? Taking babies to such a place?"

Patty and Astrid dumped their lunch plates into the sink.

"Hey," Frank called, "what am I? Your dishwasher?"

"Wash the dishes, little parrot," Astrid said and let the door to the foyer swing shut behind her.

"Fucking nannies," Frank said and went back to his cooking. Liam picked-up a monologue about Europe and antiques while I worked my way through the Tupperware buffet. I opened the crab cake container and saw there was only one left. I asked Frank if I could have it. He said to eat everything; it was getting thrown out at the end of the day. There was enough food in the combined containers for five people.

The kitchen, like the basement, was bright and sunny. There was a six-burner gas range on the cooking island and a hanging selection of polished copper pots that clinked together lightly in the breeze coming through the open window. Since there were no stools around the cooking island, I took my plate into the breakfast nook and ate at the large butcher-block table. A sofa bench had been built into one wall of the nook. Four simple wooden chairs had been placed on the opposite side of the table. Windows and a saloon door offered a view of the well-tended shrubbery in the front courtyard.

Liam was still talking at Frank when I finished my lunch. I thanked the chef for the food, but turned him down when he started listing potential desserts.

"C'mon, dude, how about one little scoop of ice cream? It's Haagen Daaz."

I went back downstairs and Linda handed me a signed letter on heavy bond stationary with *Bailey Phelan* embossed at the top, and said I could pick up the passports. I started to walk out when I saw the letter wasn't signed. Linda took it from me and scribbled Mrs. Phelan's signature at the bottom.

"And this time," Linda said, "don't get lost."

Four: The New Economy

WHILE SHAGGING KITTY GRASS DIDN'T seem like the best way to win the dot.com lottery, my brief foray into the Phelan's house left me fairly certain that I would at least get paid. I couldn't say that about the other fleeting experiences I'd had in the San Francisco job market.

My first S.F. gig came about when a college acquaintance tracked me down to see if I'd be interested in writing for the lifestyle website he was launching. This company was trying to hit the eighteen to thirty-four year old male market, kind of like *Maxim* magazine, but on the Web. He boasted that the company was in negotiations with both Dennis Rodman and Steven Baldwin to be the company's spokespeople. That should have been a warning sign right there. My friend wanted me to put together several music reviews. I asked if he was going to send me a batch of CDs to critique.

"Nah," he said, "just pick some disks out of your collection and review them."

"New ones?" I asked.

"Whatever. New, sort of new, old ones, I don't care. I just need five reviews by next week. I've got a shitload of space to fill."

My pay for this gig would be $20 a review or fifty shares of stock in the company. My friend assured me that an IPO was imminent and my shares would be worth a fortune within months. Why not defer cold hard payment for a huge payoff?

I decided to take the cash when my employment contract arrived. There were five typos on the first page. I felt it was my duty as an employee (and potential shareholder) to call company headquarters and let them know about the mistakes. My call was answered by a young woman who sounded unsure of her role at the company. In the background I could hear music and telephones ringing. The receptionist kept putting me on hold while she searched for a Vice President. The hold music was Black Sabbath, "Into the Void." The VP ended up being just as confused as the receptionist. He didn't know about the existence of the contract I was referring to. I told him I wanted the cash.

"What cash?" he asked.

I wrote twelve reviews for them, never saw a dime and never heard back from my buddy. In the end, the site was up for all of two months before passing into start-up oblivion. Obviously Basketball Dennis and Baby Baldwin hadn't resonated quite the way they'd been expected to.

I mentioned my "work" with this company to my old college girlfriend Rumi, who'd also migrated to the Bay Area with a business plan. She immediately went into talent-acquisition mode and urged me to quit that dot.com and start working for hers. She too was desperate for content to fill her spa-finding website, and pitched me on going to a couple resorts—on the company dime—then writing something about "a man's perspective on spa treatments." She'd pay me $30 per-article and would naturally throw in options. Not being entirely confident that Rumi could reimburse me for any actual expenses, I instead took fake notes on a phantom call I made to The

National Spa Association (if there even is such a thing) and then went into Rumi's headquarters to write the thing up.

The office was located in a cement strip mall complex just off the railroad tracks in Cupertino. It had taken her four months to find this garage, and they were paying $15,000 a month for it. In the Old Economy the place had been home to a window-tinting business. The office was humming along with two dozen twenty-five year olds in fleece pullovers and GAP trousers talking excitedly on the phones. The requisite dog meandered from desk to desk sniffing ankles. It was warm that afternoon, so they had rolled up the bay door in the back and I could see two employees smoking cigarettes on the loading dock. The staff started talking more loudly when I came in the front door with Rumi, perhaps thinking I was a big shot investor. In those days you couldn't tell who had clout just by looking at them, since all the men wore the same uniform of button down shirt and tan slacks. The only way someone stood out was by how many people were kissing their ass. Or if they were driving a Lamborghini.

Rumi led me to the executive offices (a storage alcove above the main floor) and sat me in front of a computer; I took the rest of the day to tap out two pages of drivel. (Sample question to the non-existent flack at the fictitious Spa Association: What should you do if you get an erection while being massaged?) My pace was slowed by the commotion in the office that I couldn't help but eavesdrop on.

Rumi's operation had yet to "go live" but it was paying salaries, hiring attorneys and had an advertising budget—all the vital signs of entrepreneurship aside from the small detail of generating revenue. It kept her going 18 hours every day of the week. The pace was insane, but not entirely surprising. Rumi had been driven pretty hard by her first-generation Japanese parents, and she ran triathlons for relaxation. That was part of the reason we broke up.

After my first day in her office, I came to the conclusion that launching a website involved a lot of talking. Rumi and her partner, a 29-year-old New Yorker whose cachet was that she had previously worked as an assistant for the trend watcher Faith Popcorn, acted like two society hostesses arguing about a party. From their desks set on opposite sides of the alcove they bickered about shades of green for the background of the web page.

"Call the designer!" Rumi's partner screeched upon seeing the mock-up. "This color makes me want to puke!"

"What's his name again?" Rumi asked as she jabbed her stylus into the screen of her Palm Pilot.

"Jeff. Call Jeff and tell him this is going to make people vomit. This doesn't say, 'Come relax and enjoy a seaweed wrap.' This says, 'I just puked all over my iMac.'"

Rumi donned her telephone headset and called the web designer. While she was chewing him out, her partner took the laptop downstairs and showed the test page to her employees, who all agreed that it made them think "seasick" as opposed to "seaweed."

Jeff finally came in, looking like he'd just logged 36 straight hours in his basement playing Doom, and began to demonstrate other color options. This went on for six hours before they finally sent the web designer packing with no fingernails left to chew and orders to lighten the background color by two shades.

Around five o'clock, Rumi began to muse about the company's board of directors. Her partner agreed that they needed more heavy hitters, and for the next three hours they threw out names—everyone from Cindy Crawford to Bill Gates—and discussed if they knew anyone who knew them. It was like that six-degrees of separation game. They were still going at 8:30 when I dropped my "article" on Rumi's desk.

Rumi called me at eleven that night to gush about the piece of crap I'd turned in. She said she needed someone talented like me to look over their business plan and make it more readable for investors. I came in the next day for what might have been the most frustrating writing assignment of my life, even considering the unlimited fruit smoothies. You haven't suffered until you've tried to edit a business plan with two anxious women constantly peering over your shoulder saying, "What we're trying to convey here is…" I'll also need to be institutionalized if I ever again hear the phrases "Outside the box," "At the end of the day" or "Bricks and mortar."

Tinkering with her business plan had obviously frayed Rumi's nerves as well, so we decided to order a pizza back at her place. We made it to her apartment, but forgot all about the pizza because we started pawing each other the moment we walked through the door. Staring at photos of nearly naked spa models all day also apparently breeds extreme sexual frustration. Rumi dragged me into the living room by my belt as I went to work on the buttons of her blouse. Since Rumi was wearing a skirt, we were able to get down to serious action without much delay. Rumi fucked like someone had a stopwatch on her. Afterwards, we lay on the floor, catching our breath.

"That was pretty abrupt," I said, crawling over to my pants.

"Time management," Rumi said. She rolled onto her back and knocked out twenty crunches.

"Does that apply to groceries?" I asked as I peered into her refrigerator. It contained a brown banana, three ham and cheese Lunchables and a bottle of champagne. I couldn't find any glasses in the cupboards. Back in the living room, Rumi was sitting on the black leather sofa in her white lace bra and panties, waiting for her laptop to boot. From what I could tell, the only furniture in the place was that couch and a bed on boxsprings in the adjacent bedroom.

"Hey," she protested as I popped the champagne cork. "I was saving that."

I wiped the bubbles off my lip as I passed her the bottle. "For what?"

"Duh? For our IPO."

"You'll buy some furniture then?"

"I'll *buy someone* to buy my furniture." She handed the champagne back to me and took the barrette out of her ponytail. She shook her long, black hair loose.

"It's gonna happen soon?" I asked.

Rumi let out a little burp. "I'm going to New York next week to talk with some VCs."

"You don't want to keep it for yourself?"

Rumi sighed. "We talked about going public ourselves, but the whole spa search thing is too specific. I'm not learning anything anymore. I figure we get our ten, twenty million and then I can get into something really dynamic."

"Why not just retire?"

"Boring. Hey, don't finish the whole bottle by yourself!"

"You've been at this for six months now, right?"

Rumi nodded.

"So ten million—"

"Minimum," she interrupted.

"Ten million for six month's work."

Rumi did the rest of the math. "One-point-six a month for my effort. Ballpark. If the deal closed tomorrow. Split in half. Minus taxes." Rumi tapped out an e-mail. "But $10 million is an insult."

I took the last swallow of champagne. "I guess you'll be able to afford another bottle." I bowled the empty across the carpet and it thunked against the couch.

"I'll buy a vineyard." Rumi set her computer on the floor and picked up the bottle. "So what the hell are *you* going to do out here?" she asked as she examined the label. "You quit your job. Check. Broke your girlfriend's heart. Check. Now what? Rely on your good looks?"

"Relyonmygoodlooks.com."

"You better register that domain."

"First thing in the morning."

"There's nothing left to drink," Rumi said. She spun the empty champagne bottle on the carpet. It ended up pointing in my direction. "So what's for dessert?"

"I thought we were getting pizza?"

Rumi smiled. "I'm not hungry anymore."

"Don't you ever sleep?"

"Nobody gets paid for sleeping," Rumi said.

There were well-funded reverse flea circuses like Rumi's all over the Bay Area in 1999. What I mean by reverse is that you could see all the players, but nothing was happening. An entire language was created so that people could sound like they had the petal to the metal when in fact the car was up on blocks. Rumi didn't say she was arguing about the background color of her web page, she said she was "Presenting it to a test audience." And what the hell is Business Development besides trying to get Larry Ellison's assistant's e-mail address? Of course, the key element I was missing was faith. That's what Rumi and her ilk were always ranting about, how you had to "believe" that the business would take off. And how could you not believe when you saw hundreds—maybe thousands—of other kids your age striking it filthy rich with no more experience or better ideas than you? An invisible force was out there handing away money like Ken Kesey had doled out LSD in the 60's; you felt like an idiot if you weren't grabbing with both hands.

In the end, I never got a dime out of Rumi's company because they were bankrupt by the end of the year.

So while temping for the Phelans wasn't exactly the fast-track to a million bucks (or spiritual enlightenment, to keep with the Kesey/acid theme), it would get me out of the house and appeared to be something that might actually pay. It was, in other words, a first step.

FIVE: BAILEY

WHEN I WENT BACK TO the Phelans for my second day of work there was no clutch of people gabbing in the kitchen, no movers lugging antiques, and no music playing on the in-house stereo. When I met Junko in the laundry room on my way to Linda's office she said good morning in a whisper.

I reported to Linda to get that day's marching orders. She was wearing another hideous sweat suit, with Air Jordan sneakers. On a girl in their 20's the look might have passed as fresh, but on the 40-ish Linda it looked sloppy. She handed me two manifests, one typed on letterhead titled "Nursery List" and the other handwritten on a piece of yellow notepaper.

"Hey, Junko," Linda called. "Does Bailey need anything?"

Junko padded into the office in her red sneakers.

"In a way, I don't know. Bailey still resting."

That explained the quiet. The mistress of the house was still asleep at 10:30. I snooze until mid-morning and I'm a bum. Mrs. Phelan *rests*. It's all about semantics. Linda handed over another envelope of cash and sent me on my way. This was more of a grocery list, and of course, there was a different store for practically every item. The first spot, where I was meant to pick up raspberry jam, was a boutique joint in the neighborhood with a ten-car parking lot that was full. Drivers of a Jaguar, a Lexus, and a Range Rover sat idling at the entrance waiting for someone to leave. I circled the block looking for a meter and came up empty. I decided to one-stop it at the big Safeway in the Marina.

The Marina neighborhood is built on land reclamation, and separates the Pac Heights from the Bay. It also serves as the breeding ground for the city's next generation of millionaires. My brother and I referred to them as the "Young Turks". The go-getters gazed longingly at the mansions above them in Pacific Heights, and fantasized about glorious vesting stock options exploding like 4th of July fireworks.

There are two main drags in the Marina, Union and Chestnut. Both are lined with sushi joints, yoga studios, and swank bars. Between the two main corridors is Lombard Street, which in contrast is mostly comprised of shabby motels due to the fact that the Golden Gate Bridge spits the sightseers out right there. The result is a strange mix of tourists and Turks, rental minivans and drop-top Porsche Boxsters. In the start-up years the median age of the residents of this area was twenty-five, and the rents were upwards of $3,500 for a one-bedroom flat—if you could find a vacancy. Stevie, Chase, and I didn't even bother with the Marina when we were looking for an apartment.

But the Turks have to eat, right? Or at least have some brie and Red Bull in the fridge. I'd always heard the Marina Safeway was the big spot for picking up ladies. Perhaps it was on a Thursday evening, but on Thursday at 11 a.m. the only women in there either had kids or Social Security. I wheeled my cart into the baby section and loaded up on diapers and formula and butt wipes. That should have taken three minutes, but I was in foreign territory and was forced to troll the aisle for half an hour looking back and forth between my list and the shelves. To the other shoppers I must've looked like Day One of Paternity Leave or a blatant scammer trying to attract female sympathy.

After filling the nursery order, I moved over to the beverage aisle and stacked the cart with Snapples and Crystal Geyser juice drinks. The cart looked bound for an orphanage in the desert.

The rest of the list was to be procured at Whole Foods, but I figured I'd save myself a trip and picked out the fanciest comparable package of each item at Safeway.

I hit a French laundry on the way back and retrieved dress shirts. The girl behind the counter explained that they had run out of boxes the previous night, so the shirts were on hangers.

It took me three trips to lug all the shopping through the service entrance and pile it in the laundry room.

Junko adjusted her apron as she came downstairs to assess my work.

"Shirts on hangers," she said immediately.

"They ran out of boxes. Is that a big deal?"

"In a way, yes. Julie like them in box."

"Julie?"

"Julie. Mr. Phelan."

"His name is Julie?" I thought the housekeeper was mispronouncing his name.

"In a way," she said, "a girl's name, but his name, too."

"Does he drive a BMW?"

Junko was too concerned about the shirts to respond. She held them up in front of my face.

"You want me to take them back?" I asked.

"Yes!" she said.

"Okay. Where do you want me to put the drinks and stuff?"

"In a way, you should take shirts first."

When I got back to the house fifteen minutes later with the shirts in their proper boxes, I saw that Junko had taken all the groceries upstairs. I went to the kitchen and found the housekeeper staring at the scones and preserves and fruit drinks. There was a taller Asian lady in a matching apron standing next to her. The taller one offered me a nervous smile.

"The other stores were out," I lied.

Junko regarded me through her tinted glasses. "Julie won't eat." She picked up the package of scones and I thought she was going to chuck it at me. "Julie won't drink," she said, pushing the sodas to the edge of the counter. "You have receipt, you take back."

"Mr. Phelan's pretty picky, huh?"

"In a way, yes."

"You want me to put those Snapples away first?"

Junko pointed to a low cabinet by the breakfast nook. When I opened it up I found that it was already full of Snapple and Crystal Geyser. I started pushing the existing bottles to the back to make room, but Junko told me I needed to make sure the old drinks were in front.

"How do I know which ones are older than the others?"

Junko picked up a Peach Snapple and pointed to the date printed on the glass.

I was on my knees date-coding Diet Mango iced tea when I heard Mrs. Phelan come into the kitchen. The open cabinet door blocked my view but I heard her telling Junko how the babies had kept her up all night.

"I see, I see," Junko said, sounding relieved to know why Mrs. Phelan had slept in until noon.

"Who's that?" Mrs. Phelan asked.

"That errand person."

When I raised my head to look over the top of the cabinet I found myself staring right at Mrs. Phelan's crotch. She was once again wearing stretch pants, but today they were black. I couldn't help but notice a faint camel-toe.

"Hi," she said. Her hair was still wet from the shower, looking more brown than blonde today. "I'm Bailey. Weren't you here Monday? Getting the kitty grass?"

"Yes. Nice to officially meet you, Mrs. Phelan." I got to my feet and extended my hand.

"Bailey," she corrected. "Sorry I didn't introduce myself the other day. Those movers wanted to get out of here."

She wasn't exactly beautiful, but she was pretty damn cute with a slim figure, pert breasts and sexy green eyes. She couldn't have been more than five years older than me—probably around thirty-years-old. I wouldn't have kicked her out of bed for eating crackers. Like Linda the previous day, Mrs. Phelan looked me over in a way that made me feel like some essential part of my wardrobe was out-of-order.

"You busy?" she asked finally.

"No, not at all." There were two dozen bottles of Snapple on the floor around me.

"You want to do something for me?"

"Sure. What do you need?"

She smiled. "If I was you, I'd rephrase that."

I was still thinking about that one when she headed downstairs. Junko was relieved to get me away from the Snapple's and practically pushed me out of the kitchen.

Linda came out of her office immediately with a book of message slips, which she started reading to Mrs. Phelan. "Liam will be here at noon to discuss the Christie's sale," she relayed. "Then you've got a play date with Stephanie and her daughter at one-thirty. Sven will be here at three for your Pilates and Gwen called twice to see about dinner tomorrow before the museum benefit. I rescheduled your appointment with Dr. Fischer from this morning. And Clive called three times asking about Miami."

Linda kept on talking, but Mrs. Phelan didn't seem to be listening as she sat in front of her computer and pulled up her Hotmail account.

"God, my desk is such a mess," Mrs. Phelan said, taking in the heaps of catalogues and un-opened mail.

"I was meaning to organize it today," Linda said, "but I wanted to check with you first."

"We really need to come up with a way to keep all this straight." Mrs. Phelan smiled at Linda. "I meant to say 'organized.'"

"Tony," Linda said turning to me, "you should go to Office Depot this afternoon and buy some little shelves."

Before I knew what I was doing, I had picked up a pad of paper and was writing that down. "What color?" I asked Mrs. Phelan.

"What color?" Linda said, intercepting my question.

Mrs. Phelan swiveled in her chair and shot me a coy look. "What color do you think?"

I paused for a moment. "I have no idea."

"Not very original," she mused. "Maybe black."

"Black," Linda said to me and I dutifully wrote that down.

"But I don't want it to look too officey," Mrs. Phelan said.

"We could call the handyman and have him make some shelves for you," Linda said. "Build them right into the wall here."

"What do you think?" Mrs. Phelan asked me again.

"You could get some baskets from Office Max," I offered.

Mrs. Phelan and Linda exchanged another look.

Linda shrugged. "Tony, you'll go to Pier One this afternoon. Get some little wicker in-boxes."

"Sure." I scribbled *What the fuck?* on the notepad.

The phone rang—actually all four phones in the vicinity rang—but Mrs. Phelan didn't make a move for the one right in front of her. Linda dashed into her office and picked up.

"It's Wendy on line one," she called from the next room. "Are you home?"

"No," Mrs. Phelan barked as she scrolled through her Hotmail inbox.

Linda explained to Wendy that Mrs. Phelan was at an appointment. The other line rang while Linda was still talking, but once again Mrs. Phelan didn't seem to notice it. Linda got rid of Wendy and caught the other line.

Mrs. Phelan switched to the calendar on her computer and started deleting appointments as I stood behind her with my pad and pen at the ready. After a minute of being ignored, I drifted to the other side of the office to examine the stereo sitting on the counter. It was a top-of-the-line Sony with a 100 disk CD player, CD burner and 100-watt amp. There was a stack of albums next to the stereo, mostly dance music.

"Ready?" Mrs. Phelan asked, startling me.

I stepped back to her desk. Mrs. Phelan reached over to the printer and pulled out a sheet of paper with a name and address on it. She tucked it into a slim paperback book.

"Would you please write a thank you note to her for loaning me this book and then deliver it?"

"You want me to type the note?" I asked.

"No, just write it out and sign it."

"I hate to tell you this, but my handwriting is really bad."

"It doesn't matter," she said.

"And sign it for you?"

"Yes." Mrs. Phelan smiled at me again.

I was going to show her the memo I'd taken to demonstrate my chicken scratch, but saw the expletive in my note-to-self, and decided against it.

"Could you do that today?" she asked as I stood there.

"No problem."

"Thank you so much," she said, standing up. "I've got to run. I'll see you next week?"

"Today is actually my last day, I think."

"Really? Do you want to work again next week?"

"Sure. That'd be great."

"Okay, come in Monday. I'm leaving for Europe with the kids Wednesday and I'll have *tons* of errands for you."

"Sure, Mrs. Phelan. I'll see you next week."

"Bailey," she smiled.

"Right."

Mrs. Phelan grabbed her tiny cell phone and her giant Prada bag, slipped on some matching sunglasses and walked through a door off the laundry room. A few seconds later I heard a garage door open and a car start.

"Where's Bailey?" Linda asked after hanging up the phone.

"She just took off."

"Damn."

I spent the rest of the day re-doing the scones and fruit drinks and picking up baskets from Pier One. I also penned the thank you note and tried to sign Mrs. Phelan's name as fancily as possible at the bottom. It still looked like it was written by a guy. The book was about how to communicate with toddlers, and when I went to deliver it I realized that it was going somewhere on the Phelan's street. After checking the address again, I saw that it was to be delivered next door.

I had finished all my drills by three that afternoon and was sitting in the main office at the third computer, listening to Linda gossip on the phone. I checked out ESPN.com and realized I was actually on the clock for the first time since I'd moved to S.F.

Upstairs I heard quick footfalls, like people scattering. The garage door opened. I Alt-Tabbed the computer and pulled the envelope of receipts from my pocket, shuffling through them as if I was doing my accounts. From my chair I could see the laundry room door leading to the garage. When it opened it was not Mrs. Phelan, but the dick who'd honked at me my first day. He was wearing a suit, and now that he was not blowing his horn at me I could tell that he was probably in his early sixties. I considered introducing myself, but he was up the stairs and gone before I could get to the laundry room.

"Was that Bailey?" Linda asked, having hung up on her friend when she heard the garage door open.

"I think it was Mr. Phelan."

Linda blanched. "He's home early."

I asked Linda if she had anything else for me to do. She said that she didn't. I told her that Mrs. Phelan had asked me to come back Monday, but Linda was distracted by Mr. Phelan's footfalls upstairs. I handed her my envelope of receipts and leftover cash and grabbed my jacket to leave.

As I walked through the laundry room to the service entrance I saw that the door at the top of the stairs was open. Mr. Phelan was standing at the cooking island reading something, his suit jacket slung over his shoulder. The house had been subdued all day with the exception of the half-hour when Bailey was up and moving, but now the place was dead silent.

Six: Join The Staff

THE NEXT TIME I SAW Clarissa at the Perfect Fit was when I had to take my time slips downtown to get paid.

"We've sent quite a few candidates to the Phelans in the past," Clarissa said. "They all say it's pretty bizarre." The temp agent looked up expectantly. "I heard it was like the best soap opera ever."

I told her that I hadn't seen anything too out of the ordinary aside from a lot of expensive scones and boxed shirts.

Clarissa handed over my check. "What would you think about working there on a more permanent basis?"

"Is this thing going to clear?" I asked, holding the check up to the light so I could see the watermark.

"Why wouldn't it?"

"Past experience," I said, folding the check. "Like how permanent are they talking?"

"They want to buy you."

"Pardon me?"

"Linda called this morning and asked me if you were available to work three days a week starting next week. They'll put you on their payroll instead of reimbursing us. All they ask is for you to commit to at least two months."

I hadn't ever figured myself as a professional errand runner, but Clarissa's not-so-subtle interest in the Phelan residence caught my attention. A couple more weeks there would certainly help the wallet. Perhaps things might get weird.

"I don't know," I said. "They've been looking at me funny."

Clarissa laughed. "Don't worry about that."

"Worry about what?" I asked.

"Linda said Mrs. Phelan was quite pleased with your work."

I took another look at my check. $136 for two days. I'd forgotten about taxes. Still that was $136 more than I'd made since arriving in the City. It wasn't going to get me a night at the Fairmont, but it looked genuine. I told Clarissa that I'd think about the job.

"Is it true that she's beautiful?" Clarissa asked as I was leaving.

"Mrs. Phelan? She's not bad."

"I heard that she was some sort of supermodel princess type."

"I didn't say she was ugly."

I rode the bus down Geary Street towards home alongside the ancient Chinese ladies clutching their plastic shopping bags of vegetables. Geary was washed in concrete gray light cast by the fog and old buildings. Despite the glum weather, it felt good to be out and about after all those weeks stuck in my apartment, so I hopped off the bus at Stanyan and walked into Golden Gate Park. The dingy clouds parted over the park, and the pathways were suddenly dappled with bright sunlight. A couple street kids lounging on the sloped lawn by the tennis courts asked me if I wanted to buy weed, and there were two sets of Asian newlyweds posing for wedding pictures by the koi pond in the Japanese Tea Garden. By the time I exited the park through the Rose Garden at 25th Avenue, I'd decided to take the job.

But before I called Clarissa, I went to the bank and cashed my check.

———

I went back to the Pac Heights Monday morning and Linda hit me with the details of a staff position at *chez* Phelan. She added a five-dollar raise so that I'd be making $18 an hour. Quick calculations revealed that if I was working five days a week at that rate, I'd be making more than I had back in Denver. And all just to shop for their groceries! Even though it seemed like a pretty simple proposition, Linda made me sit there in her office for an hour while she described everything my job would require. She tried to make keeping the Phelan's cabinet full of Snapple seem like re-supplying the 3rd Army. I kept nodding my head in hopes that she'd run out of air and shut up. At the end of the briefing, Linda gave me a key to the house. I tried to decline, but she said that I'd be coming and going all day and it wasn't practical for someone to buzz me in every time. I looked at the large, ornately engraved key as more responsibility—and liability—than I cared for. I figured it was probably an elaborate set-up; Linda was going to have her cousin strip the house when the Phelans were in Europe, and I'd be the fall guy.

Mrs. Phelan had yet to emerge from her bedroom by the time Linda was finished with her briefing, so she turned me over to Junko. The housekeeper handed me a stuffed pillow-case and told me to take it to the dry cleaner.

"But it's just sheets," I said looking into the bag.

"Yes."

"You take their sheets to the dry cleaner?"

"In a way, yes."

Veteran's Cleaners was located on the corner of Sacramento and Presidio, an intersection on the commercial side of Pac Heights with frustratingly scarce parking, lots of traffic, and a heavy meter maid presence. The result was that I either had to double park and hope no cops prowled past, or park five blocks away and walk to the cleaners with a pillowcase full of soiled sheets, knowing instinctively that every good-looking girl in the neighborhood would be on the sidewalk as I passed.

The actual clothes went up the street to the French laundry, and although it was no easier to park there than in front of Veteran's, I felt a lot better about myself carrying a bundle of dress shirts, ties and suit jackets than I did with those pillowcases stuffed with linens.

While the Marina side of the Heights was full of Young Turks trying to get their Porsches out of second gear, the opposite base was a traffic jam of middle-aged women trolling for spots to crookedly park their Jaguars and Range Rovers so they could pop into one of the sidewalk bistros for a $15 bowl of soup. There was also an assortment of quaint boutiques selling expensive clothes on Sacramento—the kind of thing where you could have one customer a day and still meet your margins. Adding to the vehicle congestion were the schools of meter maids weaving in and out of traffic in their Cushman carts; this street was easy pickin's for the parking cops because most of the socialites couldn't be bothered to carry quarters for the meters and would simply take the $55 ticket as if it was a valet fee. While I felt sheepish navigating the sidewalk with the Phelan's dirty laundry, it wasn't because I assumed the rich ladies were regarding me negatively. If anything, I felt invisible to these hollow-cheeked women in their oversize Jackie-O sunglasses because they were too busy checking each other out to notice a lowly errand boy like myself. The crest of the Pacific Heights was like the Old Money/New Money Continental Divide, and I felt a lot better being invisible among the socialites on the slope of the Heights than I did being judged by my peers in the Marina.

I returned to the house just in time to help the nannies park the car. The rule of thumb with the kids was apparently that if you couldn't find a spot within a half block of the house, you double-parked and left it to Linda. Now, of course, Linda had me. The Volvo station wagon idled at the curb and an unfamiliar pair of nannies got out when I approached. They were both in their early twenties.

"So, this is the new one?" the driver said. She was stocky with freckles, and introduced herself as Jen. The passenger was tall and thin with a pixie face, and named Sally. They were both wearing Capri pants and low-top sneakers. The kids were in the backseat fussing, but the girls didn't seem to notice.

"We hear you're the full-time errand boy now," Jen said.

"Well, three days a week."

"That'll change," Sally said.

"How's that?"

"Oh, first it'll be three days," Sally said. "And then Linda will ask you to come in on a fourth day because she's too lazy to get off her ass. And then since it's been four days, why not make it five?"

"And why not Saturday, too?" Jen chimed in. The kids were screaming now and Sally ducked into the station wagon to unbuckle them from their car seats.

"Have you met the other nannies?" Jen asked.

I told her I'd met Astrid and Patty.

"That's not even half of us."

"How many nannies do they need for two kids?" I asked.

"We're like 7-11," Jen said. "24 hours a day."

"Hey bitch," Sally called over the Volvo. "Stop wasting your game on the errand boy and get Edward. He's about to explode."

The little boy, Edward, really did look like he was about to pop as he thrashed against the restraints of his car seat. In contrast, the little girl in Sally's arms was calm and sucking her thumb contentedly, her big brown eyes staring at me. This was the first time I'd actually seen the kids although I'd heard them caterwauling in the upstairs nursery once or twice.

"Say hi to Tony, Emma," Sally instructed. The toddler looked away. "She's being shy today." Edward was now in Jen's arms and the only way to tell the kids apart was by their outfits. Emma was in a dress and Edward was in a jumpsuit, still hollering over Jen's shoulder. They had to be twins, maybe a year and a half old.

The girls left the car running and I used my new key to open the front gate for them.

"Thanks, errand boy," Sally called over her shoulder as she walked through the courtyard to the front door.

The backseat of the Volvo was littered with Cheerios and empty juice boxes and sticky stuffed animals. The stereo was tuned to a hip-hop station and the interior was thick with the sweet noxious smell of dirty diapers and antiseptic. The gas tank was on empty.

After parking the car, I went in through the front door and stood in the foyer for a moment looking at the pictures on the front table. There was a large photo of Mr. and Mrs.

Phelan dressed up in formal wear, and the photo could have easily been of a father and daughter. Since the kids were so young, I was surprised at how quickly Mrs. Phelan had gotten herself back into shape. Perhaps that's why she wore those stretch pants, to show off how fast she'd regained her figure. Upstairs I could hear Edward still screaming bloody murder.

Frank and Junko were standing at the kitchen island talking. The room was a riot of smells—basil, chicken stock, garlic, capers. Two live Dungeness crabs were trying to drag themselves off a large cutting board.

"Hey," Frank said, "it's the new errand person. You had lunch yet, dude?" He cleanly halved one of the crabs with a cleaver, releasing a briny scent.

He washed his hands and dipped a piece of warm French bread into a vat of spaghetti sauce. He sprinkled it with fresh Parmesan and handed it to me, flexing his arm intentionally to pop his bicep muscle. Just as I was taking a bite, Mrs. Phelan shuffled in wearing her short robe. Junko moved away from the cooking island and Frank turned back to the remaining crab. My instinct was to drop the bread and head downstairs, but I didn't want to insult Frank. The chef moved the still-writhing crustacean halves to the back counter so as to shield Mrs. Phelan from the sight.

"Good morning," Mrs. Phelan yawned. Her hair was still mussed from the pillow, and I found her languorous afternoon look kinda sexy.

I finished chewing and said hello. Frank asked her if she wanted a fruit smoothie or some egg whites. She said she wanted a cappuccino. Frank started for the stainless steel Jura machine, but Mrs. Phelan waved him off.

"You make it too weak," she said.

Mrs. Phelan asked me to talk with her for a minute. I sat down at the table in the breakfast nook and waited for her to finish making her cappuccino. She left the espresso portafilter leaking on the counter, and the carton of organic skim milk open. She slid onto the cushioned bench along the wall, her robe pulling open so that I could see the top of her shapely thigh.

"So you're taking the job?" she asked.

I told her I was.

"Good. I'm glad. We've been trying to find someone for a while now. We'll keep it fun for you. I'm so busy with Edward and Emma and the studio that I don't have time for all the things I need to do. Just don't let Frank fatten you up too much."

"Hey!" Frank called out.

"So, we're all good?" she asked. She took her time licking a spot of milk foam off her upper lip.

"I guess so."

"Wonderful," she sighed, as if she'd just completed a difficult transaction.

She left her cappuccino cup on the table and slid out of the nook, her robe opening a little more to reveal her pink panties. I looked out the window.

"Thanks for the job, Mrs. Phelan."

She stopped at the kitchen door and turned back to me.

"Call me Bailey," she said.

Frank let out a low whistle when she was gone.

"What?" I asked, setting Bailey's cup in the sink.

The chef laughed. "I told them."

"Told them what, Frank? Everyone around here keeps looking at me like I've got a third eyeball."

The chef lifted the cutting board back onto the cooking island. "You'll find out soon enough," he said. He picked up his cleaver and finished butchering the crabs.

SEVEN: VACATION

BAILEY AND THE KIDS WERE leaving for Europe in three hours and utter chaos had broken out at the estate. An air raid siren would've been appropriate. Sally and Jen were frantically digging through a pile of children's clothes in the dining room, Junko rushed by trailing dry cleaning bags, and Frank was in the kitchen preparing a hamper of food for the trans-Atlantic flight. Downstairs, Linda's desk was covered with passports and tickets as she organized a binder with the itinerary for the next two weeks. I glanced at the first page of the travel plan and saw it contained microscopic details such as the name of the chauffeur who was going to pick them up at Heathrow, three different numbers for him in case they should miss each other, and how much Bailey needed to tip him upon delivery to their rented townhouse in Knightsbridge. The document was fifteen pages long—a page for each day. Linda had also worked up a cost sheet figured to the dollar and decimal based upon that day's exchange rate. Peering over her shoulder, I rounded the figures up in my head.

$25,000 for an apartment in London, $19,500 for a place in Paris. Per diems for the four nannies going on the trip totaled $3,500, salaries for them was $7,500 in London, $5,000 while in Paris. Airfare from S.F. to London and back cost $16,500. Grand total: $77,000. For a two-week vacation. And that didn't even count pocket money.

I saw on the main page of the itinerary that Julie was following Bailey and the kids two days later. He had seat 1A on the Virgin non-stop.

Linda didn't notice me snooping because she was too busy panicking. Bailey had left the house early that morning and hadn't come home to pack yet. She finally noticed me standing there and thrust a list of travel medications at me, dispatching me to the pharmacy to grab them. Before I got out of the house Sally informed me they were out of suitcases, so I had to go into a cramped basement storage space and dig out several more because she was afraid of spiders. Sally and Linda inspected the bags I had brought up and decided they were all wrong. Linda called Bailey on her cell phone and, after subtly suggesting that she needed to pack, asked her what to do about the need for additional suitcases. Bailey told her to send me to Eddie Bauer to buy ten duffel bags of different sizes. Linda didn't want to lose anything in translation, so she put me on the phone.

"Hi!" Bailey said. "God, I'm tired. Went out last night and drank too much wine. Ugh." I heard tires squeal and a car horn blare.

"So, what about these duffel bags?" I asked.

"Oh yeah. Let's get ten of them. Different sizes. How about three small, three medium and four large?" She paused, waiting for me to agree.

"That sounds good."

"What colors do they have?"

"I don't know."

"We should try to color coordinate. If they have blue, get five of them blue. If they have green, get the rest of them green." I scribbled that down. "But if they don't have blue, get red. Or black. Black is good. And if they don't have green, substitute yellow. But I hate yellow. So go for blue and green and red. And then make up the difference with black. But no yellow. Okay? What do we have?"

"Three small, three medium, four large," I repeated. "Blue and green and then…" It took me a moment to decipher my notes. "If they don't have that, then black and red."

"Red then black," Bailey corrected.

"Right. And no yellow."

"Perfect!"

Linda made frantic gestures at her watch.

"I think you better get back here pretty soon," I said.

"I'm on my way. Just a quick stop by the studio and then home."

Linda asked me again if I had a cell phone. The fact that I didn't intensified her distress as she wouldn't be able to get a hold of me on the road if the orders changed. I wanted to put my hands on Linda's shoulders and tell her to calm down because she was starting to freak me out. I told her that I'd call from Eddie Bauer to see if there was anything else I needed to pick up.

"You see why we need you now?!" Linda wailed. "I can't handle all of this stuff by myself!" The house manager stuffed five hundred dollars into my hand and told me to get moving.

I was about to drive away when Junko flagged me down with a blue dishcloth.

"Frank say that we need more cucumbers and apple juice. In a way, little plastic apple juice for babies."

I bought the entire duffel bag inventory at Eddie Bauer, picked up the Pepto and Valium prescription from the pharmacy (resisting the urge to take samples of the sedatives for myself) and bought the apple juice and cucumbers. Linda's panic had wormed into me, and I drove around the city at top speed like it was a Code-3 emergency instead of a family vacation.

When I got back to the house, I found Bailey sitting in the kitchen nook eating yogurt while chatting on her cell phone. Her hair was wet from the shower. Frank grabbed the groceries, Junko took the medicine, and the nannies snatched the luggage. Linda had a sheaf of papers for Bailey to sign and was hopping from foot to foot waiting for her get off the phone. The doorbell rang and Linda dropped her papers on the counter as she ran out of the kitchen. She came back in to tell Bailey that the airport limo had arrived, then ordered me to start carrying the baggage out to the curb.

When Linda had said airport limo I'd expected one of those shuttle buses, but idling at the curb were two black stretch limousines and a matching Town Car. The nannies had filled all but two of the duffel bags with clothes for Emma and Edward, and they each had one large suitcase and various handbags of their own. The black-suited limo drivers took all the luggage to the Town Car and filled that up like a packhorse. I continued to shuttle bags out to the curb. Every time I went inside there were more waiting in the foyer. Linda was filling out luggage tags and slapping them on.

"They were supposed to leave twenty minutes ago!" she cried.

Emma and Edward finally made their appearance as Astrid and Patty, the older nannies I'd met on the first day, carried them downstairs and passed them over to Sally and Jen. Edward looked like a miniature college boy in tan corduroy slacks and a red Polo sweater, while Emma wore a pink dress and white sneakers. Sally asked about car seats and Linda told me to pull them from the Volvo. She was busy on the phone with the Virgin Atlantic VIP desk, informing them that Mrs. Phelan and entourage were running late. They would need a special envoy to meet them curbside at the airport. Bailey was still chatting away at the breakfast table, oblivious to all the commotion.

When the car seats had been installed in the limo and the kids and nannies were loaded up, Linda went inside and pleaded with Bailey to get in the car. As she made her way to the curb, Linda held out various documents for Bailey to sign—mostly checks and wire transfers, one of which was for $150,000. In her Prada blazer and matching sunglasses she looked like a Hollywood starlet giving autographs outside the Ivy. Bailey peeked inside the limo her kids and the nannies were in to say hi, which got Edward howling, then she climbed into the remaining limo by herself after giving her staff on the sidewalk a quick wave goodbye. Frank dashed outside with two Burberry-branded picnic baskets and handed them to the driver of the nannies' stretch. Three neighbors stood on the other side of the street with their Yorkies watching the departure. The motorcade slid down the street and took a right turn. I thought a couple motorcycle cops and little flags on the hoods of the cars would have completed the picture.

Linda, Frank, Junko and I stood on the sidewalk watching the procession round the corner, a sudden calm settling upon us. And then, without a word, we filed back into the house.

Eight: Who The Hell
Has That Kind of Money?

I'D ASSUMED THAT I WAS going to be mothballed while the Phelans were in Europe, but Linda told me to come in as scheduled during their absence. The house manager said that she was going to use the two weeks of quiet to get the operation organized, but as soon as the limos pulled away from the curb, a construction gang which had been waiting in trucks across the street, descended upon the house and began to tear apart the ceiling in the foyer to install new lighting. They had their scaffolding set up by the end of the day, and in order to get upstairs you had to climb through the jungle gym-like mess. Julie was still in town and, if I'd been him, I would have told them to hold off until I'd departed; but it was a two week job and he wanted it finished by the time the brood got home from the Continent.

Home improvement was a constant endeavor in the Pac Heights. There were two or three houses on every block cocooned in scaffolding. With nowhere left to build, all you could do was spiffy up the existing homes or demolish them and start anew. During the day there was a constant background hum of cranes and hammering and the *beep, beep, beep* of dump trucks in reverse. A work crew had erased a large

Tudor down the street from the Phelan's in the span of two weeks and had begun to pour a new foundation. Compared to all that, a new lighting system seemed like small potatoes.

I met the great man face-to-face on Friday. I was walking down the driveway to the service entrance when the garage door opened and I saw him getting into his coupe. I hesitated for a moment, not knowing if I should introduce myself. I quickly decided to engage and called out a hearty "Good Morning" to him before I entered the garage so that he wouldn't think it was an ambush. He stood behind his open car door as I approached, an expression on his face like he'd been sucking a lemon. He had the whole Dick Cheney Pentagon look, which was very popular with older Republicans at the turn of the millennium. Julie was not a handsome man.

"What do you want?" he asked as I got closer.

"I'm Tony," I said, a bit taken aback but still extending my hand. "I got hired last week."

"Don't let the cat out," he growled and got into the car, leaving me standing there with my hand still outstretched.

He hit the remote as he pulled out of the garage, forcing me to duck out of the way so as to not get bonged on the head by the automatic door. I shot Julie the finger through the closed garage door as I let myself into the laundry room.

The cat, a twitchy Siamese, crouched in the corner, obviously distressed by the falling plaster upstairs. I thought about giving it a swift kick to pass along to its owner. I was leaning against the washing machine when Frank came in through the service entrance.

"Dude," the chef said, "didn't you hear me whistling at you?"

"From where?"

"I was standing across the street when you went down the driveway."

"What the hell were you doing across the street?" I asked.

"Dude, I don't come in here until I'm sure Julie is gone."

"Are you kidding me?"

"You must've run right into him," Frank said, shaking his head.

"What an asshole," I said.

"That's what I'm talking about. I call from the bus stop to see if he's still home. If he is, I wait across the street until he takes off. He's usually gone by eight."

"I'll try to remember that."

My first task of the day was to arrange magazines upstairs. Linda gave me a ten-minute periodical crash course. Ones from the current month were to be displayed on the glass coffee table. Back issues of *Time, The Economist, Architectural Digest, Sunset* and *7x7 Magazine* got filed on the shelves chronologically. Rags like *Parenting* and *Twins* went to the nursery. Linda said other titles like *W, Mixer* and *Elle* I could use my judgment on, like she was giving me a big responsibility.

All this vital organization was carried out on the top floor of the house, one flight up from the bedroom level. This was my first foray to the fourth floor, and I was stunned by the 180-degree panorama of the Bay. Up until that point, I had been rather under-whelmed by the Phelan's pad. It was a nice joint and all, and even my untrained eye could see that the furniture wasn't out of the Ikea catalogue, but it seemed way too small considering the fact that during the day there were ten to fifteen non-family members coming and going. The way it was constructed added to the downsizing effect. From the street out front you could only see about fifty feet of the house, but it was built like an iceberg—everything was hidden underneath. I started to appreciate the location as I stood at the windows with an armful of magazines looking at the cargo ships crawling across the Bay and the fog rolling over the Marin Highlands on the other side of the Golden Gate. It was the best view I'd seen in the city, even better than from the observation decks of the hotels downtown. I could've charged folks ten bucks a head to file up there and gawk at Alcatraz, which was framed by the main window.

I was halfway through my magazine duty—taking a moment here and there to skim any interesting articles—when Linda buzzed me on the intercom.

"Tony?" she said over the phone loudspeaker. "Tony?" I waited ten seconds before picking it up. She was on her fourth "Tony?" by that point.

"While the painters are here they're going to do the walls leading up to the top floor, so I need you to take down all the pictures and certificates. It's very important that you pack them away super-carefully because that's Julie's stuff." She droned on about packing materials and maximum box weight and where to put the boxes when they were secured. Linda talked in circles, and by the time she hung up the phone—and then only because a call came in—we'd gone around the track three times.

I spent the rest of the day stripping the upstairs walls, and the first thing I noticed was that the guy's real name was indeed Julie, which served him right. I'd figured that for a nickname or an abbreviation of Julius or Julian. Even better was that his middle name was Norbert. I envisioned many years of playground harassment in his past. I also saw diplomas proving that he went to the University of Michigan for undergrad, graduating Summa Cum Laude, and then got his law degree from Georgetown, also graduating with honors. A framed letter announced that Michigan had given him a scholarship. At first I thought it was for $3,000, but I looked at the yellowing paper again and saw that it was for thirty bucks. Even back in 1962, the year it had been offered to Julie as an incoming frosh, thirty dollars was chump-change. Why would a guy keep that kind of thing? There were also framed letters of appreciation from the San Francisco Symphony and the Modern Art Museum thanking him for his three years of service on their boards.

While there were no pictures of Emma and Edward on Julie's wall, there were several photos of a young girl who must've been eight or nine-years-old. Some pictures of her doing ballet and others of her on horseback. The kid had her father's pinched mouth. So there was an ex-Mrs. Phelan out there somewhere getting alimony and child-support.

I couldn't stop thinking about the incident in the garage that morning, and the more I considered it—along with the view, Julie's certificates and his trophy wife—the more curious I became about this strange bird. I picked up the phone and called my apartment.

"Shark Attack dot com," my brother answered, sounding surprised to be getting a ring.

"You think you can break out of your meeting to look something up for me?"

———

"You have no idea who this guy is, do you?" Stevie asked when I got home.

"I know he must be pretty rich, otherwise he couldn't afford to be such a dick."

"Do you really want to know?"

"Why wouldn't I?"

"Ignorance is bliss," my brother said. "You ever heard of Michael Milken and Ivan Boesky in the 80's?"

I knew Boesky had been an investment banker who used to go into restaurants and order the entire menu so he could taste each entrée to see which one he liked the best. He ended up getting busted by the SEC for insider trading. Milken was the greedhead "Junk Bond King" who sank the Drexel Burnham brokerage firm in the late 80's, almost taking the U.S. economy down with him. He was eventually charged with almost a hundred counts of racketeering and securities fraud. Julie had apparently come up the ranks with these guys, but managed to avoid their fall from grace.

"Guess how much your man's firm is worth?" Stevie asked.

"What do you mean, 'worth'?"

"How much money they've got under management."

"I dunno. 500 million."

"Try fourteen billion."

"*Dollars*?"

"I'm guessing your guy is worth at least half a billion dollars personally. Probably a cool billion."

"I guess he *can* afford to be a prick."

"It helps that he's connected." Stevie named a handful of Fortune 500 companies on whose boards of directors Julie served. He was also hooked into the GOP, sitting on the advisory board of a D.C. think tank I'd never heard of.

"I found an article in *The New Yorker* which said this group is like the Republican's version of The Death Star. Here, look at this buncha rogues." Stevie showed me the organization's website and I recognized several bigwigs on the roster who had served under Reagan and the first George Bush. That explained the Dick Cheney resemblance, but it was still difficult for me to connect the lemon-sucker I'd seen in the garage with all these prominent—and somewhat frightening—names. Perhaps Stevie was right in asking me if I really wanted to know all this stuff. Julie could probably have me whacked by the CIA if I messed up his scones again.

But there was a bright side to this.

Now I could say that I worked for an investment banker.

Nine: Storage

I suppose the staff could have taken two weeks off while the Phelans were in Europe, but since everyone was paid by the hour, we had to find some way to justify our days. So that Monday morning, in addition to the six construction guys tearing the foyer apart, there were two nannies, a chef, an interior designer, two housekeepers, a house manager, a house-boy and a junkie on the clock.

I discovered the junkie when I was filing a stack of books in the library. I didn't knock on the door, so I was taken aback when I found a lady wearing a camouflage bandana to hold back her dreadlocks and ripped jeans getting ready to fix with a hypodermic needle. She was equally startled, and I started to back out of the room.

"No, no," she said, "close the door quick and come over here, I need your help."

I put the books down and did like she said.

"You aren't allergic to cat, are you?"

I said I didn't think so. I'd heard of Ketamine ("Special K") before, but I thought you took it in pill form, not shot it up.

"Good, then we need to pull this sofa out. He's hiding behind it. Poor thing is totally freaked out by all this hammering."

"What are you talking about?"

"Max," she said. "The cat."

"You're a vet?" I pulled the leather sofa away from the wall and saw the Siamese cowering in the corner.

"No, I'm Robby, the cat lady."

"What are you doing with that needle?"

"Max needs a shot twice a week. Bad heart." Robby talked soothingly as she reached for the cat, which tried to press itself into the wall. She grabbed him by the scruff and hoisted him over the couch. He let out a low yowl. As I pushed the sofa back into position, Robby administered the shot in the loose folds of its neck. She then set Max down in her lap and grabbed a toothbrush from her basket of medicines. The cat started purring as it allowed her to brush its teeth. Robby's basket also contained a little baggie of catnip along with the hypos and prescription bottles. She would have had a lot of fun explaining that kit if she ever got pulled over by a cop.

"Chicken liver flavored toothpaste," Robby explained. "He loves it."

"How often do you brush his teeth?"

Robby looked at me like I was dense. "Every day."

"That's more than I brush mine."

Robby thought that was funny.

"No offense, Robby. But you make a living with this?"

Robby smiled as she stroked the cat. "Honey, I make a living off four blocks up here."

Down in the office, Linda had dedicated a wicker basket to the stuff she wanted me to take care of each day. First thing every day I was supposed to check the basket. This is what I found that morning:

Tony,

IMPORTANT!!!!

WHILE THE PHELANS ARE IN EUROPE WE NEED TO CLEAR OUT THE NURSERY! ALL OF EMMA AND EDWARD'S CLOTHES THAT NO LONGER FIT NEED TO BE BOXED UP AND TAKEN TO STORAGE. THEY CANNOT STAY HERE BECAUSE THE CLOSET IN THE NURSERY IS ALREADY TOO FULL!!!

ASTRID AND PATTY ARE HERE TODAY AND BOXING THE CLOTHES UP. WHEN THEY ARE FINISHED YOU NEED TO DRIVE ASTRID TO STORAGE IN THE VOLVO BECAUSE IT HAS MORE STORAGE SPACE THAN YOUR CAR AND PUT THE BOXES AWAY IN ROOM #304. THE ZIPLOCK BAGGIE IN YOUR BASKET HAS ALL THE KEYS TO ALL THE ROOMS. DO NOT LOSE THEM!!! WE DON'T HAVE COPIES!!! THE CODE FOR THE DOORS IS #00073034*. YOU MUST HIT "#" AT THE BEGINNING AND "*" AT THE END OR THE DOORS WILL NOT OPEN.

TO GET TO STORAGE...

The memo continued for another two pages with turn by turn directions and parking instructions. I was surprised she didn't tell me to use turn signals and remember to check my tire pressure.

Linda was sitting three feet away from this basket and could've verbalized all this, but I'd already arrived at the point where I was prepared to sacrifice a few trees to avoid spending half an hour listening to her explain the drill.

On the way up to the nursery, I stopped in the kitchen to talk to Frank. He was alphabetizing the spice rack with Junko and the other housekeeper, Miss Tang.

"Hey, dude," he said. "I'm going to get us lunch. What do you want?"

"How about a steak and lobster?"

"Sure." He pulled a notepad from his apron. He dedicated maximum effort to flexing his trapezius muscle as he wrote, which made his pen move slower than a third grader's.

"I'm kidding."

"You can have a steak if you want," Frank said, looking up.

"I'm not going to make you cook me a Porterhouse."

"Dude," he said, unfurling his arm like a bodybuilder changing poses, to point at the courtyard. "Look at that sunshine. You think I wouldn't like to be out there smoking a cig and barbecuing?"

"What's everybody else having?" I asked.

"In a way," Junko said, "everybody having different lunch."

"What are you having?"

"Miss Tang and I having Sushi!"

"What about Linda?"

"Her fat ass is having a salad," Frank said.

"And the nannies?"

"Let's see," Frank checked his pad. "That little *puta* Astrid is having seared ahi and Patty wants a Turkey sandwich. So look, I have to use the barbecue anyway for the fish, why don't I get you a nice fat New York strip?"

"If you're going to twist my arm…"

"Where are you going?"

I told Frank about the storage operation.

"Dude, why don't you drop me off on the way so I don't have to drive? Get Astrid's *cula* moving. It's already 10:30."

I started upstairs.

"Hey," Frank said. "How old do you think I am?"

He was probably fifty but he had the body of a twenty-five year old. His only concession to age was his salt-and-pepper hair.

"You're thirty-eight," I said.

Frank smiled at Junko. "What did I tell you?"

"I see, I see," Junko laughed.

"Dude, I'm fifty-two."

———

There was a Safeway on the way to storage, but Frank looked at me like I was nuts when I suggested he shop there. I dropped him off outside Whole Foods.

"Don't make me wait around here too long," Frank said as he got out of the car. "This place is full of pepper-sniffing homos."

"And why does *el pajaro* insist upon shopping here, then?" Astrid asked.

"*No me chingas, puta.*"

"*Hasta la vista, maricón.*"

Astrid bitched about the Phelans for the rest of the drive.

"Do you know about the kids?" she asked.

I shook my head.

"You speak Spanish, yes?"

"*Claro que si,*" I responded.

"*Vamos a hablar en Español,*" she said.

"Losing the words?" I asked in Spanish.

Astrid gave me a serious look and gestured to the dashboard of the Volvo.

"I think they record everything," she whispered. I thought about telling Astrid that speaking a foreign language didn't seem like a very foolproof way of foiling bugs. I mean, if they went to the trouble to wire the car, what would stop them from hiring a translator to decipher the tapes?

My Spanish was pretty good, but Astrid had an unfamiliar Argentine accent, so I wasn't sure I got everything straight. It sure sounded like I was missing something.

The reason Bailey looked so fly so soon after having twins was because the babies had been adopted. But I don't think "adopted" is what Astrid said. What she said translated to "created", but I guess that could also apply to adoption. After the baby talk, she went on about Bailey and Julie's terrible relationship; how Bailey was out all night, every night, and Julie insisted upon being in bed by nine o'clock. That would explain why Bailey was such a late riser.

Astrid continued jabbering after we'd parked at the huge storage warehouse by the freeway. A bum wandered into the garage and tapped on my window. I rolled it down and told him I didn't have any change. I wondered if there'd always been as many panhandlers in the city, or if they were just following the cash like everyone else. If there was a stoplight in town that didn't have some dude standing there with a cardboard plea and a shopping cart laden with all his possessions, then I hadn't stopped at it. One bum even made the newspaper with his Sparechange.com sign. In the article the guy said he'd been getting dollar bills instead of quarters with that one. Probably had a business plan, too. Even the panhandlers were getting rich in 1999.

By opening my door, I conveyed to Astrid that our employee gossip session was over, but she kept ragging Bailey as I tried to figure out how to get through the storage facility's first security door. I also had to punch in a code to get into the elevator. We finally made it to the third floor with five boxes of baby clothes loaded onto a cart. I pulled the Ziplock full of keys from my coat pocket, and only then did I realize that there were a dozen of them in the bag. The Phelans had rented twelve different rooms, practically all the storage units in that wing of the building. I unlocked the roll-up door to the baby room. It was less than half full of clothes, strollers and toys.

Astrid rummaged through the boxes. "So many babies who could use these clothes and they just sit here in this room. *Que lastima.*" She threw her shoulders back. "We should take these boxes to the Salvation Army!" she declared.

"Sounds good to me," I said. "Which ones need to go?"

Astrid giggled. "Oh, no. We would get caught."

"You really think they're that on the ball?"

Astrid thought about that for a moment before turning to me with a playful smile. "You have all the keys?" she asked. "Let's open another room!"

I told her that we were late to pick up Frank.

She clapped her hands. "Yes, yes! Let's open another room!"

I figured one more couldn't hurt.

"Okay, pick a number…" I looked at the keys in the bag. "…between two and fourteen."

Astrid walked down the hall, running her hand along the corrugated doors. She stopped in front of room 310. I keyed the padlock and yanked up the roll door. The room was empty. What a waste of $650 a month, the rate I'd seen downstairs for one of these "climate-controlled" rooms. I started towards the elevator, but Astrid yelped that it didn't count since it was empty. She moved down the line to 305. That room was full of lamps: brass, ceramic, antique, modern and standing. Even though there were forty or fifty pieces, the lamps could have easily fit in with the boxes of baby clothes. Astrid made a circuit of the room like she was shopping, and I could see her sizing up a couple Tiffany jobs to see how they'd look in her apartment. I told her we had to go.

"One more?" she asked as I rolled the door down. I was tempted myself to see what else was stored in there, but I was sure Frank was waiting in the grocery store parking lot with my steak. I told her we'd look next time.

"Such a shame," she sighed as we rode down the elevator.

Back at the Whole Foods, Frank was smoking a cigarette with six grocery bags at his feet. He crushed the butt under the heel of his tennis shoe and loaded the sacks into the Volvo. "Am I glad to see you two," he said. "I just got propositioned by some old homo to perform an unnatural act behind that Dumpster."

Back at the house we had a staff luncheon. Astrid, emboldened by her foray into the storage rooms, suggested that we eat at the long dining room table, but everyone else balked. Even with the Phelans on another continent, the staff wasn't taking any chances. Instead, we ate in the breakfast nook, six people packed in eating five different kinds of lunch (Frank mixed himself a protein shake). Frank left the top half of the saloon door to the courtyard open so the cool May breeze could blow through, and Linda turned on the stereo to drown out the hammering of the construction guys. The food was good, but the conversation stilted. After all, what did any of us have in common besides our employer? Our mutual guilt, I suppose. I think we all felt a little corrupt feasting on the company time and dime. But as I cut into my inch-thick steak, I consoled myself with the fact that Julie could afford it.

———

My task that afternoon was to drive Linda to traffic court. I guess she felt it was safe for her to abandon her post by the phone now that it was midnight in London. Linda justified requisitioning me as her chauffeur by saying there was no parking near the courthouse, and that if I drove it would shave an hour off her expedition. She left Frank and Junko in charge, but told them not to pick up the phone.

"But if it's me," she said, "I'll call and let the phone ring twice. Then I'll hang up and let it ring twice again, hang up and then call right back." These were the days before caller i.d.

"So I pick it up after three rings?" Frank asked.

"No! After three times of two rings."

"Okay," Frank picked up a pad of paper. "Pick up after three rings, two times and tell Julie you're getting off with a vibrator in his bed."

"*Frank!*"

"I'm just screwing with you. Don't worry."

"In a way, don't pick up phone," Junko said and walked out of the kitchen with her feather duster.

On the way downtown, Linda force-fed me her life story. After getting a divorce from her college sweetheart, she moved to L.A. where she started working as a personal assistant. She rattled off the names of famous actors she'd been employed by and a story about hanging out on the set with Dustin Hoffman during the shooting of *Ishtar*, which might've been one of the reasons it bombed at the box office. The Phelans' offer came in at the same time as a position with 20th Century Fox opened up, but she wanted to get out of Hollywood and away from all the crazies. Besides, the Phelans offered more money than the studio. In retrospect, she thought she might have made the wrong decision; Julie was a tyrant and Bailey acted just like the childish Hollywood actresses she'd been trying to escape.

She kept this monologue going throughout the ride, and when I double parked in front of the dry cleaners, Linda was in the middle of a story about the date she'd had with an "English aristocrat" who didn't know how to do anything useful because he was gentry. I was thankful to get out of the car with my stuffed pillowcases. (Dry cleaning was still a daily errand even with the Phelans out of town. Junko was sending out every towel and washcloth that week.) When I returned three minutes later, Linda picked up exactly where she'd left of. It was like this:

"…and then I asked if he could maybe just light the barbe—"

Get out of car, drop off towels.

"—cue. And he's says that he doesn't know how because he's always had somebody to do it for him. Besides, they don't barbecue in England. I swear, the men in this city. Either they're gay or they can't tie their own shoelaces. At least in L.A. the guys would fake it. I'd be better off flying down there for dates twice a week." Linda gave me another one of those weird looks. "You know what I mean?"

Traffic court looked like an oasis by the time we arrived. Linda handed me a pager and said she'd beep me when she was through. I bought a newspaper and enjoyed the peaceful sounds of a utility crew tearing apart a sidewalk with jackhammers.

"And in L.A. at least they have the decency to set up valet parking everywhere," she said when I picked her up. "I swear, this city is killing me."

During the drive back to the house, Linda switched over to shop talk and mentioned that she was leaving for Spain in a week and would be gone for two months. The Phelans would be out of town for most of the summer, so she figured she could afford not to be there. Still, she was going to hire a replacement for herself.

I spent the rest of my day making new labels for the basement cabinets, picked up cat food and more kitty grass, ran around like a valet moving the Phelans' cars to avoid street sweeping tickets (the construction guys were using the garage for their tools), shredded some old employee time sheets and set the time on the kitchen VCR for Junko. I also made five, 89-page copies of a book called *How to Sell on the Internet*, which Linda said I was supposed to deliver to Bailey's studio when I came back on Friday. I wanted to ask Linda what the studio was all about, but figured my eardrums would rupture if I heard another sentence from her that day.

Ten: Marina Boys & Marin Locs

I WENT TO THE GIANTS game with my boys Collins and Riley on a Thursday night, which guaranteed Friday would be my first day in the office with a hangover. The Giants were playing the L.A. Dodgers, which guaranteed a heated baseball game. I knew Riley and Collins from my college years, and they were your prototypical hard drinking, Dodger-hating, San Fran natives. Both had season tickets that had been handed down from generation to generation, but this year had started off under a cloud because the Giants had moved from Candlestick Park to Pac Bell Stadium. Up until that season, games had been held ten miles south of the city at a brutal concrete bowl whipped by the freezing winds off the Bay, affectionately known as "The 'Stick". Candlestick had attracted a distinctly working class element, partially due to the quasi-ghetto that surrounded it. That year however, Barry Bonds and his teammates were whacking homers out of the shiny new Pacific Bell stadium, which had been erected on the waterfront a few blocks from downtown. The land the new stadium stood on had previously been occupied by wharves and warehouses, but as soon as the site was designated, a forest of shiny condos and office buildings sprung up around it. The athletic gentrification wiped out most of the old time bars, but the Boondocks was an exception. It had been a fishermen's hangout when the wharf was still active, and years after the last mackerel boat had docked, it still smelled of moldy boots and turpentine. While most of the game crowd packed into the swankier places like Momo's, which was right across the street from the new stadium, Collins and Riley insisted upon taking their pre-game refreshment at the Boodocks with the other die-hards, who drank draft beer and played $2 Hot Spot lotto games until first pitch. But even the Boondocks was on its way out. Property values around the ballpark had risen so much that the bar owners could no longer keep up with their taxes while selling cheap Pabst Blue Ribbon and frozen fish sticks.

Every surface inside Pac Bell had been branded with some dot.com's trademark, right down to the cup holders attached to the seats. But the most insidious amenity of the new stadium was the Club Level, a glassed-in concourse which was as sterile as an airport terminal. There were several bars and restaurants inside this members-only area, which relegated the game into background noise as the Marina Boys and Young Turks swapped business cards and bindles of cocaine while charging vodka Red Bulls to their corporate AmEx cards. With the game simulcast on TV's every fifteen feet, it was easy to forget that there was actual play happening within heckling distance.

Sitting in our outfield seats under the giant neon Coke bottle, Riley and Collins would begin every other sentence with the phrase, "Back at the 'Stick…"

"Back at the 'Stick, you wore a Dodgers jacket like that and the gutters woulda been runnin' with blood!" Collins barked upon seeing a pair of yuppies in L.A.-blue walk past our seats unmolested. "If I was sure none of my students were here, I'd rip that shit right off their backs!"

Collins was a grade school teacher.

"Fuckin' Tommy Lasorda could sit in the stands now and nobody would knife the bum," Riley added. "Fucking terrible. Get that shit outta here." Riley was a stockbroker. The two of them made kind of a Mutt and Jeff team as Collins was 5'11" while Riley stood 6'4". Stevie's girlfriend had dubbed them "the barking seals" for the way they carried on in their eternally hoarse voices.

"You do so much as boo the other team these days and fifteen fuckin' ushers show up to kick you out," Collins complained. "God, I miss the 'Stick," he added wistfully.

That night the Giants whipped up on the Dodgers, and we decided to extend the night with postgame drinks. As we were headed out of the stadium, we spotted a friend named Larry and a couple of his dot.com associates.

"How was the fuckin' Club Level, you fag?" Collins said by way of greeting.

"They put enough Red Bull in your Goose?" Riles asked.

"Fuck you guys," Larry said, slapping fives all around. He was wearing jeans and a blue blazer along with penny loafers that had dimes in the slots where the pennies were supposed to go. Larry's deep secret was that he was actually a local and had gone to San Rafael High with the guys. He was employed as a Vice President for Business Development at an e-commerce operation in Palo Alto. Larry had so much faith in his stock options going ballistic when the company had its IPO that he'd deferred his entire salary. That explained why he was still living in his grandmother's basement in San Rafael. According to Collins and Riley, Larry had been avoiding them as of late in case they decided to blow his cover. As we spoke to him outside the ballpark, Larry edged us away from his waiting co-workers. "Where are you drunks headed?" he asked.

"Figure we'll hit up the Trad'r for a scorp," Colls said. "You want to come along?"

"You guys need to find a new bar," Larry laughed. "I put the screws to every good-looking chick in there five years ago. My buddy's got a party going at Mas Sake. I could probably get you in if you had shirts with buttons." Mas Sake was a sushi joint in the Marina that was exceedingly popular with the Young Turks.

"Fuck Mas Sake!" Riles shouted.

Larry's cell phone buzzed. "Suit yourself," he said, checking the number. "But there's going to be some seriously nice ass down there."

"Yeah, but are there gonna be any girls?" Collins asked.

"Nice one," Larry said as he headed back over to his friends, who were climbing into a Town Car.

The three of us splurged and got a taxi to the Trad'r.

The Trad'r Sam is allegedly the oldest continuously operating tiki bar in the country, which says less about its pedigree and more about its condition. Located deep in the Richmond District and walking distance from all of our apartments, the Trad'r was the only bar in the neighborhood that wasn't an Irish pub or a Karaoke palace. Bamboo-framed nooks were arranged around the horseshoe bar bearing names like Tahiti and Samoa. There used to be thatch screens separating these "Islands," but they'd all been torn down long before we started going there. The cushions on the bamboo furniture spilled foam shreds and the carpet was so threadbare that you could see the concrete foundation. Riley and I established a beachhead in Hawaii while Collins ordered a scorpion bowl—the house specialty that combined a splash of every liquor behind the bar, which was then churned to a froth in a blender. They served the concoction in a large plastic salad-bar bowl, with miniature umbrellas hung on the rim for authenticity. We each got our own straw and took turns sucking it down.

"I told you my old man still has that job for you if you want it," Collins said, swiping his lip with the back of his hand.

"In Vallejo? I don't want to be making that kind of commute every day."

"It's better than hauling some dude's shit-stained underwear to the dry cleaners," Riley pointed out.

"Sheets," I corrected.

"Give us a break," Collins said. "That's a total bitch job."

"Eighteen bucks an hour," I said.

"So what?" Collins scoffed. "Taking care of kitty cats and groceries all day?"

"The only excuse to have that job is if you're planning on spearing the wife," Riley added. "Otherwise, you gotta get the fuck outta there."

"From an observer's point of view, it's pretty interesting to see how—"

"Bad the old man's socks stink?" Riley cut in. "Dude, if you want to observe laundry, get a job at a Laundromat."

Collins siphoned up the last of the scorpion bowl. "Yeah, don't give us that shit about wanting to stay there to get some kind of insight into the upper class. I'm with Riles—the only reason to hang around is if you're gonna nail the old lady. Otherwise, you spend too much time in the Pacific Heights and you'll end up like Larry."

"How's this for a reason?" I asked, slapping a couple twenty dollar bills on the sticky table. I'd received my paycheck that afternoon.

Collins and Riley looked at each other.

"Fuck it," Collins said, snatching the money off the table and heading back to the bar.

"Forty bucks still doesn't mean it's not a total homo job," Riley said.

Eleven: The Studio

I was still reeling from the postgame scorpion bowls when I walked into Linda's office the next day. The thick carpet sucked at my feet like mud, the lights burned my eyes and Linda's voice was about as welcoming as a crying baby on an airplane. I was thankful to get my assignment and get the hell out of there.

The errand was to take a cab across town to deliver paperwork and software to Bailey's studio. I was taking a taxi because after handing over the documents, I was supposed to repossess Julie's ex-wife's Mercedes SUV, which the studio employees had been using surreptitiously while Julie's ex was in Italy for the summer. Given my weakened state, I allowed myself the question, "Why?"

Linda swiveled around in her chair and told me the tale. I went into a state of shock after thirty seconds, but before zoning out I heard her say that the ex's Benz was still on Julie's insurance policy, and that he was supposed to have had a dent fixed while she was in Europe with their daughter. Before the SUV made it to the shop, Bailey had requisitioned it for the employees at her studio. They'd needed it for a weekend but they'd had it for a month. The ringing phone snapped me out of my trance, and I hightailed it out of there with the pager Linda insisted I carry, a wad of cash and one of Linda's detailed memos about how to find the studio and what to do when I got there.

When I got to the top of the Phelan's driveway, I saw my Nissan alone on the curb with a parking ticket wedged under the windshield wiper. I could hear rush of the street sweeper and the beeping of the meter maid down the block.

Hangover 2, Me 0.

The studio turned out to be a residential house in a neighborhood just south of the city. It was actually pretty close to the 'Stick, and the unkempt yards, sagging fences and abandoned vehicles lent a South Central L.A. crackhouse vibe to the area. The house was peeling paint and had iron bars installed over the blacked-out windows. As I knocked on the door, I tried to picture Bailey hanging around there in her Prada. I heard movement inside followed by people arguing about whose turn it was to get the door. Several locks clicked and the portal swung open to reveal a skinny kid about my age with tousled hair, no shirt, and wild eyes. He was wearing Adidas track pants and both nipples on his sunken chest had been pierced. This guy made me feel instantly better about my condition as he was obviously paying for the previous night with twice as much compound interest as I was. Then again, his night might not have ended yet. Marijuana fumes wafted out to the porch.

"Hey," he said. He paused a full five seconds before adding, "What's up?"

I introduced myself and the fact that I worked for the Phelans. He said his name was Jerome, but he had to think about it. I told him I was dropping off papers and picking up the Benz.

"Shit, that's today?" He turned to holler into the house. "Hey, where the fuck are the keys to Bailey's truck?" He told me to step inside because it might take a while.

I stood in the entryway, feeling very square in my khakis and polo shirt, while the kid disappeared into a back room. I heard him rifle through drawers while cursing a girl I couldn't see.

"How the fuck do I know where they are!" the unseen girl yelled back at him. "Binky drove last night! Go wake her ass up!"

While waiting for the keys, I wandered into the living room. It was packed floor to ceiling with stereo equipment and speakers. Wires had been crudely bundled with masking tape and snaked out of the living room into the dining room where they hooked into several humming computers. Black plastic trash bags covered the windows. This probably kept the light out, but also prevented any neighborhood entrepreneurs from peeking inside and seeing the high-tech bounty. There was a typed sheet posted on the wall titled "24-7djs. com House Rules." Rule number one was "No Drugs" and somebody had penned *yeah right* next to it. Rule number two was "Respect the Neighbors" and the same joker had written *'coz they sell us our drugs.*

Jerome came back with the keys, which were sticky. Just as he handed them to me there was a minor explosion somewhere in the house that caused both of us to jump. It sounded like somebody had dropped an M-80 into a toaster.

"Holy shit!" a different girl yelled from downstairs. "I just scared the fuck out of myself!"

"Female DJ night," Jerome explained. "A couple of them crashed here after the session and now I can't get them out. Bailey's idea. Classic that she and Clive aren't here to deal with it."

"Yep, that's Bailey," I said, nodding in agreement even though I had no idea who Clive was.

"She comes up with all the marvelous ideas and then Clive forces us to do the stupid shit. Then he takes off for Miami to party while we pick up the fucking pieces."

The kid suddenly realized that I wasn't a turntable jockey in my square outfit, and that I was working for Bailey because I'd come for the keys. I could see his mental tires spinning, trying to get traction.

"So, um, you work for Bailey?" Jerome asked.

"Kinda. I actually work for Mr. Phelan."

"Really?" Jerome realized he wasn't wearing a shirt and crossed his arms over his chest to cover his nipple rings. "Um, what do you do for him?"

"Security."

What little blood Jerome had been able to keep in his face drained out.

"Dude," I said, "I'm totally messing with you. I'm Bailey's runner."

Jerome started breathing again.

I told him to have good weekend and let myself out. I found the SUV parked on a steep street a block away, doors unlocked, headlights on, parking brake not set, and tires not blocked to the curb. The interior was strewn with cassette tapes, CD jewel cases and half-filled juice bottles. The gas gauge was below empty.

I gassed up at the first station I could find before driving downtown and getting purposely stuck in the mid-day traffic on Market Street. I popped in one of the mix tapes and slid the sunroof open. Linda could page me if she needed something.

Mercifully, I got to spend the rest of the day delivering the ex's SUV to the body shop. Usually, taking the car to the garage is one of my least favorite ordeals, but when it's not your car and you're not paying for the repairs, and—best of all—you're being *paid* for all the time you waste sitting around the shop reading two-month-old *People* magazines, the operation takes on a whole new dimension. On the way to the shop, I stopped by the apartment and picked up Stevie so he could enjoy the afternoon through the sunroof. We took the longest possible route to the body shop, playing the mix tapes and beeping the horn at hot chicks. The mix tapes were all very up-tempo dance stuff that probably only sounded good when you were tripping your balls off on ecstasy.

To kill more of the day, we stopped at a coin car wash and cleaned the SUV's interior before taking it to the shop. Both of the seatback pockets in the rear were filled with sand and seashells. We also discovered six crumpled parking tickets in the glovebox.

From the garage we walked a few blocks before catching a cab, timing it so that I'd get back to the house right around quitting time. Stevie waited on the sidewalk while I punched out.

"I don't know why you're bitching and moaning so much," my brother said as we drove my car back to the apartment. All afternoon I'd been telling him about Collins and Riley giving me grief for taking Julie's sheets to the dry cleaner. The truth was that I'd started feeling pretty silly about being a professional errand runner when there were so many other golden options out there. Take Bailey's studio, for example.

"You just got paid sixty bucks to drop a car off at a body shop," my brother continued.

"Before taxes," I reminded him.

"Whatever. Would you really rather be stuck in some cube staring at a computer with a boss breathing down your neck?"

"Depends on the stock option package."

"If I was you, I'd ride this one out and see what happens. You can always get a desk job."

"But you can't always get a job as an $18-an-hour lackey, right?"

"Exactly."

Twelve: Reinforcements

A YOUNG WOMAN NAMED WANDA would fill in as house manager while Linda vacationed in Spain, and I saw immediately that Wanda was going to be a problem. 28-years-old, about 5'6", bleach blonde and constructed in the classic hourglass format—big breasts and an equally large (but apparently firm) posterior separated by a slim waist. Wanda's look was topped off with bright red lips and wicked blue eyes.

"Nice to meet you," I said upon meeting her, trying to keep my eyes in the right place.

"Oh," Wanda said huskily, "the pleasure is all mine." There was so much sexual static coming off her that I thought for a moment that she might be a man dressed in drag.

Linda sat Wanda and me down in the office for a thorough review of our duties in her extended absence. To wit, we spent fifteen minutes on how to properly restock the drinks, ten minutes on avoiding fruit decay, half an hour on shelving auction catalogues and magazines, and a full hour on sorting the mail. She also gave us codes for the alarm system, which seemed like a very bad thing. Wanda played along like a professional, taking notes and asking questions throughout the shakedown, but when I peeked at her notepad I saw that it was full of sketches of big loopy hearts and buxom women. We then had to sit around until the phone rang so Linda could demonstrate the finer points of phone answering. After she'd covered all that ground, Linda gave me a sheaf of papers to shred while she taught Wanda how to make wire transfers in and out of the Phelan's accounts.

Most of the documents were old receipts which didn't seem very interesting or shred-worthy, but then I came upon a multiple page report titled "Household Expenses 01/99 – 03/99." The review detailed every domestic expense incurred that quarter, including, but not limited to, gardener, cat care, alarm system, car washing, interior decorating, food, drinks, gifts, and staff. I was about to feed the last page into the shredder when I saw the grand total: $1,534,311. I re-read the final tally to make sure I'd seen it correctly. *A million and a half dollars! For three months?* No wonder Julie wanted this document destroyed. For a guy who framed a $30 college scholarship, seeing something like this must've been akin to food poisoning.

As I continued shredding papers, I realized that it was time to ask for a raise.

———

I drove out to Linda's place in San Rafael to take her to the airport in Bailey's BMW, so I could then take the car into the shop for a tune-up before the lady of the manor got back from Europe. S.F. was lousy with BMWs that season and this was the only day Linda could schedule an appointment. It was amazing to see the proliferation of luxury rides in the city over just one year. There had always been a lot of nice cars around, but with the stock market soaring on IPO fairy dust, every other car was European. I remember when my dad had a BMW back in 1984 and the cool thing to do was to flick your headlights when you saw another guy driving one. Well, if you did that in S.F. in 1999, you'd need a strobe light on your grille to stay friendly. I was rather content behind the wheel of Bailey's 740 as I popped a Nirvana CD into the stereo and crossed the Golden Gate Bridge to Linda's condo in San Rafael. I was able to get the car up to 90 mph on the 101 and wasn't too concerned about crashing because the previous week Linda had added my name to the insurance policy covering all the Phelan vehicles.

Linda had enough luggage to give five bellboys hernias, and she kept remembering important things to impart to me about running the Phelan's estate in her absence. She was as nervous as a parent leaving the house with the kids, and I suppose I would've been as well by the looks of me and Wanda. It really was weird to think that this sexpot Wanda and I were going to be at the helm of a multi-million dollar enterprise for the rest of the summer. With that in mind, I was grateful Linda had hired Wanda so that I'd have at least one scapegoat higher up the chain of command than myself. Linda told me seven times to call her day or night in Madrid if I had any questions. I understood her anxiety because among the documents I'd shredded earlier that week were a batch of Linda's old timesheets. She'd been getting $35 an hour the previous year, so she must've been pulling down at least $40 now. Assuming she worked forty hours a week, that meant she was earning over eighty grand a year. I would have been nervous leaving a cash cow like that, too.

I unloaded Linda at the international terminal and gave her a hug goodbye, mostly because I was just so damn happy not to have to hear her voice until September. She stood there for a few moments, muttering, "What else? What else?" She was still standing there talking to herself when I drove away from the curb.

Wanda shuttled me back to the BMW shop later that day when the car was ready to be picked up. It turned out that she was also a candidate from The Perfect Fit and had scored this choice gig because she was an old friend of Clarissa's. Bailey's original plan had been for *me* to take charge for the remainder of the summer, but a week before her departure, Linda got freaked out that I wasn't qualified to handle the whole she-bang. They did a hasty search and came up with Wanda. Bailey interviewed her over the phone from Paris and hired her. As Wanda chatted about her fondness for tequila and samba dancing, I started to wonder exactly what kind of qualifications the Phelans specified when they put their job postings in with the temp agency. I wouldn't have hired Wanda and me to manage a Circle K. Yet there we were—possessors of keys, security codes, insurance, and banking information. I'd only been on the job for two months.

"Oh God," Wanda said, firing up another Marlboro 100 Light. "I took the *best* ecstasy last night."

Thirteen: Welcome Home

THE PHELANS WERE DUE THE following afternoon, but the house was still a work in progress. The main problem was that the construction guys hadn't finished putting the foyer back together. I couldn't even tell what they'd done because the room looked the same as when they'd first taken their saws to it. At any rate, they were busy with last-minute electrical touches and getting their scaffolding broken down. Two lighting engineers were then going to focus the new lights, and until they cleared out we couldn't bring the Persian carpet and furniture up from the garage and then replace the BMWs in their proper spots. The vehicles and furniture were my two tasks for the day, and until the entryway was clear all I could do was sit around and read magazines. I wasn't complaining about that, but as the day wore on, I started to get nervous. The last thing I wanted was to be in the process of putting the place back together when Julie walked in the door.

The fact that Wanda, Junko, and Frank were losing their minds didn't help matters. Wanda had seemed pretty nonchalant the previous day about meeting her new bosses, but now she was scurrying around the house making heart-shaped "Welcome Home" signs and hanging them on all the door handles, including the portal to Julie's lair on the fourth floor. I got rid of that one when Wanda wasn't looking. Downstairs, the computer was tuned to the Virgin Atlantic web site so we could track the Phelan's flight over the North Pole. Seeing that red line creep towards S.F. added to the general unease. Wanda decided that the house needed flowers. She thrust $200 into my hand.

"Um…" I said, looking at the crisp bills. "Any particular kind of flowers?"

"Oh shit," Wanda said. "Clarissa told me about you."

"Told you what?" I asked.

Wanda snatched the money from my hand. "Don't worry," she called over her shoulder as she hustled out of the office. "I won't tell anyone."

"Tell anyone what?!" I hollered after her. Wanda ran out the service entrance without responding.

Frank was in the process of fixing an elaborate homecoming meal and, in order to make sure he was getting it right, he'd had me fax a menu to London the previous night so the Phelans could check off the dishes they wanted. The fax never came back, and Frank, who had been working there for a year, couldn't seem to remember what they liked to eat.

"If you just came back from London," he asked me, "what would you want for dinner?"

"A pizza."

"Fuck, dude, I can't cook them a pizza! You sure there's no fax downstairs?"

"I just checked, Frank. How about some fish? A nice piece of salmon?"

"I dunno, don't they eat a lot of fish n' chips in England?"

"That and pudding. How about some steaks?"

"You think?"

"No, maybe not. Aren't they having that mad cow disease over there right now?"

Wrong thing to say to Frank. Guy looked like he was going to faint. I left him in the kitchen with six cookbooks open on the counter.

Junko, meanwhile, was standing in the living room with her vacuum watching the construction guys pack up their gear. She had the rest of the house ship-shape, but the foyer was going to need some work. When I said I was going out to get some sandwiches, she grabbed me by the arm.

"In a way, I need you here to help with furniture."

And downstairs, huddled over the computer screen featuring the Phelan's flight, was Gladys, the house accountant. Gladys was a skinny Taiwanese lady who handled all the Phelan's bills and the staff payroll. I'd only met her the previous Friday because up until then she'd done all her work off-site. Bailey and Linda had decided she should start coming in on Fridays to pick up that week's bills, hand out the paychecks and have a weekly meeting with Bailey so that she could approve and sign all the checks that needed to go out. She'd also make sure Wanda and I didn't get too loose with the finances in Linda's absence. Gladys was 35-years-old with the nervous energy of a squirrel and an absolute terror of Julie. When I'd met her the previous Friday she'd asked me twice if Julie was *really* in Europe. The first thing she did upon coming through the service entrance every Friday was peek in the garage.

"Three week ago," she explained in her shaky English, "I come in early to leave check for everybody, and I look in garage to see if Julie home. His car gone, so I go upstairs to kitchen to get bagel and I'm standing by toaster when he walk into kitchen in his robe! I swear I have heart attack! I forget bagel and run downstairs."

I told the accountant that if she was this nervous, she should just go home. She was practically in tears when she said she had to have Bailey sign a stack of checks so she could put them in the mail. She said that some of the bills were going to be past due if she didn't get them out that day.

"Only thing Julie tells me when I interview for job. No past due bill! And he very serious." She rubbed her fingers together. "You no play around with man like Julie." The flight line on the computer screen inched forward. Gladys sprang out of her seat. "Oh my God! They just cross Canadian border! Oh God, what if Julie want to talk to me?!" The phone rang and Gladys dashed into the laundry room.

Wanda was on the line, asking me to come out to help her with the flowers. Her Saab looked like someone had set off a tulip bomb in the backseat.

Astrid and Patty arrived at one o'clock to take over for the four inbound nannies just as the lighting engineers finished and the builders removed the last of the scaffolding. Junko went into Hirohito mode, and we had everything back in place by the time Gladys came upstairs to announce that the Phelan's plane had landed. Junko and Miss Tang did one last run through the house, tweaking flowers and fluffing pillows, while I took both BMWs to the gas station and topped off the tanks with super unleaded. Frank had decided upon a whole roasted chicken, parmesan herb crusted lamb chops, tuna nicoise and a cucumber tomato salad. He had it laid out beautifully on the kitchen counter. For once he wouldn't let me sample anything.

We then stood around the kitchen (except for Gladys, who continued to hide out in the basement) waiting for the hurricane to arrive. I ducked into the bathroom to check my hair and tuck in my polo shirt.

We heard them before the doorbell rang, Emma and Edward shrieking and car doors slamming. I was debating whether to rush out and greet them or hang back and play it cool when my feet took over and propelled me out the front door. The rest of the staff was right on my heels. I came out of the courtyard to see the same limo formation as before. Julie blew past me without responding to my hello, then Bailey skipped into the house looking as if she'd just come back from the spa, not a ten-hour flight from Europe. Astrid and Patty took Edward and Emma from the very thankful Sally and Jen, who looked as if they were about to collapse. The other two nannies never even got out of the limo. Frank and I helped the drivers carry all the baggage inside while Sally and Jen went downstairs to get paychecks from Gladys. Julie disappeared to the top floor and slammed the door behind him. When I went back to the curb for more luggage, I saw Bailey pull out of the driveway in her Beamer and speed away.

Sally came outside with a handful of envelopes and ducked into the remaining limo to give them to the other nannies.

"Fired," Sally explained as the cars pulled away. Then she asked if I could give her and Jen rides home. I was happy for an excuse to get out of there.

I went back inside to get the keys for the Volvo and found Frank in the kitchen looking dejected. The Phelans hadn't touched the food. He started to pack it away in Tupperware. Upstairs in the nursery, Emma and Edward were still howling.

I drove Jen and Sally to their respective homes while they told me about the voyage and how awful it had been. Things started off badly when one of the now dismissed nannies told the customs agent at Heathrow that she was there working and proceeded to give the agent all of the Phelan's travel information, having apparently forgotten Julie's stern instructions to tell anyone who asked that they were in London on vacation so as to avoid work visa problems. The following day a crew of immigration officials "raided" the Phelan's posh apartment and the nannies had been forced to hightail it out of there with the kids while Julie threw the cops off the scent.

The kids were terrors, Julie was grumpy and Bailey was out every night at the clubs and slept all day. The only consolation was that both teams of nannies had been granted 72-hour shore leaves and plenty of spending cash by Bailey. Jen and Sally used their time off kid patrol to hit up Italy. The time off, however, was tempered by having to work for three days straight at a time.

By the time I'd taken the girls home, lugged their 200-pound bags up several flights of stairs and secured a couple hundred bucks worth of diapers and wipes, it was almost six o'clock. The house was dark and empty-looking, but, since I'd taken the Phelan's Volvo and left my key ring inside, I couldn't unlock the door to the house. I stood on the sidewalk for a few moments, not wanting to ring the bell. When I finally sucked it up and punched the doorbell, Julie came on the intercom. I explained who I was and he buzzed me in without comment. Bailey met me at the front door looking loopy. While I took the baby stuff upstairs to the nursery, she chased the cat around the new foyer. Bailey blew me a kiss as I let myself out, and I was sure she was hopped up on something. There's no way a person could be that happy coming off a flight with two screaming babies and an ultra-grouch husband.

But as I drove home, her delight made sense. I mean, what would I be acting like if I just got back from a kick-ass vacation to find my house remodeled and stocked with all my favorite food and drink? The last time I came back from a trip to Seattle I was ecstatic to find two Sprites and a frozen pizza in the freezer.

Fourteen: In The Closet

By June I was a full-time Phelan employee. Errands I was supposed to run on Monday spilled over to Tuesday, and arrangements for Wednesday were re-scheduled for Thursday. When dealing with Bailey there was no choice but to remain fluid. Appointments were canceled with regularity, meetings were missed, schedules got scrapped. The only exception to this rule was when Julie called and made a demand—he did not make requests—that superseded everything else. Ninety-percent of the time, the staff served at Bailey's pleasure, but when Julie left a sticky note on the kitchen counter or had his secretary call from his office with orders, that became Priority Number One. Still, despite his negative six personality rating, the man wasn't really that much of a pain in the ass. All he really wanted from his staff was for us to keep his special Trad'r Joe's oat cereal in the cupboard, his shirts folded in boxes from the French laundry and that we stay the hell out of his way.

I arranged my work schedule (a la Frank and Gladys the accountant) to avoid Julie. I showed up at eight in the morning, knowing he left for the office at 7:45. I tried to vacate the house no later than 5:30 because he got home from the office at 5:45. It worked out so that I only saw the master of the house once or twice a week, and usually it was just the back of his balding head as he came into the laundry room from the garage and headed upstairs. If he wanted something specific from me—like for me to program his VCR—he'd leave a Post-It note in the kitchen.

The rest of the staff wasn't quite so sanguine when it came to the lord of the manor. Gladys continued to tremble at the possibility of a finance charge, Frank was convinced that he was going to get fired for making a dish that offended Julie's taste buds (despite the fact that the chef faxed a menu to Julie's office every weekday so that the boss could check off the items he wanted), and the nannies hustled the babies into the nursery closet when they started crying lest Julie think they were being abused. At first Wanda had tried to seduce Mistah Phelan with sultry voices and her heaving chest, but he remained oblivious. Wanda kept hurling her useless flirts like apples against a concrete wall, and then, after two weeks of no acknowledgment from Julie, Wanda got scared; any man who didn't stare at her marvelous tits was something to be feared.

Junko was the most comfortable around him because she had worked for the man for ten years. She knew better than anyone else (including either of his wives) what Julie wanted in his cabinets, closets, and refrigerator. So I quickly learned that the real boss of the house during the day wasn't Bailey. It sure as hell wasn't Wanda. The daytime boss was Junko.

The head housekeeper never felt safe unless there were four times as many Snapples in the house as could be consumed over a long weekend. Same for every other sundry item: paper towels, toilet paper, detergent, cat food, paper coffee cups, sugar cubes, sponges, Tupperware containers, clean sheets, bottled water, kitty grass, milk, Trad'r Joe cereal, cottage cheese (another of Julie's favorites), hand soap, light bulbs, paper napkins. All that trivial junk normal people run out of and have to make a trip to the corner store for, Junko needed to have stored in the tall white cabinets in the laundry room. I knew that if there was ever a major earthquake in S.F., I would head straight over to the Phelan's and loot their pantry.

Even though I appreciated her motivation, Junko still drove me bonkers with her specific requests. Like the scones and jam I bought on the first run for her, if they weren't the right brand, the right size and from the right store, they got bounced. If I brought home coffee cups for Julie to take with him when he drove to work that were two ounces too large, she made me take them back. If the lids for the coffee cups didn't have the correct sipping aperture, she made me take them back. If the paper napkins were square and two-ply, I had to return them and get ones that were rectangular and three-ply. If I bought sugar packets instead of sugar cubes, she sent my ass back to the store.

I would purposely buy twice as much of everything so as to save me having to make a trip to places like Trad'r Joe's every week. The Trad'r Joe's was a total nightmare. They had a parking lot that fit twenty cars and there were always fifty neo-hippies in their Saabs and Volkswagens trying to get in. So if I happened to be driving past Trad'r Joe's on the way to another errand and saw there was no bottleneck in the parking lot, I'd swing in and buy five boxes of Julie's cereal plus ten six-packs of the Key Lime soda Junko was always asking for.

Equally elusive were the scones. To solve that one I finally gave the bakery woman at Whole Foods twenty bucks so that she'd put aside five packs of the regular flavor ones when they came in. I gave her my pager number so I could get them fresh.

I'd come back to the house and lay these provisions at Junko's feet, thinking that it would keep her off my ass for a couple weeks and maybe even blow her circuits trying to stash the stuff. Alas, she was always able to salt the stuff away in every little nook and cranny like some sort of deranged packrat.

———

Bailey, on the other hand, didn't seem to know anything about what was going on in her house. If she opened the refrigerator and found that there was no more low-fat raspberry yogurt, she'd act genuinely surprised and say, "Hey, there's no low-fat raspberry yogurt in here." Frank would overhear Bailey's puzzlement and quietly tell Junko, who would then dispatch me to the grocery store to buy ten yogurts. Bailey was spacey like that, almost as if she thought things appeared magically and then just as mysteriously disappeared. If she cared about the how or why, she didn't say anything about it.

About the only thing that did get to Bailey was that she had to make what she called the "Walk of Shame" every morning. When she married Julie, she decided that the master bedroom closet wasn't big enough for the two of them, so she let him have the one upstairs and moved all her shoes and clothes into a massive basement storage room that she had converted into a walk-in closet. An adjacent room was filled with accessories and purses. She'd had a lock installed so nobody could walk in on her while she was changing. Although no one ever specifically told me not to disturb her while she was in the closet, it was an unspoken rule around the house that if the closet door was closed, Bailey was out of pocket until it opened up. The same mandate applied to Julie's hideout on the top floor.

Luxurious as a walk-in closet might seem, the arrangement meant that Bailey had to navigate the kitchen bottleneck of household servants in order to get dressed. Making it even worse was the fact that everyone always needed to talk to Bailey about something. You'd think with ten people working for you full time you'd never have to make a decision, but the opposite was true. Junko and Frank needed to know if there were dinner guests coming over, Wanda had to ask about RSVP-ing for parties and doctor's appointments, Gladys needed her to sign checks, nannies needed to know if she wanted to spend time with Emma and Edward before they took the kids to the park. Bailey put off all her decisions until the last minute, and since you couldn't very well chose a dinner menu for guests or schedule her for a pap smear without her okay, there were always staff members chasing her around the house with questions. Everyone knew that if you waited for an opportune time to ask Bailey something, she would disappear on you. Who knows where she went, but the garage was only ten feet from her closet and, more often than not, once she was dressed, the next time you'd see her she'd be tearing out of the driveway in her BMW. The end result of all this was that every morning Bailey was bombarded with questions while half-naked and groggy—and this directly contributed to the fact that she habitually forgot about things that she'd okay'ed.

Once she'd escaped the house, you could try to hit her on the cell phone, which was usually dead despite the fact that I kept two fully-charged spare batteries on her desk and one in the glove box of her car. This touch-and-go communication drove Linda mad and it was starting to get to Wanda as well. I thought it was ridiculous to care so much about talking to the woman. Let her be free, I thought. She'd have to come home to change shoes at some point, wouldn't she?

Every few weeks (usually after she'd managed to attend a couple of her psychiatric appointments in a row) Bailey would decide that her life needed more order. She'd send me to Computer World for a new scheduling program and try to get it working. She usually did these computer experiments at two or three in the morning. While Julie left Post-It notes for what he wanted done, Bailey left time-coded messages on a dedicated voicemail. I could tell there was going to be a spate of late-night messages on the phone for me if there was a half-empty bottle of Cakebread chardonnay on Bailey's desk when I arrived in the morning. At midnight she'd leave chipper new directives for me about how to take care of her merchandise returns; around 2 am she'd relay a rambling list of new organic ingredients for me to pass along to Frank; at 2:45 am she'd boozily pontificate improved methods for the house manager to contact her via carrier pigeons.

The following day we'd go over the schedule with a hungover Bailey and see huge blocks dedicated to "Family Time," "Working Out" with her trainer and "Learning Italian." The whole thing looked great on paper, but without fail it was shot to hell within three days and we were back to chasing a robed Bailey around the house.

Still, the house had a rather pleasant vibe when Bailey decided to stay home and adhere to her new directives. Sure, she was scatterbrained and left a wake of unfinished projects and half-consumed drinks in her path (Bailey never finished any beverage whether it be wine, water, espresso, or juice), but sometimes when she put in a day at the house you actually got things settled. These in-house days always coincided with Julie being on a trip.

I got swept up into one of Bailey's in-house projects the week she returned from Europe. That afternoon our priority was re-arranging her shoe rack, and we spent two hours sitting on the floor of her footwear annex inserting shoehorns and separating pumps from loafers. An old girlfriend once told me that no self-respecting woman had less than ten pairs of black shoes. Bailey had thirty-six. Gucci, Prada, Michael Kors, Jimmy Choo, Christian Louboutin. All told, she must've had a hundred thousand dollars' worth of kicks. And who knew what she had in storage.

She queued up a Buddha Bar compilation CD on the closet's Bose stereo after ordering Wanda to hold all her calls and closing the door. Bailey referred to new purchases as "fresh kill," and she looked even younger than usual sitting Indian style on the floor of her closet in her stretch pants and a hoodie sweatshirt surrounded by all the finery she'd bagged during her European vacation. She was having so much fun with her shoes that she told me about how her stepfather had set her up with Julie at a Christmas party. After the party Julie started calling her twice a day, every day, until she finally agreed to go on a date. They were engaged five months later and married within a year.

"You shoulda seen the rocks in the earrings Julie gave me after our second date," she said. "I was embarrassed to wear them, they were so huge."

I handed her a strappy gold sandal.

"That's the one great thing about Julie," she said.

"His taste in jewelry?"

"The fact that he's recession-proof."

"I can see that advantage."

"It almost cancels out the fact that he's one of the most boring people in the world."

I pointed out that she seemed to keep herself entertained.

Bailey placed the last pair of shoes on the rack and shot me an innocent smile. "I do my best." Her smile morphed into a more devious expression as she sat back on her heels. "Wanna see my new Prada?"

I was trying to figure out how to respond to that when Bailey popped to her feet and skipped over to a cluster of garment bags that had arrived via FedEx the previous day. She leafed through the fresh kill until she found the pencil skirt she was looking for. She unzipped her sweatshirt, revealing a lacy black bra. She tossed the hoodie onto the floor and started to wriggle out of her pants.

"I better wait outside," I said, standing up. I was thankful for my baggy khakis as my hard-on—just like Bailey's Prada—had arrived Express Mail.

Bailey paused with her stretch pants lowered to mid-thigh. Her skimpy panties matched her bra.

"What's the problem?" she asked with that devilish smile still spread across her face.

"I just don't think it's appropriate for me to be watching you change."

"Why not?" she asked, getting all innocent.

"It's just… you know… you're a good-looking woman."

Bailey yanked her pants up and started pogo-ing around the closet. "I knew it, I knew it, I knew it!" she exclaimed.

Bailey's odd reaction eased the stiffness in my groin area, but there were still signs of life down there since she hadn't bothered to put her hoodie back on.

"Knew what?" I asked.

"YOU'RE NOT GAY!"

"Whoever said I was gay?"

"Linda owes me twenty bucks!" Bailey laughed. She slipped her foot under the sweatshirt and kicked it up in the air so she could grab it. She didn't seem in too much of a hurry to put it back on, though. "Frank said you were straight right away, but Linda swore you were homo. Sally and Jen couldn't decide if you were or not. I was pretty sure, but you calling that espadrille a flip-flop sealed it." Bailey zipped herself up. "I guess two gay men in the house would've been too much."

"Who's gay?" I asked.

"You didn't know Frank was gay?"

"Really?"

"Don't tell him I told you. He'd be furious. He tries to act so macho around you to cover it up. But he knew right away that you were straight. Kind of strange to find a hetero guy who'd take a job as an errand boy. "

"I think the proper title is 'houseboy.'"

Bailey hooted. "Oh, that's even better. Definitely houseboy."

Bailey gave me a sock on the shoulder as she went to the closet door. She put her hand on the doorknob, but didn't turn it.

"Still…" she said, smiling over her shoulder. "I'm not *completely* convinced. Maybe I should go ahead and try on some of my outfits to find out for certain. If you get more excited about the Prada than me in my underwear, we'll know you're just in denial."

I tried to come up with a clever retort to that, but my tongue had taken on the dimensions of a wooden block.

Footsteps in the hallway broke the moment.

"We better get out of here," she laughed. "It's so classic, though. Here we are in the gay capital of the world and they send me a straight guy." She opened the door while I lagged behind to let my erection die down completely.

Wanda was waiting in the hallway to let Bailey know she was late for a doctor's appointment that she'd already rescheduled three times. Bailey grabbed her purse and slipped into the garage.

Wanda arched her eyebrows. "So, how was it?"

Bailey poked her head back into the laundry room. "Can you help me for a second?" she asked.

Wanda smirked as I followed Bailey into the garage.

"I've got a little shoe bonus for you," Bailey said when the door closed behind me. She handed me five hundred-dollar bills. "Our secret," she winked. She was into her car and pulling out of the driveway before I could say thanks. Even if I'd been able to express my gratitude, I didn't know what exactly I was supposed to be thankful for.

Fifteen: Dissed Jockeys

When Bailey said that she managed to keep herself entertained, she wasn't talking about stripping down in front of houseboys to confirm their sexual preference (not at that point, anyway). Most of her spare time was spent at the studio. But saying "spare time" makes it seem like she had a lot of obligations to attend to. Occasionally she'd be forced to sit through a formal event with Julie, or she'd get blindsided with guilt about ignoring her children and attend a play date with them, but other than that, if you wanted to locate Bailey, the studio was the first place to check.

As that summer went by I had to make increasingly frequent trips across town to 24-7djs.com headquarters, shuttling documents and checks. I knew Bailey was around because her car was parked outside, but I hardly ever ran into her because she kept herself off the main floor and therefore removed from the DJ hoipolloi. Despite her unseen presence, there was no doubt that 24-7djs.com was her show. I deduced from all the contracts and tax forms I delivered that my boss was bankrolling the outfit for the benefit of a British guy named Clive, code name DJ Channel.

This patronage might've made sense if DJ Channel didn't absolutely suck. Jerome, the kid over at the studio I dealt with when I made my deliveries, clued me in to his handle and I subsequently found one of his tapes in Bailey's music pile. It sounded like Lionel Ritchie getting hit by an ice cream truck. I managed to listen to it for five minutes before the blood vessels in my brain started to hemorrhage.

"If you think he's bad," Jerome hollered over the sound of two DJs spinning in the living room, "check out hers." Jerome offered me a joint, but I declined since it was only ten in the morning.

"Hers?" I shouted back.

"DJ Feelin'!"

"Who?"

"Bailey. Between you and me, she makes Clive sound like Kruder and Dorfmeister."

"Bailey? A DJ?"

"Yeah. Have you seen her studio at the house?"

I shook my head.

"It's off the garage. You should check it out."

On the way back to base I popped in a DJ Feelin' tape that Jerome gave me. For a moment I thought it was Madonna's "Like a Prayer" played underwater at 78 rpm. Upon returning to the house I went to look for the secret room. I'd never given the door much notice as it was in the back of the garage and had a "Water Main" sign on it, which had made me believe that it just led to a bunch of hoses. The door itself was small, like something out of *Alice in Wonderland*. I ducked through the portal into the 15' x 5' nook. The shelves on one wall were full of hundreds of records. There was plenty of junk along the lines of New Order and the Pet Shop Boys, but she also had some decent LPs by artists like Tricky and Massive Attack. There was a two-foot walkway between the record racks and the top-of-the-line turntables, double CD decks, CD recorder, mixing board, amplifier, dual tape player and four speakers.

I also found a half-empty package of Marlboro Lights and a pipe packed with high-grade marijuana.

The next morning, when I had her alone, I addressed Bailey as DJ Feelin'.

"Pardon me?" she asked, a nervous smile playing across her face.

I told her about Jerome's dish.

"Well, a girl's got to have a hobby," she said.

Gladys didn't think so.

Although the skinny accountant might have been frightened of Julie that was about all she was sacred of when it came to money. She came into the house on Fridays and usually spent the first hour calling up contractors and credit card companies to dispute charges. She'd buck her way up the chain of command, rattling cages all the way, over a $10 finance charge that she didn't feel was warranted. When she got off the phone from these battles, she'd smile serenely.

Bailey's studio wasn't so easily accounted for. From what I overheard in the conversations between Bailey and Gladys, 24-7djs.com ran at a hundred percent negative cash flow: all spending, no profit. Jerome had explained that the concept behind the studio was to sell records mixed by the in-house DJs over the Internet. This profit would be augmented by advertising for local clubs and music stores. Even at the peak of the dot.com madness, this was a moronic idea, especially after a couple visits to the studio during business hours, which, despite the "24-7" tag, were wildly erratic. I'd log onto the website from the home office and sometimes all I'd see on the screen was the empty living room. Occasionally and if I was lucky, I could watch a wacked-out DJ crawl across the floor in real time.

"How we supposed to deal with taxes?" Gladys wailed during her weekly budget meeting.

"I don't care," Bailey said. "Just deal with it."

"Try and write anything off?"

"Can we?"

"Not unless you let me audit! I don't understand any books over there."

"I don't want to get into that. Julie would freak."

"But how I supposed to account? You spend four-hundred thousand dollars in year and a half! For what? Nothing sold! No profit!"

"Gladys, you worry too much. Forget the write-offs. Just treat it like I threw the money into the Bay, okay?"

"Threw money into the Bay?!" Gladys asked, her eyes bulging.

"That's right. Into the Bay."

Despite Bailey's desire to keep Julie oblivious, Gladys was unable to completely bury the line item on the next quarterly expense report. Julie demanded an explanation. Gladys and Bailey called the studio employees into the home office for an interrogation the following week. Only Jerome made the trip to the Pac Heights in person, but Clive, the co-conspirator, agreed to talk via conference call. I'd met Clive once when I needed his signature on a tax form. He was a piece of rough trade with dreadlocks and a heavy Cockney accent. I suppose he was handsome in a grungy, unshaven way.

The main issue that day was how to account for $50,000 that had been charged to the company credit card over a long weekend in Miami. Jerome perched on the filing cabinet while Gladys and Bailey sat in the Herman Miller chairs.

"Look 'ere, Bail," Clive said over the speakerphone in his thick Cockney accent, "you know bloody well where that money went, so why don't you deal with Gladys and leave us the fuck alone to run the shop?"

"I'm not accusing you of anything," Bailey said, trying to calm him down. "It's just that we need to get all this straight for Gladys so she can get the books in order."

"Okay, fine. Then put down that we spent 'alf of that fifty thousand in Miami at the music conference and put down that we spent the other 'alf on studio equipment and promotion."

"But I need receipts!" Gladys hollered into the speakerphone.

"I fuckin' told you that I don't 'ave any! I thought that's why everything went on the bloody credit card!"

"I need receipts!" Gladys repeated.

"I don't fuckin' 'ave 'em!"

"How you spent $50,000 and have no receipt?"

"How do you mean? Are you saying I spent this money on myself? Bailey you better sort your girl coz she's pissing me off."

"You pissing me off!" Gladys yelled. "This my job!"

"And this is mine, innit it?! Bailey asked me to go to that fuckin' conference to publicize the company and if she don't like the way I did it, she should 'ave come along and done it proper!" Clive banged his phone on something hard, which made the speakerphone squawk with feedback.

"Clive," Bailey said, "Gladys is trying to help us."

"Well, I don't like the way she 'elps, do I? This is bollocks over the phone. Childish, the way you think you can just stop funding when it gets dodgy. You come over 'ere in person and we'll talk about it, but I ain't having it over the phone with the bloody accountant and Jerome sitting in. This is between you and me. Cheers." Clive hung up. There was silence in the room.

"That was productive," Jerome said finally.

"I so sick of this," Gladys moaned. "What is bollocks?"

"I hate to tell this to you, Bail," Jerome said, "but this is totally getting away from us. Clive refuses to deal. When we try to sit down with him, he says it's between you and him and that the rest of us should fuck off. I'm telling you, I don't like being over there any more. The vibe is all wrong. Clive's been punching holes in doors."

"All right," Bailey sighed. "Tell him I'll come over tomorrow."

———

Bailey didn't go over to the studio the next day or the day after that. Wanda had been instructed to tell Clive the boss was busy whenever he called. He rang again one morning when I was alone in the office.

"Phelan residence," I said. This was my standard pick-up-the-phone greeting.

"Bailey, please." The "please" part was more spit that spoken.

"Sorry, she's in the shower." I never said Bailey was asleep. She was always in the shower or dressing or at an appointment, never asleep. This proved problematic at times, especially when Julie called. He'd call back an hour later and ask incredulously how his wife could still be bathing.

"Well, tell 'er Clive called."

"Will do."

"Is this Tony?" he asked before I hung up.

I told him it was.

"What's up, mate?"

"Still living that dream."

"Yeah, innit it?" Clive's tone turned friendly all the sudden. "Listen mate, can you 'elp me out?"

"With what?"

"Gettin' 'old of Bail. She's refusing to speak with me. I obviously can't run a bloody business without her go ahead."

I told Clive I'd see what I could do.

"I swear I never should 'ave opened shop with 'er. Totally unreliable."

"Women."

"Yeah, well this whole thing is crumbling because she refuses to deal, innit it? I know she 'as the money, it's just that she doesn't want to 'and it over. I've got bills to pay, you know?"

"Sure."

"She agrees to fund the studio through the first two years—until we show a profit, yeah?—and then eight months into it, she decides she doesn't want to be in the music business no more. People 'ave made sacrifices for this company, given up other careers and the like. But for 'er, it's just a bloody 'obby, innit it? You can't run a business like that now, can you?"

"No, you can't."

"Mate, 'ave her call me, okay? You're the only one over there with any brains. She said so. She'll listen you. That bitch Wanda. And that other gash, that Linda. Useless, those women. Treating me like I'm some sort of fuckin' birk!" Clive was getting worked up and I heard him pause to light a cigarette, or more likely, a joint. "Sorry, mate. It's just the pressure getting to me. Can you 'ave Bail call me?"

"I'll do my best, Clive."

"All I can ask for, mate. Cheers."

When Bailey emerged from her closet two hours later, I told her about Clive's call. She slumped into a chair and stared at the wall without speaking for so long that I was about to walk away. She finally asked what I would do in her position. I told her that I didn't know what her position was.

"Will you come over there with me?" she asked. I remembered what Jerome had said about Clive punching holes in solid objects, but I wasn't really in a position to decline. We went into the garage and Bailey headed straight for the passenger side of her Beamer, which meant I was driving. She just sat there silently for the first couple minutes of the ride, taking occasional sips from her bottle of Evian. I stopped at a gas station to fill up. The pump slowed down when I still had a few cents of gas to pump. Bailey called out to me to forget it.

"I've got fifty cents here," I protested.

"Leave it."

I hung up the pump.

"You men are such babies," she said when I got back into the car.

"That's a quarter gallon of gas."

"I'm not talking about gas. I mean the moment you don't get what you want, you start crying. Clive didn't show any concern about the studio finances until I said I didn't want to be with him any more. And now all the sudden he's some sort of businessman and all he's worried about is the company. He told me that if I didn't keep paying for the studio, he'd blackmail me."

There were several big questions in my head, but I kept my mouth shut.

She laid her head against the window. "He thinks Julie gives a damn that I was sleeping with him."

"Doesn't he?"

"Well…" she smiled faintly. "It's kind of like the military."

"How's that?"

"Don't ask, don't tell."

"Oh."

"I would never have had an affair if he didn't have one first. Julie was on a trip to Stockholm—business trip supposedly— and I called the hotel. He didn't pick up when I connected to his room, so I transferred down to the front desk. The woman tells me that Mr. and Mrs. Phelan just went up to their room. So I said two can play at that game." Bailey looked at me long enough so that I became sort of uncomfortable. "I shouldn't be telling you all this, but I don't care anymore. If Clive wants to blackmail me, then let him. There's no way I'm giving him any more money. The jerk says it's for the company, but he's driving around in a brand new Cadillac. I tell him I can't go to the Winter Music Conference in Miami because I'll be in London with Julie, so he goes off and blows $50,000 at the W. Such goddamn babies, you men."

"You're just going to let him tell Julie?"

"What else can I do? Keep paying him $10,000 a month? Gladys would kill me. And that's just what he calls his 'salary.' I'm not even talking about all the other shit. But the thing is that he's got all that equipment over there. I want that stuff back. That's like $200,000 worth of gear. If I stop paying him, he'll sell it.

"God," Bailey laid her forearm across her eyes dramatically, "I wish he'd just go back to England and leave me alone. He wasn't even a good lay. Between him and Julie I'm gonna be in therapy the rest of my life. I wish I could get a divorce."

"You can't?"

Bailey stared out the window for a few moments. "You ever been to Vegas?" she asked finally.

We were coming over the top of Bernal Heights and the city was laid out beneath us like a travel brochure. The city could sneak up on you like that because of the way it was nestled in between the hills and the Bay. You'd come over a rise and there it was all the sudden, looking so tidy and serene.

"A couple times," I answered to Bailey's question about Vegas.

"You like it?"

"Vegas is okay. I'm not a very good gambler."

Bailey laughed. "Neither was my dad."

I didn't say anything.

"Vegas, the track, hell he even played the stock market like it was blackjack. A real optimist, my dad. I guess you can afford to be optimistic when it's not your money. I had to drop out of college, you know?"

"Where'd you go to school?"

"Dartmouth. I had to take a semester off and get financial aid before I could go back. My mom made me swear I'd never tell anyone, like it was some kind of stain on the family name."

We arrived at the studio and I saw Clive's black Escalade parked on the curb. I pulled up behind it and killed the engine. We sat there in the car for a moment while Bailey applied lip-gloss.

"Julie would never lose my money on a fucking horse," she said finally, smacking her lips in the vanity mirror. "But he sure as hell isn't gonna hand it over in a divorce."

She got out of the car and started across the street. She motioned for me to roll down the window. "You're coming inside. You're my bodyguard."

Clive was not happy to see me. He ushered Bailey downstairs through a door marked "Private" while I sat in the living room and watched a dj spin. As usual, the place reeked of sweat, smoke, and burned microwave popcorn. Bailey was right about the equipment, it would be a shame to lose it all. As I flipped through a *Fader* magazine, I thought my roommates and I could easily clean the place out in an hour. If we hit it early in the morning when everyone was still cashed out, they'd never even know we'd been there.

I wondered to myself why I even cared—about Bailey, about her money, or her troubles with Clive and Julie. She was such a spoiled little brat, but I could also see something vulnerable about her, as if she was trapped in a situation that had stopped being fun and had taken a more sinister turn. On the ride over, I'd been shown a part of her that I could finally relate to—that overwhelming feeling of things spiraling beyond your control. And there was also a sudden sense of rapport. Bailey had bared her soul to me for a moment, and sitting there in the dank studio, I realized what she might need more than anything was a friend. Her honesty had made me feel kind of special. Then again, Bailey was no dummy. The way she referred to Julie's money as her own left me feeling that her sudden honesty might have a hook. If it came right down to it, I could see myself being left holding the bag on this whole studio meltdown; I didn't want to be that sucker who fell for the damsel-in-distress act and got burned for covering up her foray into techno music.

The office door swung open, and Bailey stepped out. "Ready?" she asked.

I dropped my magazine and followed her back to the BMW.

"Well that was fun," she said once we were underway. "He said that he bought a gun." Bailey smiled to herself. "I really know how to pick 'em."

I nodded.

"By the way," she added, "he thinks I'm sleeping with you now."

"Great," I muttered.

"Hey, I'm the one that's supposed to be depressed. Let's get a drink. Where should we go?"

I suggested the Blarney Stone. An Irish Car Bomb sounded appropriate for the situation.

"The what stone?" Bailey laughed. "Seriously, Tony, if people are going to assume we're sleeping together, you're going to have to start hanging out at nicer bars. Let's go to Mas Sake. First round's on me."

———

"Very nice," Larry said, as he continued to give my boss the eye. It was no surprise that we'd found him at the bar when both Bailey and I arrived. Mas Sake was like Larry's second office. We'd been at there for two hours now, and my boss was on her fourth Cosmo. I'd just dropped a sake bomb with Larry at the bar and was waiting for the bartender to bring more drinks. "You get in her pants yet?" Larry asked. "Because if you haven't, I think I'll give it a shot."

"That's my employer you're talking about," I burped. The sake wasn't sitting very well in the pit of my stomach.

"Whatever," Larry said, flagging down the bartender to order two Red Bull and Grey Gooses for himself on Bailey's AmEx Black.

Mas Sake was packed with Larrys that afternoon, a mob of 20-somethings in their uniforms of chinos and un-tucked dress shirts. It was only six-thirty on a Thursday evening, but the Turks and Turkettes were already running under full steam. No one was eating sushi.

"You missed a spot," I said, pointing to a dab of white powder under Larry's right nostril.

Larry rubbed the smudge away with the back of his hand. He and two of his buddies had been running a bucket brigade operation into the men's bathroom: One of them would emerge from the toilet, low-five a fat bindle of cocaine into his partner's hand and then that guy would take the handoff into the john. Repeat as necessary.

"Does your boss party?" Larry asked, tapping his nose.

"Jesus, man, I've still got to get her back to the house at some point." I looked over to Bailey at her table in the corner of the bar. She waved her empty martini glass at me. Bailey had handed me her phone along with her credit card, and Wanda had called twice to ask where the hell we were. Since our trip to the studio, Bailey had missed a Botox appointment, her Pilates instructor, and a neighborhood play date with the kids. Wanda didn't sound too happy about the fact Bailey and I were out boozing while she deflected Julie's questions about his wife's whereabouts. The bartender delivered the drinks and Larry headed off to the bathroom with his two highballs. I held Bailey's Cosmo at shoulder level as I wove through the throng to get back to our spot.

"Wanda called again," I reported. "Julie's pissed."

"Will you forget about my fucking husband for a second?" Bailey took a slurp of her drink. "I'll give the old ATM a blow-job when I get home and he'll be fine."

I threw my hands up. "Do I need to hear this?"

"Jealous?" Bailey smiled.

Bailey's cell phone buzzed. It was Wanda again. "What do you want me to tell her?"

"Have another drink, for Chrissakes." She grabbed the phone out of my hand. "Hello?"

Bailey was still on the horn when I got back to the table with my big bottle of Asahi. "Hold on," she said into the handset, "he's right here."

"I'm turning the phone off now, Wanda."

"Who the hell is Wanda?" my brother asked.

"Forget it," I said. Larry slipped into the chair next to Bailey and started whispering into her ear.

"Tell me you're not really at Mas Sake," my brother Stevie said. He'd gotten Bailey's phone number from Wanda.

"Sad but true. Want to come rescue me?"

"Not a chance. Me and the guys are at the Trad'r. Get your ass over here."

"Technically, I'm still at work."

I heard a scuffle and then Riley's voice boomed over the line. "You're at fucking *Mas Sake*?!"

"It's a long story," I told him as I watched Larry nuzzle Bailey's earlobe.

"Mas Sake?!" Riley yelled.

I hung up the phone and turned off the power. I took a long pull off my bottle of Asahi.

"That's more like it!" Bailey laughed, leaning over to lay a sloppy kiss on my cheek. "Who needs a DJ when they've got a houseboy?"

Sixteen: Money

THAT FOLLOWING FRIDAY BAILEY HAD Gladys cut what she assured the accountant was the last $10,000 check for the studio. She and Clive had agreed to dissolve the company, and by the end of the month, it would all be over. That seemed a little too neat, and I told Bailey so the next time I had her alone.

"You're right," she said. "We didn't agree on anything. I'm just working on the assumption that I can figure something out before the end of October. I've been thinking about calling the INS and having him deported. Julie could have it done like that—" she snapped her fingers—"but I don't want to get him involved if I don't have to." She said Plan B was to have Clive committed to an asylum.

"He claims that he's so in love with me that he'll kill himself if I don't start seeing him again."

Although Bailey hadn't mentioned anything about our escapade at Mas Sake or how I'd had to pour her through the service entrance later that night and hightail it out of there before Julie saw me, the next day I was informed by Gladys that I'd been bumped up a pay grade to $25 an hour. Since I was also now working (or rather, on the clock—big difference) forty hours a week, that meant I was making $52,000 before taxes, $12,000 more than I had been making in Denver.

Bailey's insistence that I get a cell phone turned out to make the job even more agreeable. I'd fought the mobile pretty hard, knowing instinctively that it would become an unbreakable tether to the job. But Bailey kept pressing, saying that if I accepted the phone I could use it for all my personal and long-distance calls as well as my Phelan-related duties. The best part about the new Motorola Razr flip phone was that I was no longer forced to wait around the house in stand-by mode. I could take my car down into the Presidio—just a three-minute drive back to the house if they needed me, and off the beaten path so that I didn't have to worry about being discovered—and read a book until I was hailed. If it was a bad hangover day, I could go home and take a nap until the cell phone rang. Besides, there was no use clocking out early as it was almost certain that as soon as I signed out on my timesheet, Bailey would call with an urgent errand. Her busiest hours of the day were in the late afternoon when her brain finally caught up with her body. Now that the studio was a no-fly zone, Bailey came up with lots of projects to keep herself busy, shopping being the primary new occupation. Bailey was a stick-and-move consumer, and she liked to call me as she was leaving a store to have me come down and retrieve her purchases so she wouldn't have to lug them with her to the next kill zone. So it was more prudent, even if also more expensive for the Phelans, for me to keep the houseboy meter running all day.

Chasing Bailey's ass from Neiman Marcus to Nordstrom's was tiring, but the hard part about the job was not stealing. I'd never really been confronted by this temptation to swipe stuff until I started working for the Phelans. Sure, I hadn't been above putting personal mail through the office postal meter in Denver or liberating a couple of pens and notepads from the supply closet. That was penny ante in comparison to all the larcenous possibilities I encountered working for the Phelans.

The first way to pad my pockets would've been to take money right out of the petty cash till. The cash box was one of those little boxes you see at elementary school bake sales. There was a key that we never bothered to use, and we kept the box in an unlocked desk drawer with sometimes as much as $2,500 in it. Technically, the only ones with access to this box were the house manager, Gladys, Bailey, and myself, but everyone in the house knew where the box was and that it wasn't locked.

We were only supposed to get cash to replenish the box from Gladys so she could make sure we'd turned in receipts to match the expenditures, but since she was only around on Fridays, we usually got the money straight from Bailey. You might have to remind her a couple times, but she'd finally show up with a horse track wad of hundreds and ask how much you needed. A thousand bucks was the norm. She'd hand it over, sometimes without counting it, and you'd enter a deposit on the ledger. When Bailey was low on dough and didn't want to hassle with the bank, she'd reach into the box to pull a couple C notes. And Bailey wasn't the type to enter that transaction on the ledger. After five months watching the petty cash flow, I was sure that I could grift *at least* two hundred bucks a week without anyone getting wise.

The second way to augment my income would be to buy stuff for myself when I shopped for the Phelans. If I went to the Safeway on a regular run—which meant that I was buying forty or fifty items—was Gladys really going to see that Speed Stick deodorant thrown in with all the Snapples and diapers and cottage cheese? Highly unlikely considering the fact that every Friday I was handing her sheaves of receipts. Finally, it got so bad that Bailey and Gladys decided to get me my own company credit card with a $10,000 limit so that all my expenditures would be bundled onto one monthly statement. Most months I exceeded my limit on the credit card by the 15th, and we'd have to wire transfer more money into the account.

Once I had the credit card, there was almost no monetary constraint to what Bailey could send me out for: stereos and computers, car repairs, clothes, toys for the kids. Bailey would send me to the Virgin record store with instructions to buy every CD I thought she'd like. I'd drop five hundred bucks in ten minutes in the dance music section. Was Gladys really going to look at the receipt and know that Bailey didn't listen to Soundgarden? Not a chance.

The third way to skim would've been to have an accomplice provide fake receipts. But the first two ways were so easy, why bring in an accomplice?

I'd considered myself a fairly ethical person before working for the Phelans, but there was so much booty around it was hard to resist. And seeing weasels like Clive committing grand Cadillac larceny didn't make my desire to steal lessen.

In the end, the main reason I didn't rip them off was because it was too easy. My logic was that it had to be a trap. After all, what is virtue besides the fear of getting nailed? Hell, the fact that they were paying me over fifty grand a year to pick up Bailey's Wilkes Bashford purchases was the biggest crime of all. Still, considering the river of money flowing through the Phelan house, I was impressed that I didn't dip my beak.

You could've passed Bailey or Julie on the street and had no idea how wealthy they were. They fell somewhere between new money and old money, and, as a result, they didn't have that, how shall I say? *bulletproof* look to them. From the set of her mother's jaw, I knew that Bailey's family was old East Coast, but Julie was first generation big bucks. That left the Phelans a couple feet short of true social respectability, Board of the S.F. Symphony or not.

There was a lot of that going around San Francisco at the turn of the millennium. While the Pac Heights was full of Old Money (the Gettys had a mansion down the block from the Phelans) there were also scads of freshly minted Internet billionaires grenading the engines of their Ferraris on the steep hills of the city. Even though Julie was only one or two steps above these dot.com tycoons, Bailey still had enough East Coast blood in her to sniff at their wives and girlfriends (not many of the e-commerce wizards were female) from her perch at the top of the Pacific Heights. These young women tried desperately to break into proper San Francisco society by throwing gala benefits and fashion shows. Bailey dismissed these young women as "climbers," and tossed their embossed invitations into the trash without reading them.

Of course there were several old birds up in their Pac Heights roosts who thought Bailey was a climber herself. Nothing demonstrated this more clearly than when Julie got upset that the owner of the mansion one street below was adding a solarium to his top floor. Julie was sure that the new structure was going to impede his fourth floor view of the Bay by eight centimeters, and he did his due diligence at City Hall. When he discovered that the owner of the house had not filed a building application, Julie decided to slap an injunction on him even though the project was almost completed. It turned out that the guy who owned the house was the son of one of these old Pac Heights condors. Her name didn't mean a thing to me, but it sent Bailey into hysterics. This was *real* Old Money, the kind that gets written up in *Town and Country* when its Yorkie catches a cold. Over the next week I heard Bailey get as close to begging as she ever did while beseeching Julie to let the matter slide.

"Julie doesn't give a fuck," I heard Bailey moan to her mom over the phone. "He's starting a war over this and it won't cost him a thing because he doesn't care about social stuff. But for me, it's suicide!"

Bailey avoided high-brow social functions unless her absence would definitely put a dent in her Pac Heights credibility. Bailey's preferred method of operation was to let Julie's money show up for her. She'd buy a $10,000 table at the Orphans without Laptops benefit, never get around to calling enough people to occupy the ten seats and, as a result, never make the event. But buying a table got her name on the official program and in the newspaper advertisement. That's all anyone remembered, anyway. Julie seemed to understand this tactic as well, and the Phelans had their very own charitable organization that doled out hundreds of thousands—if not millions—of dollars each year to various causes. I was aware of this because whenever a donation from The Julie & Bailey Phelan Fund was made, the foundation faxed a press release to the house. For smaller, less socially prestigious, things like the S.F. Boys and Girls Club they might kick down five-hundred dollars. If the grant was for something with more social cachet—the Modern Art Museum, for example—half a million dollars was in order. That didn't even get them a plaque, but I'm sure Julie appreciated the tax write-off.

But the week Julie filed his injunction against the neighbor, Bailey had Wanda RSVP for every piddling cocktail party and fundraiser in the neighborhood (and one in the Marina) so as to get her side of the story into the right ears. She finally ran into her nemesis (the mother of the guy who was building the solarium) at a breast cancer benefit. According to Bailey, it wasn't so much a run-in as an ambush.

"So," Bailey related to her mother the next morning, "I'm in the bathroom and turn around and all the sudden there's Selena with her new nose, dripping diamonds as usual. She comes over and hisses, 'If your husband continues with his course of action, I will <u>ruin</u> you. You and your children will be socially ostracized in this city forever.' She actually said that. 'Socially ostracized forever.' I felt like I'd just been mugged. And then she checks herself in the mirror and walks out like nothing happened. It was the most *awful* thing that I've *ever* been through in my *whole* life. This means I'm going to have to stay home with Julie every night for a month!"

Apparently, Julie only needed a week of Bailey's constant companionship before he agreed to drop the injunction. Bailey was back to her old tricks the next day.

———

Philanthropy and all, you hang around people like the Phelans long enough and you start to realize that there's nothing divine about them except for their ability to spend $100,000 without worrying where the next $100,000 is coming from. When you're working for people like that, the $70,000 trips to Europe and the $500,000 donations to museums stop seeming unusual.

What I ended up appreciating more than the sheer amount of money they spent was the way in which that money insulated them from the mundane details of life. For example, one afternoon Bailey wrecked her Beamer on the way to her shrink appointment. She had been talking on the phone and didn't react quickly enough when the driver in front of her slammed on his brakes. Bailey wasn't hurt, but the hood of her Beamer was crumpled. Instead of waiting for the tow truck like anyone else, she called home and had Wanda and me come pick her up. I was left with the smoking car, instructions to swap insurance with the other driver, and wait for AAA. I got the car towed to a garage, then I took a cab to a rental agency and picked up a Range Rover. When I got to Avis, Wanda had already taken care of all the paperwork with the insurance agency. I had the SUV parked in front of the house before Bailey cabbed back from her appointment. She jumped in the Rover and took off for the rest of her day like she hadn't just totaled her $80,000 sedan.

Money makes it so that you are in one room and your everyday problems are in another. Your help scurries back and forth making peace between the two.

Of course there were still moments each week when the frugal side of my brain got jolted. An enormous AmEx bill would come in (like the one with the $45,000 charge from the Prada store in Milan) or I'd get wise to one of Clive's $50,000 weekends in Miami. One of my daily jobs was to open all the packages that came in from UPS and Fed Ex, so I was sort of the doorman checking off all the Phelan's extravagances. None of that prepared me for the monstrous crate that arrived one Friday in July.

The box was so big that it took up an entire parking spot in the garage. My first instinct was to leave the crate un-opened until Monday, but I knew Julie would not take kindly to finding his parking spot occupied. So many boxes arrived for the

Phelans that even with two garbage pick-ups each week there was still too much refuse for the house's four trashcans and three big recycling bins. The result was that I'd have to drive around to the neighborhood construction sites and look for open Dumpsters. Usually, I could ask one of the workers if it was okay—hey, I was just another grunt like them, right?—and toss the stuff in. If I had an old bookcase or something like that, I'd pick up a six-pack of beer and pay the construction guys off with that.

The problem that Friday was going to be getting rid of the crate. The construction sites closed down around three and they usually locked the lids of their Dumpsters for the weekend. I could see myself driving around with this huge container strapped to the roof of my Nissan looking for a spot to ditch it. My happy hour with the guys at the Boondocks before the Giants game was getting shorter and shorter.

I started pulling the screws out of the crate with a power drill, but they were sized wrong and the drill bit wouldn't fit; the crate was from the UK so it must've been a Limey metric thing. After stripping four out of the twenty screws, I gave up on the drill and went for the crowbar. Someone had done an ace job on that crate because it was highly resistant to my prying. By that point, I sweating full-on and the garage floor was covered with splintered wood. Frustrated, I took a few caveman swings at the crate with the crowbar before I finally broke through. The lid of the crate was now in seven or eight pieces. The next layer was a sort of polyurethane and I'd torn the hell out of that, too. I took a box cutter and slashed my way through. Under that was a solid Styrofoam lid that had been seriously injured by the crowbar. I ripped this off, saw the contents nestled in another cocoon of foam, and almost puked.

It was a painting. A very, very old painting. I'd gotten a B- in Art History, but even before I looked at the manifest I knew that I'd almost made a serious mistake.

It was 1863 Manet landscape with an invoice attached for $319, 935.21. A ring of black started to close in on my peripheral vision, and I thought for a moment that I might pass out. Then I saw that it wasn't a dollar sign next to the price but Pounds Sterling. I wasn't up on the exchange rate, but that had to be something well over $600,000. A bead of sweat dropped off my forehead while I was leaning over the painting, and in my terror I was able to actually catch it in my palm before it hit the canvass. I sat down amid the wreckage on the garage floor and took some deep breaths, remembering my overhead swings with the crowbar. Judging by the state of the Styrofoam, I had been inches from putting a nice hole in Mr. Manet's painting. There was a terrible ringing in my head.

I went upstairs to get Bailey after clearing away the splintered wood and other signs of violence.

Frank was flipping grapes into her mouth. "What's the matter with you?" she asked after swallowing.

"There's some *very* fresh kill in the garage," I reported. "I think you should check it out."

Down in the carport, Bailey asked me to lift the painting out of what was left of the crate so she could see it better. I hesitated to touch it.

"C'mon," she said, spitting a grape seed at me, "pick it up."

It was the lightest thing I'd ever held. Even though it was the size of a large desk calendar, it felt like it might float out of my hands.

"Hmm," Bailey said, "not as cool as it looked in London. Oh well, let's bring it upstairs."

"You want me to carry *this*?"

"What's your problem?"

"This thing's worth more than my life."

Bailey laughed like I'd made a joke.

She led me upstairs, opening doors ahead of me while I had visions of tripping over the cat. A friend of mine had worked for an art handling company in New York and I remember him telling me about moving Picassos. The key to not freaking out, he'd said, was to treat every piece of art as if was equal; the five-dollar Snoopy lithograph the same as the $5,000,000 Van Gogh. I tried to think of the Manet like it was a Joe Montana poster, but my brain wasn't buying it.

We went into the living room and Bailey told me to set the painting against the wall.

"That's good," she said and turned to leave.

I protested that this might not be the best spot for the Manet. The cat could claw it, Emma might make alterations with her Crayon, the humidity level in the room might make the paint dry out.

"What's the matter with you today?" Bailey seemed truly concerned.

I finally made it to the 'Docks an hour later after dumping the remainders of the crate in a mercifully open Dumpster.

"You look like you just got carjacked," my brother observed.

Even though I pounded five beers in the thirty minutes we had left before the game, I could not forget the weightlessness of that painting in my hands; there was no logic to something that light being worth so much.

Seventeen: Nightclub

At the end of the fourth inning, I told the guys that I was going to the bathroom and just kept walking until I was standing outside the stadium listening to the crowd's disembodied roar. The whole deal with the Manet had really messed me up, and I still couldn't put my finger on why. It was like my nearness to ruining something that valuable had mixed with the weightlessness of wealth and the indifference of money and the terrible thought that this poor sap Manet had put his heart and soul into a 3'x3' painting and now some loopy socialite in a distant country had bought his work and set it on the floor in her living room where a cat was probably pissing on it. And watching millionaires prance around in matching uniforms while drinking $8 lukewarm beers hadn't lightened the load any.

I grabbed an idling taxi and was halfway home before the phone started ringing. It was Collins. I debated whether to pick it up, but decided that the guys were just going to keep dialing if I didn't.

"Yeah," I said.

"Where the fuck are you?" Collins barked.

I told him I wasn't feeling good.

"Sure, sure. I bet you're up there in the Club Level with Larry. Too good for us bums in the outfield now?"

My call waiting beeped. I told Collins to hold.

"Oh, houseboooooyyy," Bailey cooed. There was trance music playing in the background. "Get a limo and pick me up. I need an escort tonight and you're it."

"That sounds fun, Bailey, but I'm not really feeling that great. I was just about to go to bed."

"Not acceptable," she said.

"What's the limo for?"

"We're picking up some people and going out."

"So it's 'we' now?"

"Yes."

"I'm not dressed for going out."

"Like it matters. You're with me. There won't be any problems. Thirty minutes, my house. You've got the credit card. Use it." She hung up.

Collins rang back. "You're hanging up on us now?"

"I'll call you back later."

"What the fu—?"

The cab stopped at the light at Geary and Van Ness, right on the edge of downtown. I considered my outfit. Jeans, Polo shirt, black leather jacket, Adidas sneakers and a black knit cap. I figured Bailey would want to hit strictly dress code spots, and this outfit wasn't going to cut it. Well, we'd see how much clout she really had. I told the driver to pull over. I went to a pay phone kiosk to look up limo companies in the shredded phone book.

I called Bailey from the stretch a half-hour later as it idled outside her house. Amazing how quickly you can pull things together when you're not spending your own money. I'd secured a black Lincoln with room for eight and, sensing that we were not headed for the library, stopped at a liquor store to pick up Grey Goose, Veuve Clicquot, fresh-squeezed orange juice, and Heineken. Bailey click-clacked her way out of the courtyard, and I could see the light on in the nursery and the shade drawn slightly aside so that whoever was in there could spy on what was going on.

Bailey slid into the car wearing the usual stretch pants along with a glittery Prada top, Jimmy Choo pumps and a short leather jacket by Tod's. Her hair was done up in a wind-swept fashion and I must admit that in the dim limo interior she looked pretty damn good.

"Vodka or champagne, boss?"

"Oh, you are houseboy supreme!" she laughed. "Champagne!" She scooted up to talk to the driver through the lowered partition while I worked the cork. She crawled back to me and emptied a plastic bag containing CDs.

"Music, houseboy!"

We drained one bottle of champagne before we arrived at our destination. Since the windows of the limo were tinted, I had no idea where we were. Bailey used my cell phone to call inside and three guys and a woman skipped down the driveway to the car. The woman was Wanda, the guys I didn't know.

"DJ Feelin' are you feelin' it tonight!" Wanda shrieked when she got inside. "And you got Tony to come. Oh my God, I'm so fucking happy!" Wanda was wearing a short, short leather skirt, fishnet stockings and a bikini top that covered perhaps a third of her ample breasts. Over this she had modestly thrown a feather boa. Wanda squeezed into the space between me and Bailey, immediately placing her hand on my thigh and kissing me full on the mouth. I felt her tongue prod my lips experimentally. She introduced the guys as they ducked inside. I forgot their names as quickly as I shook hands with them, but there was no question from their leather pants and open shirts that these fellows were members of the community the fair city by the Bay is notorious for. They were gorgeous men, slender and with faces so angular and defined that they might have been wearing make up. I looked like a goon in comparison. They tapped into the Grey Goose and ignored the orange juice while Bailey and Wanda debated where to go first. It was a little before ten and obviously too early to hit the serious clubs.

Thankfully, we got stuck in post game traffic around the stadium, and that gave me time to try and catch up with everyone, intoxication-wise. Bailey and Wanda were slithering all over each other to such an extent that I figured they had to be hopped up on something more exotic than champagne. They ground against each other to the music as we inched along in the traffic. I tried to ignore the lesbian show by chatting with the guys, who were digging hits of cocaine out of a glass vial. They were nice, but obviously not interested in wasting witty banter on someone playing for the other team.

I spotted my brother and the fellas in the post-game throng. My first temptation was to ignore them and keep this action for myself. But then I realized some hetero male back-up might be nice. I was about to ask Bailey if we could stop, but didn't get a chance because Wanda saw my brother first. They'd met once when he'd picked me up at the house.

"Oh my God!" she screamed. "It's Tony's brother! We have to grab him!"

She pointed him out to Bailey, who slid down her window and whistled. When Stevie turned around Bailey waved him over to the car. Collins and Riley watched in stunned, gape-mouthed, silence. Stevie tried to walk over confidently, like being hailed by a sexy blonde in a limo was normal for him. Bailey opened the door and told him to get in. He hesitated until he saw me. Collins and Riley watched in amazement as the limo turned down an alley to escape the gridlock.

After a short pit stop at a murky cocktail lounge that brought to mind a chest cavity illuminated by a flashlight, we piled back into the limo and drove to a club. There was already a line at the door, but Wanda walked right to the front and started fondling the doorman. Stevie, Bailey, the gay guys, and I brought up the rear, my 6'5" brother and I boxing Bailey in like bodyguards. Having negotiated a group, no-wait-in-line, fuck-your-dress-code price with the doorman, Wanda returned to get $300 from Bailey. Bailey reached down the front of her stretch pants and pulled out a fold of hundreds. She peeled some bills off for Wanda and handed the rest to me for safekeeping.

Bailey, Wanda and the boys dove into the crowd on the dance floor while Stevie and I pushed our way to the bar to order beers, tequila shots, and a bottle of champagne for the dancers. I dropped two C-notes on the bar, feeling pretty slick.

This was not a club I would've come within a half mile of on my own. The music was 170 bpm humping rabbit techno and the beers were $6 apiece. Although there were some good-looking girls in the crowd, the ladies had obviously come to avoid *homo sapiens* like my brother and myself. We were all but invisible to the men. It was like we had big, flashing neon "Straight" signs over our heads.

Bailey and Wanda broke off their bump and grind to rush the bar and spill the bottle of champagne. Bailey told me to give Wanda a hundred bucks and Wanda made a beeline for the men's bathroom. She came back to hand Bailey five purple pills.

"Recharge!" Bailey yelled over the din. "You want?!"

"Okay!" I yelled in her ear. She handed them around, popping two herself. Bailey grabbed Stevie and me and dragged us onto the middle of the dance floor. For the next hour she and Wanda convulsed around us as the music and lighting and my bosses became increasingly appealing. Although I was doing nothing more than the New York Torque combined with a little Roger Rabbit, the overall effect of the booze and the ecstasy and Bailey grinding her crotch into my thigh made me feel like a goddamn All-Star. Wanda had cornered Stevie by the DJ booth where she was forcing his face into her cleavage. When we broke away for more beers, my brother turned to me at the bar as I shucked another of Bailey's C-notes. "Keep this job!" he yelled. "Whatever you do, keep this fucking job!"

The hours after we left the disco are hazy. I recall having to stop at an ATM because we needed more money. Bailey didn't have her card with her, so Stevie and I both pulled $300 of our own on my boss's assurance that she'd pay us back with interest. I know we ducked into the famous 1015 nightclub after once more paying our way past the block-long line at the door. I remember standing in an open bathroom stall with one of Wanda's gay friends snorting coke off a plastic collar stay. Around 3 a.m. Bailey suggested that we take the party back to her house. I was drunk enough to forget for a moment that her house was also the place I went to work five days a week.

Bailey broke out the champagne and Glenlivet, cranked up the stereo and threw open the fridge for an all-you-can-eat buffet. Julie was most definitely out of town, but it still felt like a high school party where the 16-year-old hostess can't remember which night her folks are coming home. I also thought about the babies trying to sleep upstairs and the poor nannies wondering if they dared come downstairs and investigate the ruckus. There was also that $600,000 painting on the floor in the next room which somebody might step on.

The initial excitement of partying in somebody's mansion quickly wore off and we settled down into the plush leather chairs of the library and drank like respectable drug-addled folk. Perhaps it was because the ecstasy had run its course, but I started to feel depressed. The house may have had a killer sound system, but it was not a place that inspired high spirits. Everything from the heavy Baccarat crystal highball glasses we were drinking from to the elegant carvings on the doorframes suggested *Masterpiece Theater* rather than *Miami Vice*. I was brought down all the way when I pulled one of Julie's college yearbooks off the shelf and flipped to his lone picture in the thing. It was a club called "Tomorrow's Achievers Society" and there he was, standing in the back row with the same dour expression on his 19-year-old face. I put the yearbook back on the shelf as Bailey and Wanda slipped away to the basement. I soon heard a separate set of thumps start up. I excused myself after giving Stevie instructions to keep an eye on things.

I followed the beats through the garage to the little *Alice in Wonderland* door. I opened it to find Bailey and Wanda standing in front of the turntables, locked at the lips and hips. I made a quick reverse out of the room and was halfway through the garage when Wanda caught up with me.

"Don't leave," she said, grabbing my hand. Her pupils were as big as .45 bullet holes.

I let her pull me back into the DJ room and sit me down on a milk crate holding LPs. Wanda went over to Bailey and slipped her arm around her waist. They started kissing again and running their hands over each other. Bailey unhooked Wanda's bikini top up and ran her tongue around one of her erect nipples. She fumbled for the half-full bottle of champagne and poured a measure over Wanda's breast.

My two superiors continued to lick each other for another couple minutes before remembering I was in the room. When they swung their attention towards me, I was reminded of the Velociraptors in *Jurassic Park*. I felt rather low on the food chain.

"C'mere," Wanda slurred.

I stood up and took the three steps to close the distance. Wanda started working on my ear while Bailey brought her lips to mine. There was no preamble to our kiss; our tongues were immediately mixed and I put my hand on the back of Bailey's head to pull her into me. Wanda had gotten my shirt raised and had one of my nipples in between her teeth while her hands worked on my belt. Just when I thought she was going to pull my pants off, she stood up and poured more champagne over her exposed breasts. She then guided my head down to lap it off. The record on the turntable came to its end. As Bailey started another one, we were enveloped in a fuzzy silence where the only definite sound was Wanda's moaning and the quiet *thunk, thunk, thunk* of the record needle. I dropped to my knees and moved my tongue into her belly-button, my hand running up and down the inside of her thighs. Her fishnet stockings were on the floor and she wasn't wearing any panties.

"Yes," Wanda moaned. "Just like that."

Bailey got the record playing again and started kissing Wanda while I raised her tiny skirt up and lapped at her shaved pussy. We went on like this for the length of one song.

When it ended, Bailey tugged me up by my hair so Wanda and I could trade places. Wanda finished undoing my pants and began giving me head. I slipped my hand under Bailey's shirt and cupped her small tits. Bailey was biting more than kissing now.

I'm still not sure if I was overwhelmed by my first three-way or the fact that it was, in fact, with my boss and co-worker. Perhaps the fear stemmed from the feeling that I was being eaten alive. All that I was certain of was that if I came in Wanda's mouth I was going to be in big trouble.

Without being too abrupt, I backed my groin away from Wanda's hungry lips and got her up from her knees. She and Bailey started kissing again, and as soon as their attention was focused back on each other, I folded my dick in half and ducked out of the room. I buckled my belt at the bottom of the stairs and went back to the library where the gay contingent was chalking up lines of coke on the antique coffee table. I told Stevie that it was time to leave. He didn't protest as it was now quarter to five in the morning and his eyes were half-closed.

I only felt my chest unbind when we were a few blocks away from the house. I used my cell phone to call a cab and we waited for it on the corner of Divisadero and California. I expected Stevie to ask why we had to leave so suddenly and what I'd been up to in the basement, but he was tired to the point of silence. The cab showed within a couple minutes and took us home as the sky over the Bay started to leak the Saturday morning sunset.

I woke up that afternoon with a sour champagne stomach, an echoing head and a hard on that could've driven nails. There was also the acute feeling that I might soon be out of work.

Eighteen: Test Tubes

I developed a depressing post-ecstasy cold over the weekend, and considered calling in sick Monday morning. I finally decided there was no use in putting off the inevitable. The house was always quiet around eight when I arrived and—after checking the garage to make sure Julie's car was gone—I went upstairs to fix myself an espresso and toast a bagel. The newspaper was where Julie had left it in the kitchen nook along with his dirty breakfast dishes. I tucked the paper under my arm and went back downstairs to enjoy the hour of silence before the rest of the staff arrived.

There wasn't much news in the paper, so I folded it up and took it into the garage to throw away. I looked at the small door to the DJ room. Part of me had begun to suspect that Friday night's debauchery had been a crazed ecstasy hallucination, so I slipped inside. The turntable was still spinning and I could hear the white-noise hum from the speakers. The bottle of champagne had an inch of flat liquid left in the bottom. The floor was sticky from spilled liquids. I turned off the stereo and collected the empty bottle. I then locked myself in the bathroom off the office and quickly jerked off to the lurid images of Bailey and Wanda still vivid in my head. I came on a wad of tissue and flushed it down the toilet. I caught a brief glimpse of my reflection in the mirror as I washed my hands. I looked away, feeling an awful tinge of guilt.

The rest of the staff showed up in a rush. Junko, Miss Tang, Frank and the two day nannies came through the service entrance together at nine, talking about their weekends like it was a GM plant. All they were missing were hardhats and lunch pails. They congregated into the office to b.s. with me and I was happy they were still crowded in there when Wanda arrived in her typical rush, trailing a cloud of Marlboro Light smoke. Frank asked her how many times she had gotten laid over the weekend.

"C'mon, you slut," he kidded, "how many dudes did you bag?"

"Frank!" she exclaimed.

Junko covered her ears.

"Really. I bet you got two. Whattaya say, Tony? Two fucks this weekend for Wanda?"

"I'm staying out of this one." I had the awful feeling that Wanda had already told Frank about Friday night. But then again this was pretty much the typical Frank/Wanda repartee.

"Frank," Wanda said, "why don't you tell us how many cocks you sucked? I think that's the better question."

"I'll tell you the truth: none." Frank had given up on his hetero act now that the word was official about me being straight. "And I'm ashamed of that. I swear I can't find a decent man in this town. Supposedly fags on every corner, but I can't find one good one."

"So what makes you think I can?" Wanda shot me a sly look.

"Because you're a slut and don't care. Quantity over quality is your motto."

I knew from experience that this could go on for a while, so I took the opportunity to slip out of the room and talk to Junko about shopping lists. We were inspecting the contents of the cupboards when Bailey descended the stairs in her pink satin robe, a tiny cup of espresso in hand.

"Good morning," she yawned. "How was your weekend?"

"Pretty good."

"God, I went out Friday night." She smiled. "Still recovering."

"Yeah," I said. "I feel like I'm coming down with a cold."

"Hmm. Me too. Must be something going around." She continued into her closet and locked the door behind her.

The Phelans left the next day for two weeks at their lodge in Jackson Hole, and the whole scene with the limousines before the trip to Europe was repeated. Julie was on the intercom paging Bailey every ten seconds, saying it was time to leave, while she and I were down in the basement getting her electronic gadgets in order. To survive a week in Wyoming she had to bring more high-tech gizmos than a CIA agent. She handed me an envelope when she was finally ready to head out the door.

"The money I owe you and your brother. Plus a little bonus for all your, um… hard work."

When she was gone I opened it up to discover sixteen, crisp hundred-dollar bills.

———

The thousand-dollar bonus rattled me not just because of its extravagance, but because it showed that Bailey remembered that I'd sucked on her nipples; I'd been hoping that she might've blacked out before our three-way in the DJ room.

The fact that she was also conscious of the six hundred she owed my brother and me from our big night out was proof that she hadn't. I would've gladly taken the three hundred dollar hit and paid Stevie out of my pocket in exchange for Bailey's obliviousness. But I also got the feeling that Bailey had planned our party to coincide with her imminent departure. This was also Wanda's last week, which seemed consistent with Bailey's plan to kiss and run.

Wanda wasn't as subtle as Bailey when it came to talking about our night out. She kept throwing exaggerated winks and double entendres at me. There were times when she'd stare at me then shake her head as if to clear all the nasty thoughts. I now knew what sexual harassment felt like, even though I wasn't exactly regretful about Friday night as far as Wanda was concerned. It seemed inevitable since she had first arrived that we would hook up. Some people just have that kind of overt sexuality to them, and if you get close enough you will be sucked in. But Wanda and I shared something else too, which was the camaraderie that comes from working together in an unusual and somewhat demanding situation. I realized that she'd made my days at the Phelan's more entertaining, and she really did have a good heart. Plus, those tits of hers should have been bronzed.

So now, as far as Wanda went, the question was not if we would ever finish that act, but when and where. I certainly didn't want it to happen in the Phelan's basement with Junko in the next room. In order to avoid such a sordid catastrophe, I gave Wanda a wide berth, which in the end didn't prove difficult because she spent the majority of her final days up in the kitchen talking with Frank about what she was going to do with her life after this job.

One afternoon Wanda started crying. Frank put his arm around her waist and walked her out into the courtyard to light her a cigarette.

"Hey, Tony," he called from outside, "stir those shallots, okay?"

I manned the stove for a few minutes until Wanda and Frank came back into the house. Wanda's mascara was smeared and she bolted downstairs without a word while Frank reassumed command of the kitchen.

"Drama," I said.

"Poor little *puta*," he said. "I'd hate to be a temp. She's been rotating from job to job for two years."

"Does she realize that part of the reason she gets so attached is because she knows she's gonna have to leave?"

"What are you?" he smiled "Some kind of shrink?"

"Nah, it's just... You know?"

"Yeah. I shouldn't give her so much shit for all her boyfriends. Different symptoms of the same disease."

"And you're calling me an analyzer?"

Frank looked at me seriously. "I used to be a priest," he said.

I told him I was surprised.

"Well, I never got out of the seminary because of this," he pointed his spatula at his groin. "But that's part of what a priest is supposed to be, a shrink. It's too bad, I think I might have been an okay priest. The key is listening. Amazing the things people tell you if you just shut up and let them talk. Like the babies. I know the Church would excommunicate Bailey for what she did, but I really respect it. I guess that was another part of the Catholicism I couldn't handle. So fucking judgmental."

"What do you mean?" I asked. "How she adopted them?"

He looked surprised. "Nobody told you?"

"Yeah, I mean, I know they're adopted. What so big about that?"

Frank left the stove and looked around the corner into the foyer. "You never heard about how they made them?" he whispered.

I shook my head.

"Dude," he said, "it's science fiction. They bought the eggs from this Nobel Prize scientist and the sperm of an Olympic athlete and then hired a host female—a tri-athlete or something—to carry them to term. It's like Frankenstein." He lowered his voice two more notches. "I heard they paid the mother a *fortune*."

"So what's the point?" I asked.

"Dude, you are seriously slow when it comes to this kind of shit. Those kids are Bailey's pension."

At first, the story didn't seem so bizarre. Test tube baby, big wow. But then I started thinking about how the Phelans decided they didn't even want to use their own chromosomes, opting instead for buying super sperm and eggs and then letting someone else be pregnant for them. And Frank's revelation certainly helped explain why Bailey was so unattached to the children.

The fact that she never had to care for them must've only widened the existing maternal gulf. The Phelans insisted on having two nannies on duty at all times, including the overnight shift. In addition to Sally, Jen, Astrid, and Patty there were an additional four nannies backing them up and filling holes in the schedule to insure double-coverage at all times. The kids were always sort of a rumor to me, and I never saw much of them because the nannies had a fairly solid routine which kept the toddlers on the move throughout the day. The only occasions when things got really screwy was when Bailey decided she wanted to see her kids.

Since Bailey wasn't competent enough to watch Emma and Edward at the same time, there was a single car seat in the back of her BMW. When she called to say she was coming home to "pick up a baby" it sounded like she was accessorizing. Grab a handbag, some pumps, and a toddler. To avoid the usual bawling and brawling, Bailey would phone from the street and have a nanny bring one of them out, usually the youth who was having the best behaved day.

On one such excursion with Edward, Bailey asked me chauffeur so she could make phone calls. When the baby crapped his pants and started crying, she turned the stereo up.

"This usually works to quiet him down," she said over the music.

When that didn't do the trick, she handed him her cell phone and that seemed to appease him. I kept hoping she'd ask me to pull over so she could change the diaper because the smell was making me nauseous. The longer we went on in that awful stench, the more panicked I became that she might be waiting for me do it. When we finally arrived at Circuit City, she broke out the diaper bag and ducked into the backseat to handle the change. I couldn't believe she actually had a diaper bag in the trunk.

Inside the store, Edward tottered around pushing buttons with his sticky mitts as Bailey's picked out ten thousand dollars worth of stereo equipment in five minutes. I did my best to hedge Edward in between his mother and myself.

"He's adorable," the saleswoman said as she rang up Bailey's purchases. "How old is he?"

Bailey smiled sweetly at me. "Honey, how old *is* he? I always forget."

"Two?" I offered.

The clerk gave us a questioning look.

"Sorry," Bailey said when we were back in the car. "I'm just sick of people thinking ATM is a grandpa every time we go out with the kids. Once in a while it's nice to pretend I'm actually married to someone my own age."

Ever since Bailey's strip-tease in the closet, she'd become increasingly candid with me. I'm not talking so much about our lost evening with Wanda or getting drunk at Mas Sake with Larry, but in our day-to-day contact. Increasingly, Bailey had begun to talk to me like I was her friend as opposed to her employee. She didn't seem to expect advice as much as a sympathetic ear. In some ways it was titillating to be privy to Clive's blackmail attempts and her continuing dissatisfaction with Julie (aka "ATM"), but there was also a part of me that wished that I could just do the grocery shopping and be left out of the emotional entanglements. Because every time I accepted one of Bailey's "bonuses"—$500 here, a grand there—I realized I was getting paid-off, and I wasn't sure whether the bribes were meant to ensure my continued sympathy or if they were Bailey's way of telling me I had better keep my mouth shut. In the end, it was probably a little of both. But this was the first time she'd said anything about her relationship with Emma and Edward.

"I know I'm going to be held responsible for how screwed up they're going to be," Bailey continued as we made our way back to the house from the stereo store.

I kept looking straight ahead at the road.

"But what the hell?" she added, brightening a bit. "They're almost two now, so it's too late to do anything about it."

Bailey was running late for an appointment, so she asked me to take Edward inside the house. Edward wanted to walk, so I had to bend down to hold his hand. He was gurgling about something and I kept on saying, "Right, right" as I led him slowly up the sweeping staircase. I knocked on the door of the nursery when we got to the top, and Sally opened up.

"Look," the nanny smiled, "the two men of the house. Did you have fun with Tony and mommy?"

The kid pointed at me and said, "Daddy."

"Don't worry," I told the kid, "it's going around today."

Nineteen: Special Assistant To The Houseboy

Speaking of parental issues, Frank was catering a meal for Bailey's parents, who were having a party at their crib down the street that night. They asked Bailey to send me over to help them move things around beforehand.

"You might want to bring someone else," Bailey's mom said. "Some of it is pretty heavy and Bill's golfing this afternoon."

Wanda started to call the movers so they could send a man over, but I told her that I knew a guy who needed the work.

As usual, Stevie was setting a new record on Atomic Cannon and waiting for the phone to ring. I told him I had cash-money work if he was interested. He was.

Bailey's mom, Wendy, was delighted to see us when we showed up at her spacious apartment, looking like Rent-a-Frat-Boys in our chinos and Polo shirts. I explained to her that my brother had put off several meetings because he needed a break. "Conducting business by cell phone," was the way I put it. Wendy seemed to think that was reasonable, to want to trade white for blue collars as a relief from dot.com stress. Wendy was wearing a pair of blue Capri pants, docksides and a white Yves St. Laurent blouse, looking like she'd just returned from the San Francisco Yacht Club. The only feature that betrayed her as old enough to be Bailey's mother was the noticeable tightness of her facial features—the Pac Heights facelift look. She led Stevie into the kitchen and handed him a pair of yellow dish gloves so he could start polishing silver. Stevie looked at me like, *this is what you do for a living?* but he played along for the next four hours as we got things cleaned up and rotated out the fine antiques for more party-proof furniture from the basement storage area. When we finished, I was expecting Wendy to kick down some cash for our services, but she made no move for her purse when walking us to the door. At the last moment, she ducked into the den and came back with a bottle of Dewar's. The seal around the neck had been cracked, but the bottle was still 90% full.

"Thank you so much," she said, handing over the Scotch. Stevie looked at the bottle of Dewar's and shrugged. It was more than he would've made sitting around Sharkattack.com headquarters changing every "that" in his business plan to "which." I took him back to the house and Frank fed us a late lunch with the leftovers from the catered meal he had prepared. I showed my brother the Manet, which I had moved to a safer spot on top of a table.

"Six-hundred grand for that," he said. "I'm in the wrong racket." This from a dot.commer, no less.

Wanda found us on the top floor admiring the view of Alcatraz. She asked if Stevie had been paid for his time at Wendy's. Stevie told her about the bottle of Scotch.

"I can't believe how cheap rich people are," Wanda said. "You get paid $25-an-hour, right?" I nodded. "Okay, I figure four hours... How about $150 with tip?" She had the cash in her hand. Stevie shot me a questioning look.

"Is that not enough?" Wanda asked.

"No," he said quickly, "it's—"

"Fine," I cut him off. "But tell him he has to buy me dinner."

"Buy him dinner," Wanda said.

Stevie started down the stairs before Wanda could change her mind.

"Are you nuts?" I asked, once he was out of the room. "I was going to suggest paying him fifty bucks."

"What the fuck do you care?" Wanda asked. "Besides, that's half of what we'd have had to pay the movers." Wanda ducked her chin and shot me a wolfish grin. "And don't you worry, sexy. I haven't forgotten about *your* tip."

Twenty: Unfinished Business

Wanda picked Friday, her last day, for her farewell luncheon. She laid the dining room table, lit candles and opened bottles of Chianti. Junko even allowed her to break out the linen napkins and place mats. Wanda told us all to sit down so she could serve. It was me, Frank, Junko, Miss Tang, Robby the Cat Lady, Gladys, Astrid, Patty, and the kid who worked on the computers. (Bailey screwed the computers up so often that we had to call the computer kid in once every two weeks.) The nine of us sat around the polished walnut table as Wanda dished out the pasta and poured the wine. Wanda took the chair at the head of the table and proposed a toast.

"To all of you who have made my two months here the best job I ever had." She started to tear up. Frank put his hand on her shoulder. "Ah, what the hell?" she snuffled. "*Bon appetite!*"

There was polite talk about what Wanda was going to do next and speculation about if Bailey was going to give her a "goodbye bonus." Gladys refused to say yes or no and that was as good as a yes for the rest of us. As the accountant, she always knew about these things ahead of time. But aside from those topics, we had nothing else to discuss. It would have been difficult to round up such a diverse group if you'd tried. We had a South American (Astrid), a quasi-nympho (Wanda), two

African Americans (Patty and Robby), a homosexual (Frank), a Chinese (Miss Tang), a Taiwanese (Gladys), a whiteboy nerd (the computer guy), a Japanese (Junko), and me.

I would have gladly downed a couple more glasses of wine, but like the rest of the group (perhaps with the exception of the computer kid), we all expected the Phelans to come crashing through the front door at any moment, back home early from their trip to Jackson Hole. Ten minutes into the meal I pretended my cell phone rang (vibrate mode) and got up from the table to speak to the imaginary manager of the BMW shop who was pretending to tell me that Bailey's car was ready and needed to be retrieved immediately because they were out of space in the lot. In reality, the BMW was ready, but in no hurry to be picked up. I held this conversation within earshot of the dining room, and, after hanging up, explained to Wanda that I had to run. I expected everyone else to stay put, but people began to take their plates into the kitchen. I think the feeling was that if we were going to get nailed, it was going to be as a collective. The only person who didn't get up was the computer kid, who kept shoveling pasta and slugging vino.

I started to call for a cab, but Wanda said she'd drive.

"Is that okay?" she asked Frank.

"Sure, honey. We'll take care of the dishes. But what about the cake?" Wanda said we'd eat it when we got back from the garage.

"That didn't go off very well," Wanda said when we were in her Saab and she had a cigarette lit.

"It was delicious."

"I'm not talking about the meal. I just wanted everyone to relax for a little bit."

"Hard to do at work. Maybe if we were in a restaurant."

Wanda laughed. "You imagine trying to get all those people together outside of that house?"

"Impossible," I agreed.

It was a semi-cloudy but beautiful September afternoon. This was my favorite time to be out and about, early afternoon in between lunch and rush hour. Traffic was light and the stores weren't crowded. At the BMW shop I asked Wanda to wait before she went back to the house. I backed Bailey's big sedan out of the garage and pulled up alongside her.

"You ever driven a 740?" I asked

"No."

"Want to drive this home?"

"Really?"

"Yeah, I'll follow you." I was about to add "drive carefully" but figured she'd do that on her own.

"Can we take the long way?" she asked.

"Your choice."

Wanda took a moment to fix her hair in the vanity mirror, adjust her sunglasses and tune the radio to a Latin station. I saw her looking for the sunroof switch and went over to open it for her. She headed away from the garage. Wanda looked good in the car, loose strands of hair blowing in the breeze and shaking her shoulders to the music. She turned up the stereo and poked her head out the window at a stoplight to yell something back at me that got lost in the traffic and stereo noise. There was a middle-aged suit in a Mercedes alongside her and he smiled at what she'd said to me. It struck me that this guy wouldn't be able to guess in fifty tries what was taking place. In his eyes we were anything but a couple of domestics bringing the boss's car home the long way. We could have been a husband and wife taking the BMW for a test drive, or maybe a couple swingers getting it on in traffic. Whatever the guy thought, it couldn't have been reality.

I followed her to the park at the Palace of Fine Arts. Wanda got out of the car with a huge smile.

"It even turns off slow," she said. "I love it!"

We'd been gone for almost an hour by that point and I was starting to worry what the rest of the staff back at the house was thinking. But what the hell? The Phelans were in Wyoming and it was a beautiful day. A little foggy but just the right temperature. The park wasn't crowded.

"Have you ever been here before?" she asked.

I told her I hadn't.

"I've always wondered what those women up there are doing." She pointed to the stone columns on the other side of the lake. Carved women leaned against the top of balustrade. I said that they looked like they were crying. Wanda didn't think so. In the pond the seagulls bathed themselves like ducks, splashing water and nuzzling their feathers with their beaks.

"Too bad it's foggy," she said.

"Nah," I said, "if it was clear it would be too perfect. It's better with a little flaw."

We crushed our cigarettes out and took the extra time to throw the butts into a garbage can. We spent a few minutes looking up at Pacific Heights trying to spot the house, but couldn't decide if we saw it or not. I said we should get back to eat Frank's cake. Wanda handed me the keys to the BMW and gave me a gentle kiss on the lips.

"Thanks for that," she said. "My first Beamer."

I stopped at a liquor store on the way back to buy a bottle of Patron tequila. I gave it to her later that day, and she looked like she was about to cry—but in a good way. I didn't want to ruin it by telling her I'd charged it on the company Visa. It was three o'clock, and since there wasn't much else to do, I clocked out and said goodbye to Wanda and Junko, who was in the office dusting. Wanda handed me a note that read, *Are you going to be home later?* I nodded.

My brother, Chase, and I were into our usual Friday afternoon routine of drinking beers and playing cards when Wanda showed up at 6:30 with the bottle of tequila. We put down some shots and Wanda was sitting on my lap by the time Collins rolled in around seven. We decided to walk to a neighborhood pizza joint named Giorgio's. There was a half hour wait for a table, but the owners let us drink wine and eat appetizers on the sidewalk, using a newspaper box for our table. Chase and Collins found a tennis ball and started tossing it back and forth across the street, trying to lead each other into parked cars.

Wanda pulled me around the side of the building.

"Now tell me the truth," she whispered into my ear. "Did that party the other night turn you on?"

"Well, I…"

"I hope it did." She bit my earlobe before turning my head so she could kiss me on the mouth. We held our glasses of red wine away from our bodies in an attempt not to spill. We broke the kiss after a few seconds.

"The hardest part about my job has been keeping my hands off you," she breathed.

"Yeah, well, it's been, uh…"

"You don't know how many times I've wanted to lock the door to the office and fuck your brains out right there on the desk."

"That would've, um, been…nice."

She slid her free hand down the front of my pants. "Did you ever think about that, too?"

"Hey, break it up," Collins called. "Our table's ready."

"I'm not hungry," Wanda said. "How about you?"

"I could, ah, skip it, I guess."

She took my wineglass inside and we headed back to the apartment. I walked backwards so as to flag any cab coming our way. When I was about to run into a bus shelter, Wanda darted forward to guide me around it. It felt like we were doing the tango on the sidewalk. By the time an empty cab stopped for us we were only two blocks from my apartment. The driver flipped us the finger when we waved him along.

Back at my flat we dropped onto the sofa in a frantic search for buttons and zippers. We were both down to our skivvies when I got up to put on some music. Wanda poured two glasses of tequila. We drank them off and Wanda peeled off her bra to reveal her full breasts. She held the back of my neck tightly as I licked her nipples. I tried to pull her back to my room, saying that my roommates might walk in on us.

"They're eating," she said as she reached into my boxers. I leaned back on the couch as she gave me the best blowjob of my young life, cupping my balls as she looked up into my eyes. When I groaned that I was about to come, she got off her knees and stood above me on the sofa with her hands flat against the wall, pressing her pussy into my face. I could feel her whole body vibrating as she climaxed. She pulled me onto the floor and used her mouth to unroll a condom over my cock before guiding me inside her. I came within seconds.

"Now," she said, taking my hand, "we can go back to your room and do it again."

She left me in bed, wrung dry, at four in the morning.

"See you around, houseboy," she said as she kissed me goodbye and tip-toed through my brother's room. He'd wisely decided to spend the night on the living room couch.

Twenty-One: Pasty Kittens

I'D BEEN WITH THE PHELANS a little more than five months, but that Monday was the first day I was scared to come into the office. The Phelans and Linda were back in town and I didn't want to face any of them. I crept through the service entrance and ran smack into Wanda in the laundry room.

"What the hell are you doing here?" I asked, my first thought being that she was making a final pillage of the petty cash box before turning in her key.

"Crazy," she said, shaking her head. "Bailey called last night to ask if I'd help transition Linda back."

"I can't believe you agreed." I peeked in the garage to make sure Julie's Beamer was gone.

"Hey, a week's money is a week's money, honey." She smiled, "Besides, DJ Feelin' has to give me my severance. Espresso? I'm going up."

Linda came in early as well that morning with a look in her eyes that betrayed her confusion as to how everyone had grown so attached to her temp. She was dressed up like a Spanish Gypsy hooker (obviously the latest fashion from Madrid) and as the day wore on, the outfit added to her vengeful demeanor. I kept expecting to see the flash of a dagger being pulled out from under her four-inch wide paisley belt.

159

The first thing Linda did that morning was erase all signs of Wanda from the office. All the baskets with loopy Wanda-written signs on them—"Invites," "Bills," "Correspondence"—went into the garbage. The pastiche of sticky notes stuck on the side of the computer and on the window was taken down. The only thing left was a single envelope with Wanda's hand-writing on it, which was pushed all the way to the far corner of the desk. Half the envelope was hanging over the edge.

Meanwhile, Wanda was hamming it up, playing best friend to everyone and acting way too happy for a Monday morning. She kept giving me little pinches on the ass, which, under normal circumstances, I would have attributed to hold-over affection from Friday night. But this, I could see, was all about Linda.

Even Junko got into the act, coming up to Wanda in the kitchen and giving her a hug.

"So nice to see you!" the housekeeper said. "In a way, I thought you gone."

Things really ramped up when Bailey came into the office at ten. Linda and Wanda both made a huge show of welcoming her back from Wyoming, and if I'd been judging I would have given the medal to Linda. The three of them stood around gab-bing for several minutes, and since neither Linda nor Wanda would break away and let the other have solo face time with the boss, Bailey was forced to stand there in her robe. The phone finally rang and Linda and Wanda had an-honest-to-goodness showdown as to who was going to break off first and pick it up. I used the fact that I was on my knees changing the toner cartridge in the copier as my excuse not to make a break for it. I could see the calculations working in Linda's mind. By the second ring (and believe me, when around Bailey, not picking up the phone on the first ring was a demerit) I think Linda realized that there was more benefit in letting the caller know she was back in the office—and in command—than in making Wanda pick it up as her proxy. It's amazing how much workplace struggle you can fit into two telephone rings.

Linda tried to drag me into the fray, going so far as to engage me in Spanish, and even though I knew she was making a serious effort, all I could say in reply, in English, was, "Nice tan." I could tell by the disappointment in her eyes that she thought our goodbye hug at the airport two months earlier had guaranteed my loyalty. Well, she'd never put her hand down my pants outside Giorgio's, had she?

Mercifully, I had to pick up a crate of silver polish for Junko, and that got me out of the house for an hour. When I returned, I found Wanda sitting on the curb out front smoking a cigarette. She was pulling about a quarter inch of tobacco into her lungs with each drag.

"Goddamn, I'd like to paste that bitch," she said when I sat down next to her.

"Paste?"

"You know," she made a fist and jabbed it in the air, "punch her."

I lowered my voice. "She's not the one you should punch." If someone was in the courtyard, they'd be able to hear us on the street.

"Bailey?" she asked.

"Well, don't you think this could have been avoided?"

"I guess." Wanda lit another cigarette off her stub.

I helped Wanda to her feet and we walked down the street. "She shouldn't have let Linda take off for two months in the first place and then she shouldn't have let you get so settled into the job. It just seems like this and the whole fiasco with Clive—"

"What do you mean with Clive?"

I brought myself up short. "You know, the studio falling apart and all that shit." Wanda nodded. "It's all caused by her refusing to make any decisions. It's easier working for Julie. He doesn't try to make you think he likes you."

Wanda shook her head. "I still don't get what you're saying."

"It's just that Bailey tries to make everything so easy—so non-conflicting—that she just ends up making it harder." I put my arm around Wanda's shoulder. "Hey, you should be happy you're getting out now. Summer's over and they'll be home all the time and it's gonna get nuts. Take your fat severance and chill out for a little while."

"The only thing I'm not going to miss are those fucking nannies."

"They can't be that bad."

"Oh, you have no idea. Everything else I'll remember fondly. You and Frank and Junko and all that food. Emma and Edward trying to explain the Barney show. The view from the top floor on a nice day. You ever just go up there and look at the Bay?"

"Up there you kinda forget where you are," I agreed.

"I'd kill for that view."

"I think you're crazy," I continued. "You're getting out clean. If I was smart I'd walk right now, too."

"Why don't you?" she asked. "I don't know how you're gonna deal with that bitch Linda."

I thought about that on the way back to the house. Although the whole idea of getting a job in the first place was to put myself

into a position to grab some of the start-up glory I'd seen floating around the city, I had quickly gotten used to living off the
Phelan's spoils. I was nowhere near rich, but I was definitely
comfortable. Every week I brought home a check for over $700,
after taxes. A check and a half covered my rent and the rest was
all gravy. I didn't save any of the money, but I sure felt flush.

"Bailey's letting me go early so I can finish getting unpacked," Linda explained when we returned to the office.
Bailey had also disappeared for the day and the rest of the staff
was upstairs.

I wanted to clock out, too, but Wanda asked me to stick
around. Since Julie wasn't due back from the office for a few
hours, I turned up the basement stereo and got a couple Negra
Modelos from the wet bar in the library. We spent the rest of
the afternoon in the office, just Wanda and me down there sipping our beers, putting stamps on envelopes and finally, after
the sexual tension got too thick to take any longer, locking
ourselves in the bathroom where I set Wanda on the edge of
the sink and hiked her skirt up so we could fuck. Afterwards, I
had bite marks on my hand from Wanda chomping down on
it to keep her from making too much noise.

After we'd straightened ourselves up, Wanda went into the
petty cash box and handed me $300.

"What the hell is this for?" I asked.

Wanda slapped me on the ass. "I think you deserve a nice
bonus."

———

"Where are you going dressed like that?" my roommate Chase
asked that evening. He and my brother were lounging on the
living room sofas in basketball shorts and flip flops

"Like what?" I asked, checking myself in the hallway mirror. I was wearing Armani slacks, a salmon colored Canali dress shirt and my new Ferragamo loafers. "I thought we were going out for dinner?"

My brother laughed. "To Buffalo Burger, dude. You don't have to wear pants unless you plan on going to a Young Republicans meeting afterwards."

Chase checked my outfit again. "He does look kinda like Alex P. Keaton, doesn't he?"

"And what's the matter with your hair?" my brother asked.

"What are you talking about?" I asked.

"It's all...*guido.*"

I'd slicked my hair back with a little mousse; it was hardly as bad as they were making it out to be.

"Are we going to eat, or are we going to stand around and be jealous of my outfit?"

"I could go for some dim sum," Stevie said.

"C'mon guys," I said. "Let's get a decent meal for once. I was thinking Harris's."

The guys looked at each other. "Harris's?"

"If you two bums will put on some pants and deodorant, I'll buy dinner."

"Shit," Stevie said, getting off the couch, "you should have said that in the first place."

Harris's steakhouse was on Van Ness a couple blocks up from the Marina, and usually a place we only went to eat when one of our parents was in town to foot the bill. Slabs of prime meat were displayed to the sidewalk in a huge glass-walled refrigerator, and a jazz trio played softly in the dark, walnut paneled bar. Its location made it a popular place for the Pacific Heights gentry and businessmen closing deals. Unbeknownst to my roommates, I'd taken a couple dates there because I thought it was classy to eat in the lounge while listening to the piano player. Since Chase and Stevie refused to wear anything but jeans, that's where we ate that night. The bastards both ordered soup, salads, appetizers, entrées and dessert along with two $50 bottles of Cabernet. The check came out to $500, not including the tip.

"Not bad," Chase said, leaning back in his chair to pat his stomach.

"Average," Stevie offered.

"You guys are ingrates," I said, signing the tab. "The least you could do is offer to buy me a couple drinks now."

"That seems fair," Stevie said. "A little Trad'r run?"

"I was thinking someplace where we might actually be able to order a drink that didn't come in Tupperware."

"The Blarney?" Chase offered.

"How about the Owl Tree?" Stevie said.

I suggested the Balboa Café.

"In the Marina?"

"Shit, may as well go to Mas Sake," Chase said.

"Guys…"

"Mas Sake is so super cool," Stevie mocked. "I feel like a player just waiting in line to get inside."

"There's not going to be a line tonight."

"Oh, so that means you know what nights there *is* going to be a line?" Chase challenged.

"Marina Tony," my brother said, nodding to Chase.

"Marina Tony," Chase agreed.

"Okay, I give up. Where do you two guys want to go?"

"The Blarney," they said in unison.

Twenty-Two: Spawn Of Julie

I WAS WOBBLY FROM THE four Irish Car Bombs my room-mates pushed on me the previous night, so I neglected to check for Julie's car in the garage that morning. I staggered up to the kitchen to make my morning espresso and grab his discarded newspaper off the kitchen table. I was back in the office reading the sports section when the intercom buzzed. It startled me so much that I dribbled espresso down the front of my shirt.

"Tony," Julie's disembodied voice called over the speaker phone.

I picked up the receiver. "Yes, sir."

"Where is my newspaper?"

"I have it."

"Bring it back upstairs."

I quickly folded the paper into shape and hustled it to the kitchen. I found Julie wearing gray sweatpants, slippers and a white undershirt. As I handed over the *Chronicle* I considered making the excuse that I'd thought he was gone for the day. I elected not to because it might indicate that I read his old paper every day, therefore wasting his money and my time keeping up on current events not pertaining to the Phelan residence. I scuttled back to my office and chastised myself for not checking the garage as usual.

Junko and Frank came into the office in short order. "Dude, what's up?" Frank asked. "I just saw Julie in the kitchen window. Is something wrong?"

"I don't know why he's here," I said. "It is his house, you know?"

"In a way, he usually gone by now. Sick?" Junko asked.

"He didn't look sick," I said.

Junko hurried upstairs.

"You *talked* to him?" Frank asked.

"Yeah, he's up there in his sweats."

"Oh shit, dude. I'm not going up."

"Maybe he wants you to make him waffles."

Frank ducked into the bathroom to check himself in the mirror.

"Dude, I wore shorts today."

I wished Linda would haul her sorry ass into work so I could split.

"What do I say to him?"

"Good morning?"

Frank thought about that one before leaving the office. I heard him exchange good mornings with Julie as he opened the door at the top of the stairs. Despite the fact that I called him "Mr. Phelan," everyone else, despite their discomfort, called him by his first name. My reasoning calling him Mr. Phelan that first day was that I'd been schooled to use a formal address until you were told otherwise. Well, Julie never got around to requesting the informal, and I didn't see how I could stop the "Mr. Phelan" bit after six months.

Bailey dashed into the office a few minutes later with pillow marks on her face. "We've got *major problems*," she announced. "Julie's daughter is coming over tonight—that bitch ex-wife of his decided to come home from Florence a week early—and I haven't done a thing to get her room ready. Julie is furious." She sat down at the desk and started making a list. "Fuck, I haven't seen Madeline in four months." She looked around the office. "Where's Linda? Where's Wanda?"

I told her they didn't usually come in until ten.

"I bet Wanda never called Dawn Lindsay while I was gone. Did Dawn Lindsay ever call when I was in Jackson Hole?"

"Who's Dawn Lindsay?"

"Where's Junko?"

I told her she was upstairs.

"Okay, get in the database and find Dawn Lindsay and ask her if she has the curtains ready for Madeline's room."

I called the interior designer's office and the receptionist said she would be in around eleven. I reported this to Bailey.

"What?! Eleven? Does anyone fucking *work* in this city? Call her cell phone."

I tried her mobile, but Dawn didn't pick it up. I left a message for her to call the Phelans immediately.

"Okay, okay," Bailey said, calming down a bit. "Here's the list. First, you need to go to storage and bring Madeline's toys back. In one of the rooms there are a bunch of boxes with her stuff in them. What kind of toys do eleven-year-old girls play with?"

I shrugged.

"Barbies?" Bailey asked.

"I guess."

"Okay, bring back all the Barbie stuff. And the horses. And all the art supplies. No, we'll buy new art supplies. Just bring everything that looks like eleven-year-old girl."

I looked at her incredulously but she was staring at her list again. Well, I'd wanted to get out of the house… I grabbed the keys to the storage unit.

My phone rang before I was out of the Pac Heights. It was Linda, trying to sound supremely efficient.

"This room should have been ready weeks ago," she said loudly enough for Bailey's benefit. "I told Wanda about this before I left. It's very important that you bring home all Madeline's toys. We sent them to storage when she left for Europe and we re-did her carpets. So we need all that stuff back. Then you need to go to Lilly's downtown and pick up the sheets for her bed. Here's the address."

"Hold on, Linda. I don't have paper." I flipped open the glove box and rummaged around for a pen and then wrote on my hand while running a red light and almost getting t-boned by a van.

"According to them," Linda continued, "everything's been ready for weeks and Wanda never picked it up. It's very important to get the toys and the sheets back here before Dawn shows up at 11:30." It was 10:15.

"Got it."

"I don't understand why Wanda never took care of this. Did she ever tell you about Madeline's room?"

"I'm at storage. I'll see you soon."

"11:30."

I parked and dialed Wanda's cell phone.

"Hey sexy," she breathed.

"Where are you?"

"I'm almost at work."

"Has Bailey given you your severance yet?"

"No. Why do you ask?"

"Too bad. You're walking into a total shitstorm." I relayed the morning's events to her like it was some kind of emergency. Between Julie's newspaper and this I was really starting to lose respect for myself.

"Linda never said a goddamn thing about Madeline or this Dawn bitch!" Wanda exclaimed. "I didn't even know Madeline existed until you just told me! I swear I'm gonna paint that cunt."

"Get your pay-out first. I gotta go find eleven-year-old girls."

"Eleven-year-old what?"

I hung up and said to myself, "Thirty dollars an hour, thirty dollars an hour." I did that sometimes when the job started to get to me. Those pay numbers helped keep me from getting too pissed off.

It took me forty-five minutes to get all the toys packed into my car. At first, I sifted through the figurines and books looking for newer things. But then I remembered how kids sometimes get attached to old or broken toys and realized that it would be my ass if the little princess got home to discover that her favorite headless horsey was missing. So, like Bailey said, I ended up bringing everything. It was almost eighty degrees, and I had worked up a nice sweat by the time I headed cross-town to pick up the bed sheets. I had fifteen minutes to spare.

If you're going to work for a billionaire, you might as well act like it, so I called the store as I idled at the curb—scanning the rearview mirror for meter maids because I was in a bus zone—and told the clerk to bring the linens out to me. Apparently, Linda had been on the horn with them multiple times and they were expecting me. A young swifter hustled out and handed several packages through my rolled down window along with the invoice. I pulled away from the curb just as a bus came whooshing up behind me with its horn blaring.

At a stoplight I grabbed the invoice so it wouldn't fly out the window and saw that Bailey had spent $1,494.73 on two sets of sheets for the kid.

I figured Wanda could use some points, so I called her cell a few blocks from the house. She was waiting for me on the sidewalk when I pulled up to hand her the sheets.

"I swear I'm gonna kill that bitch before the week is over," Wanda said with a demented smile. She ran back into the house.

There wasn't a parking spot within two blocks of the Phelans, so I put on my flashers and double-parked so I could convey the boxes of toys inside. It would have been more practical to leave the front gate and the front door open, but knowing Julie was home, I decided not to make it easy. When I got the first box upstairs I found Bailey, Wanda, Linda, and a blonde who must have been the interior decorator standing around watching Junko put the new sheets on the bed. The sheets had purple flowers embroidered around the edges that matched the curtains the decorator had brought over. I set the box in the hallway and went back for the rest. It took me three trips to get it all upstairs, and by that point I had sweated through my shirt. The women were standing around commenting upon the fit of the sheets. Bailey wasn't entirely pleased with the way they matched the new drapes. Dawn said she had other samples in the trunk of her car. The four women looked at me and I headed off for them.

I returned to hand the samples to the decorator, who actually went down on bended knee in front of Bailey as she flipped through the book. I could understand her willingness to prostrate herself if she was charging for the curtains like she'd charged for the sheets.

Julie walked into the room and surveyed the scene. He had changed into jeans and a dress shirt, but still looked like he was starched. It occurred to me that it was only the second time I'd seen Bailey and Julie in the same room together.

"What do you think, sweetie?" Bailey cooed.

"It looks fine," Julie said in his usual monotone.

"I think I like this dark pink better than the purple." Dawn held her breath because she didn't have the curtains ready in dark pink.

"The purple is fine," he stated. "I just talked to Susan's woman and she wants to know where the SUV is."

Julie posed this to Bailey, Bailey looked at Linda, Linda looked at Wanda and Wanda turned to me. Then everyone looked at me, Dawn and Junko included. I was glad that I was already sweating.

"It's being detailed." I said. "I was going to drop it off at her house this afternoon." I had no idea where the Benz SUV was. I hadn't seen it since I'd left it at the body shop after re-possessing it from Bailey's DJs. The tale about detailing was just a time buyer.

Julie scowled. "Fill it up with gas before you drop it off." He walked out of the room and everyone took a deep breath.

"Is it really being detailed?" Bailey asked as soon as we heard Julie close the door to the top floor.

I told her I'd take care of it.

"Oh, God," Bailey wailed. "I can't believe this is happening. Madeline will be here in two hours."

I called the body shop.

"Yeah it's ready," the guy said. "It's been ready for three weeks. I called you four times."

I told him I was on my way.

"Hey," he added before I hung up. "I'm gonna have to charge you for all those days we kept it on the lot."

I dipped into petty cash for hundred dollar bills before climbing back upstairs to tell Bailey I was off to get the car.

"Thank God," she said. "You shouldn't be responsible for things like this, you know?"

Linda glared at Wanda. "I agree."

"No, this is my bad," I said. "Wanda gave me a note that the car was ready but we didn't know what to do with it. I'm guessing Susan is Julie's ex-wife?" Wanda winked at me.

"You didn't tell them about this?" Bailey asked Linda.

"I swear I did before I left." Linda looked at Wanda and then me. "I'm sure I told you where to take the car. Didn't I?"

"I don't remember," I said.

"You didn't even tell me about Madeline," Wanda said, sticking that one in and twisting it.

"You must've forgotten," Linda said. "I'm…I'm sure I told both of you all about this."

"Well, it doesn't matter now," I said. "I'm going to get the car. Anything else while I'm out?"

"Art supplies," Bailey said.

"I'll get those," Wanda said.

"Okay, good."

"So what do we think about the purple?" Dawn asked, still on her knees.

The guy at the shop charged me $500 for storing the SUV. He was surprised when I paid him without argument. I took the Benz to a big car wash on Divisadero that employed half the Mexican state of Sonora, and had them give it the deluxe treatment. I tipped the car wash guys with some of the petty cash I had left over then drove the sparkling SUV back to the Pac Heights to search for Julie's ex-wife's house. The place was so big that I almost passed right by it. It was done up like an Italian Villa, complete with vaulted arches and a fountain in the front yard. It took up a third of the block and was probably twice as big as the Phelan's. There was a "Welcome Home" banner strung over the marble entryway. At least someone was hitting the bastard where it hurt.

I left the keys with the ex-wife's house manager, a stern Filipino lady with tattooed eyebrows, and headed back to the house on foot. I was halfway to the Phelans when Linda called.

"What are you doing?" she asked.

I told her that I'd dropped the car off and was on my way back.

"Well, hurry up. We need to return those toys to storage."

"*What?*"

She hung up without offering to come get me. It took me twenty minutes to make it back walking double-time. I passed my car on the way and saw a parking ticket under the wiper. I'd been in such a rush to get to the body shop that I'd forgotten to check for street sweeping. I stuffed the ticket in my pocket and realized I hadn't even had lunch. It was 3:30 p.m.

By the time I'd taken the toys back to storage (Bailey had selected five items from the whole load) and grabbed extra scones from my girl at Whole Foods, it was past six. I was hungry, exhausted and I smelled like the three coats of sweat I was wearing. Driving home, I realized that this was the first day I had worked straight through in a long time. Earning your pay can be a real bitch.

———

I expected to meet the young princess the following morning, but the only evidence of Madeline was a half-eaten scone on the kitchen counter. Bailey got out of bed after lunch, and I asked her how it had gone.

"Fan-fucking-tastic," she moaned, "her mother has her thinking I'm the anti-Christ. Other than that, she's just like a little Julie. Thank God that's over for another month."

"She's not living here?"

"God no."

"So…she was only here for one night?"

"Mercifully," Bailey said, before disappearing into her closet.

What a waste of thousand dollar sheets.

Twenty-Three: The Dragon's Lair

WANDA HAD HER SECOND GOODBYE party that Friday. There was a heavy dose of false mirth as she opened her gifts from Bailey (silk scarf, a pair of tickets to the ballet), but the only thing I think Wanda really cared about was the envelope Gladys had containing her last paycheck and severance. The person who seemed to be enjoying themselves the most was Linda, who couldn't keep the smile off her mug knowing that the coup had failed and it was once again her show. The thing that made me feel the worst was Wanda giving Bailey a painting she'd done.

"Ah," Bailey said, "I'm supposed to be the only one around here who gives gifts."

Bailey did a convincing job of pretending that she liked the acrylic portrait of a samba dancer, but I could already see it making the slow slide down the house's chute for unwanted items. So many random objects flowed into the house in the form of gifts and freebies and impulse purchases that there was a shortage of space for all the crap. When items first arrived, they were taken upstairs for Julie's inspection, mostly for him to see that someone was vying for his patronage. Then he'd leave the wreath or fruit basket or tote bag in the kitchen the next morning so Bailey could offer it to the staff. Nothing was quite as degrading as carrying home one of the Phelan's cast off cracker tins like some bum who's found a half bottle of Gallo in the Dumpster. But one day I scored a new Bose Wave CD player (retail price: $499) that Bailey was giving away because she didn't like the off-white color. That was a good score, but most of the castoffs were useless.

If nobody claimed the stuff or Bailey thought she could re-gift, it was brought to the basement where I stashed it in one of the overfilled closets. When those closets reached maximum capacity, I loaded up the car and took all the brand new junk to storage.

So as Bailey fussed over Wanda's painting, I knew it would end up in one of the basement closets, and eventually in storage. In 2020 the new houseboy would come across it like an artifact from another civilization. *Hmmm, yes. Must be something from Mrs. Phelan's Late 90's techno-bisexual period.*

My reprieve from the maudlin events of that afternoon, which promised to drag out for quite a while, was Julie's secretary calling to have me deliver a sheaf of documents to his office. Usually they employed a courier service for this type of thing, but it was late Friday and he needed to lay his hands on the papers before the weekend. His secretary gave me a fifteen-minute window to hit so as to not throw the Great Man off stride. I found the forms on the Chippendale armoire in the master bedroom. This chest of drawers and a spot on the kitchen counter next to the phone were the only two places in the house we were allowed to exchange correspondence with Julie. I headed out the door while Frank was decorating another farewell cake.

Unfortunately, I was in my Friday casual attire of shorts and a T-shirt. I considered stopping home to change, but knew that if I did I would be cutting my ETA dangerously close. It seemed fitting that the one day I looked like an absolute scrub was the day I got called into Julie's HQ. I made it to his Embarcadero high-rise with a few minutes to spare. The mirrored glass structure rose above the older buildings around it to dominate the skyline; a shimmering monolith of commerce. I wedged my Maxima between a Bentley and a Mercedes CL600 in the garage then ducked into the closest men's room to try to make myself more presentable. I tucked my shirt, slicked my hair, evened my socks above my sneakers and counted myself lucky that I wasn't wearing my Jesus Lizard shirt that day. Luckily I'd also made a Friday exception and shaved that morning. My appearance could have been worse, but not by much.

Julie's office was on the second highest floor of the skyscraper (the top was a private club) and he shared it with a law firm whose litigation viciousness I recognized from articles in the newspaper. There was a small plaque on the wall next to the two frosted glass doors of the suite's portal indicating that deliveries should be brought around to the side entrance. I followed the hall to a nondescript door by the stairwell and buzzed the intercom. An attractive young woman in slacks and a blouse cracked the door to ask me what I wanted. I explained that I was from Mr. Phelan's house and she stepped aside to permit my entry. She led me past the kitchenette and copiers to the secretary I'd spoken to on the phone, who turned out to a mousy woman with short brown hair and jug ears. I'd been expecting Miss Moneypenny. She told me Julie was still in a meeting and that I should wait in the kitchen. She mentioned that there were newspapers out front if I wanted to take one back to the kitchen with me. I picked a *Wall Street Journal* off the etched glass coffee table in the waiting area and took a survey of the facility as I made my way back to the holding pen.

The place was not as big as I had expected, maybe ten private offices in a wheel formation with an equal number of cubicles in the center. The view of the Bay Bridge, however, was almost as good as the one of the Golden Gate back at the house. Unlike the Phelan estate, which was cluttered with dark rugs and antiques, the interior of Julie's office was decorated Scandinavian style with blonde wood paneling, lots of glass, and sleek lamps. There were monochrome photos on the walls of gold rush era San Francisco, but not much else in the way of art. The doors to all the offices were open. The place was subdued, but since the markets had already closed in New York, I supposed there wasn't much to get excited about. A guy about my age sauntered out of one of the offices and leaned in the doorway of his neighbor. They were talking about the Giants game, and I distinctly heard the words "Club Level." The dude was dressed like all the other Young Turks downtown: chinos, dress shirt, tasseled loafers, and a little cell phone in a hip holster. When he was done recounting the game, he ambled past me without so much as a nod. Everything about my get-up—from the T-shirt to my lack of a clip-on cell phone—made me feel inferior.

I was fantasizing about throwing a reverse chokehold on the Turk when Julie emerged from an office at the other end of the hall and started walking towards me. Correction. He didn't walk: he *swaggered* down the hall, a toothpick stuck jauntily out of the corner of his mouth; a corporate Tom Sawyer on a lazy Friday afternoon. His whole body language was so at odds with what I'd seen at home that it was like seeing a Julie twin who didn't suck lemons and who'd had the stick removed from his colon. I detected a slight hitch in his pimp roll when he spotted me in the hallway. The pause only lasted half a second.

"Good afternoon, Mr. Phelan." I resisted the urge to salute.

"What are you doing here?" he asked around the toothpick.

"Your secretary needs me to take something back to the house. She has it for you to sign."

He turned around and ambled back down the hall. I followed at a safe distance. When I got to his secretary's desk, Julie was reviewing phone messages that she handed to him one by one. She nodded towards a manila envelope on the desk. I waited for a moment, thinking Julie might say thank you or "dismissed," but he kept right on scanning the phone logs. The man obviously considered duty its own blessing, and therefore it required no acknowledgement. His secretary, however, smiled and mouthed, "Bye." I headed for the back door, leaving Julie to his universe.

I passed the young investment banker in the outer hallway and managed not to chop-block him. I shuffled to the back corner of the elevator to make room for people getting on as we descended to the garage. All of the sudden, I experienced such a powerful sensation of sadness that, had the lift not been so crowded, I might've actually let loose a couple tears. Something up there in Julie's roost had awakened a terrible dissatisfaction in my soul. Taken separately, Julie and the Young Turk and the high-sheen of the office didn't seem to be anything I wanted for myself, but when combined, it had put a collective foot right in my ass.

It was only as I pulled out onto Embarcadero that I remembered that it was me—not Julie or his little office gimp—who'd taken ecstasy with Bailey. That knowledge made me feel slightly better, but I knew there was still some bigger problem out there that I couldn't understand, let alone grasp with my own two hands. In the end we are all servants to something, but at that moment I felt it more acutely than I ever had before. After months of catering to the whims and banalities of the Phelan's day-to-day existence, I realized my life had devolved into nothing more substantial than stocking the refrigerator and delivering dirty laundry. Any feelings associated with the intimacy inherent in these tasks had been wiped out in the face of Julie's complete indifference to my service. In the end, I was, like my friend Riley had pointed out a few months previous, just a rich man's bitch.

I realized on the drive back to the Pac Heights that I was going to have to demand another raise in the very near future. I'm not exactly sure where this idea came from, but when I asked myself what might make me feel better about my life, the only thing that popped into my mind was money. It seemed to work for the Phelan's. Why couldn't it work for me, too?

Twenty-Four: Antiques

On Bailey's summer jaunt to Europe she'd bought enough antiques to fill a small castle. It became my job to track the furniture as it arrived in New York via the slow boat across the Atlantic. The operation got especially confusing because the antiques had to be divvied up when the vessel landed; one set of furniture was bound for the Phelan's ski house in Jackson Hole, another directly to storage, and the last bunch to the house in Pac Heights. I was on the phone three mornings in a row trying to sort out what was going where. This should have been Linda's job, but since she didn't get in until ten, I was the guy who dealt with everything on East Coast time. Part of my problem was that I wasn't familiar with the verbiage. Highboy, lowboy, commode—they all meant "chest of drawers" or "card table" to me and the mooks on the dock in New York.

The shipment of antiques finally arrived in S.F. and I was dispatched for champagne and caviar to celebrate. When I returned there was a moving truck double-parked on the street, and men were carrying large crates into the garage, where they unpacked each item. Liam, the antique consultant, fluttered around the process, keeping up a constant banter as each piece was revealed. The old fruit oohed and aahed to himself like a hick watching a demolition derby. Bailey was upstairs in the library drinking with her mom. Liam periodically popped up there to flap his hands and tell Bailey how wonderful everything turned out and how smart she'd been to buy this past summer because prices were now heading for Jupiter. He also made sure to keep her champagne flute filled. My guess was that he was trying to get her drunk to avoid any pangs of buyer's remorse. I was enlisted to carry the new stuff upstairs and, like the Manet painting, it all felt too light to be worth so much. I caught a glimpse of the invoices on Liam's clipboard and saw that the wobbly end table I was holding cost over $40,000.

"You really think this shit is worth that much?" I asked.

Liam gaped. "Oh, my! Definitely! These pieces absolutely sing!"

I put my ear to the wood. "I don't hear anything."

"Philistine!" Liam hissed.

By the end of the day, there was a half-million dollars worth of old junk on display in the living room, everything from little ceramic saucers and hand mirrors to a massive armoire (which I now know means "Chest of Drawers" in American). When Liam had arranged all the goods and the moving guys had departed, Bailey strolled through the room with her flute of bubbly.

Despite Bailey's invitation to sit with her in the library along with Liam and her mom after the showing, I took my glass of champagne and a caviar-heaped toast point into the kitchen. I perched on the marble counter where I could still overhear Liam hamming it up. I understood his compulsion to justify his commission. We all did that around Bailey, telling her what we were working on or what we'd accomplished that day even though I'm sure she usually didn't give a damn. I heard Bailey say that they were out of Dom Perignon, so I popped another bottle and took it into the library to pour, seizing the opportunity to cadge another bite of caviar. Liam's enthusiasm was still too much for me to bear, so I retreated back to the kitchen. Junko was polishing silverware, and I asked her if she wanted a drink.

"In a way, I'm working," she said. "But okay."

I doled out half a glass of champagne and we toasted quietly.

"In a way, very good," she said after taking a sip.

I ditched my flute and filled a water glass with champagne and topped it off with orange juice. I took my mimosa to the basement.

The antiques party broke up a little before three when Linda informed Bailey she had an appointment in ten minutes. This would be her twice-weekly shrink session, which she was habitually late for it. Now she was going to show up for it tipsy *and* late. Someone besides Liam was going to earn their money that day.

After Bailey said goodbye to her mom and Liam, she paused to ask what I thought about the fresh kill. I smiled and said, "Decline comment."

"Being a consumer is such tough work," she sighed.

"But the capitalist system—and the London antiques market—thanks you."

She offered me a crooked smile. "Don't forget the Prada store in Milan. They thank me, too."

The following day the regular movers came to the house and took everything but two antique end tables away to storage. Bailey had decided that the array she'd visualized while buying in Europe didn't seem to fit the actual space. All the way from London just to be put back in the dark. The Manet painting, thankfully, had finally been hung in the library.

Twenty-Five: Test Drive

THINGS STARTED TO UNRAVEL FOR Linda as soon as she re-assumed command of the Phelan operation. Two months away had been just enough time for the house manager to forget how hopelessly chaotic everything was, and now she was losing her mind. She fought for her sanity with constant memos and the repeating of every order. She stopped-up each leaky crack in the Phelan Dam by stuffing it with paper. But the more she tried to fill every hole with a memo, the more water sloshed over the top or around the sides.

"The woman's crazy!" Sally the nanny screamed, her pixie-ish face reddening in frustration. A new directive had just been issued forbidding the nannies to close a door between themselves and the babies—not even when they were going to the bathroom.

"I won't work for her," Jen said. "We're going to tell Bailey that we'll quit if she doesn't hire Wanda back."

I agreed with them that Linda was going a bit overboard. "But we also got a little sloppy with Wanda," I added.

Little Astrid stormed into the office to join the gripe session. "I quit!" she fumed. "The woman is crazed. Absolutely crazed. If she doesn't get fired I promise you I will leave this house."

All this quitting talk was nonsense. Nobody ever quit the Phelan house because if you quit you didn't get your pay-out. You had to find a way to get fired so you could get a severance.

"You should take over," Sally said to me.

"It's a good idea," Astrid agreed.

"Read my lips, girls. No. Fucking. Way."

"I'm gonna suggest it to Bailey," Jen said.

"Please don't," I begged.

Linda entered the office and the nannies scattered. When they had all disappeared, Linda told me she was on the verge of firing the lot of them.

"And how do you plan on finding eight new nannies?" I asked. "We've been short two since Bailey canned those girls after London."

"Bailey already has me looking," Linda said. "She says either Patty or Astrid has to go because they can't get along. But that's between you and me." She flopped into a chair.

"Wanda spoiled them," she continued, "letting them change their shifts all the time. Look at this." She held up the October schedule. It was a mess of crossed out names and arrows to indicate people trading spots. I thought about the revolutionary concept of a mother taking care of her own two children, but kept it to myself.

"And I swear if that faggot Frank makes one more comment about my ass, I'm going to cut his balls off."

For the past week, every time Linda came into the kitchen to get a snack, the chef would crouch down and squint at her butt like he was taking a survey. Linda would shoot back some comment about chicken-flesh on Frank's arms and Frank would be driven to the brink of tears. The guy worked out six days a week and looked like a Greek statue, but after one of Linda's zingers, he would spend the rest of the day flexing his arms for anyone who passed through the kitchen, nervously asking them how his guns looked. It had gotten to the point after three weeks with Linda back in charge, that every time she left the kitchen this 50-year-old man would stick his tongue out and make a face.

"See that bad, bad lady in the movie," Frank asked Emma and Edward, pointing to the TV in the kitchen nook. The nannies had queued up the *Wizard of Oz*. "The Wicked Witch? What's that bad, bad, nasty, ugly lady's name?"

"Winda?" Emma offered.

"Right! What's the nasty witch's name, Eddie?"

"Winda!" he laughed.

Frank gave them each a cookie from the pocket of his apron.

"In a way, Linda makes job harder," was Junko's only comment about the situation.

As a result, the staff began to skirt the chain of command and come to me directly if they needed anything. Slowly but surely Linda was being phased out of day-to-day operations.

Linda was aware of what was happening and started to put the screws to me. I came upon a sheet noting my stated time of departure every day compared to when I actually left the house. I'd gotten into the habit of rounding up, putting down 5:30 even if I shoved off at 5:20. After finding Linda's secret log—and starting to make precise checkouts on my timesheet—I began my own campaign to make her life more difficult. If she sent me out to the store for a certain kind of iced tea she wanted for the mini-fridge in her office, I came back two hours later saying the stores were sold out. When she paged me on the house intercom system, I let her buzz three times before I picked up, knowing how much she wanted me to spring for her calls like she hopped for Bailey's. During her briefings I made a point of turning my back and pretending to work on something.

"Then Bailey asked me to have you go to storage and pick up…Hey, are you listening to me?"

"Yeah," I'd say, my back still turned to her as I leafed aimlessly through a file cabinet pretending to look for a document. "Bailey wants me to go to storage and pick up that rug. She told me yesterday."

So Linda was understandably gleeful when she discovered that I'd botched a job and almost cost the Phelans thirty grand.

———

I came back from my morning errands with my stomach growling for a big lunch of jumbo prawns left over from the previous night. Frank bought these suckers that were more like lobsters than shrimp, each one as big as your fist. Throw one of those in the microwave with a couple slices of leftover sirloin and—pow!—surf and turf for lunch. I was so preoccupied with getting to my meal that I'd failed to notice the memo in my office basket reading:

TONY: SEE ME IMMEDIATELY!!!
IMPORTANT!!!

I was polishing off my prawns when Linda stormed into the kitchen flourishing the note.

"Did you see this?" she demanded.

"No."

"Did you open that crate?"

"I don't even know what crate you're talking about."

"THIS CRATE." She thrust a memo in my face. It was from the previous day. I vaguely recalled seeing it in my basket. It concerned the movers, a chair and a crate.

"I left this for you yesterday," she went on. "You must have IGNORED it. I told you to use the electric drill to open the crate in the garage and take out the chairs. You seemed to have told the garbage men to take the crate away without opening it and they just called to say that they found the crate—with the chairs still inside—AT THE DUMP."

My stomach soured as I remembered the moving guys coming over the previous afternoon with a load of antiques and one big crate. When we finished swapping furniture, there was the usual mess of packing materials lying around the garage, which I asked the fellas to take with them in the truck and toss.

I sort of recalled Denard, the head mover, asking, "What about this fuckin' crate?"

I started to explain to Linda about the garage being full of other boxes and that she must be thinking of a chair that had been next to the crate not inside it, but the phone rang. Before she picked it up, she told me that the chairs were valued at $30,000. Frank let out a whistle.

I examined the note. The first (of five) paragraphs said to open the crate and take out the two chairs. I started to wonder if Linda had already told the Phelan's about my gaffe. I pictured Bailey huddling with Gladys at that very moment writing up my severance check. I could see them calling me into the office and asking me to hand in my badge and gun (cell phone and credit card.)

The doorbell rang and snapped me out of my funk. I needed some air, so I walked out into the courtyard to open the front gate. Denard was standing there with the two chairs.

"Jesus," I said. "I'm glad to see you with those bad boys."

"No sweat," he said. "We had to come back over here for another job."

"How did you get them back from the dump?"

"What dump, homes?"

"The dump where you threw the crate."

"Ah, man, we didn't throw the crate in no dump. We got back to the warehouse and Rafael saw that the screws was still tight and figured it hadn't been opened. So he opened it up and we brought the chairs back."

"Shit, Linda said they were in the dump."

"They right here, ain't they?"

I handed Denard a twenty, but he waved the bill off.

"C'mon," I insisted. "Take it for a couple sixers. You don't know it, but you just saved my ass."

Denard accepted the bill and thanked me. I signed the invoice and took the chairs into the house where I carefully set them down in the dining room. Looking at them I could understand why "Antiques Roadshow" was so popular. The chairs looked like you might use them to set a plant on in the corner.

I was regarding the antiques when Bailey rushed through the front door. Linda hung up the phone and met her in the foyer. Bailey saw me standing by the chairs in the dining room before Linda could speak. I hoped the presence of the furniture, unharmed, would work in my favor.

"Oh, great!" Bailey said. "The chairs made it. I was wondering where they were."

Linda's mouth started to work but no words came out. The phone rang and she stalked back into the kitchen

Linda returned a few moments later. "You got lucky," she said.

———

I spent the next morning rehearsing my resignation speech. I needed to hit just the right tone, indignation with a dash of melancholy, so that Bailey would believe I was serious. The key was to word my farewell address in such a way that the boss would be compelled to try and talk me out of it. Simply quitting was out of the question—especially since halfway through 2000 there was more and more talk about the Internet "bubble" bursting. Panic had yet to hit the streets, but I had a feeling that this was not the time to rejoin the ranks of unemployed, even if it meant having to forsake a healthy portion of my dignity. I'd also just bought myself a $1,500 Zegna suit, anticipating my next paycheck.

The cause for my histrionics was Linda. She had me on my knees scraping gunk off the basement cabinets. This might have been a semi-agreeable task if it hadn't been Linda giving the direction. We were in the middle of an autumn heat wave and it was so hot that the phones weren't even ringing. Junko and Miss Tang spent their lunch hour standing in the short hallway between the kitchen and the library where there was a gentle cross breeze. Patty called in sick (flu, she claimed) and, since we were already short on nannies, Linda had been forced to call the French Au-Pair agency so they could rustle one up for us on short notice. In the meantime, Astrid was making a heroic attempt to watch the kids by herself for a whole hour. Considering the circumstances, being in the basement with all the lights off and the windows thrown open wasn't that bad a deal. All the same, I wanted to punch Linda in the mouth.

"Awwww, is houseboy having a tough day?" Bailey cooed when she saw me on my knees with a bottle of Goo Gone, a sponge and a roll of paper towels. She looked like a teenager in Daisy Duke shorts, Gucci flip-flops and a halter top.

I tried to keep pouting, but the way she was beaming down at me kind of broke my sulk.

"Here, take some calm mints." She handed me a box of boutique Certs. I grudgingly took one.

I said that real calm mints were blue with little V's on them.

"The ones I take are yellow."

"Got any of those?" I asked.

"Not for you. C'mon, on your feet. I need your help."

Linda poked her snout out of her office, but Bailey told her to hold the thought. The house manager scowled at the incomplete goo removal project as I followed Bailey out the service entrance. We walked up the driveway to the sidewalk. With so many ears in the house the only way to have a private conversation was to go outside.

"So what's the matter?" she asked as we strolled down the hot sidewalk, picking up our pace between the shady sections. "You've been sulking all week."

I told her about the Goo Gone and segued from that into my general annoyance with everything Linda. Bailey listened to my gripes, but prevented me from going into my fake resignation spiel by saying she was having the same troubles.

"Why don't you just fire her?" I asked.

"If it was only that easy. I have this feeling that she'd fight it, say that I didn't have justification."

"What more justification do you need than that she bugs the shit out of you? It's your house."

"And who would I get to replace her?"

I said that there had to be hundreds of people qualified to do her job. "Hell, I do most of her work anyway."

Bailey smiled. "Do you?"

"What's she do that's so hard?" I asked. "She picks up the phone, opens the mail and makes appointments for you. Everything else she puts me on."

"She deals with the nannies," Bailey countered.

"I don't know why that's such a big hassle."

"I can't quite figure that one out either. But she seems to think we need to fire all of them and start over. She says the agency has been calling every week. They've got all kinds of nannies looking for work now."

"Fire Linda and I bet things improve."

"Maybe," she said. We had made it around the block and were back in front of the house. "I'll talk to Linda, okay? You just keep doing the great job you're doing and I'll try to get it straightened out. It might take a little while, but I think we can make this work. And the truth is that the ATM doesn't like Linda either. That's the kiss of death right there."

"And what does Julie say about me?"

"Not a thing," Bailey responded. "Which is good, trust me. So hold on for a little while and I'll see what I can do. Okay?"

I scuffed the toe of my sneaker on the concrete. I didn't know what I'd want Julie to say about me, but the idea that I still wasn't even crossing his consciousness was rather disheartening.

"Better now?" Bailey smiled.

"Can I have a raise?" I asked.

"You're a real go-getter, aren't you?" Bailey laughed. "What are you making now? Thirty?"

I nodded.

"That's a lot of money."

"Yeah, but I can't shake the feeling that I'm getting ripped off when Linda is getting thirty-five."

"How do you know what we pay her?"

"Timesheet shredding."

"Thirty-five, huh? Let me talk to Gladys."

"What does that mean?"

"It means okay."

"Really?"

"But we're going to have to work it out some way so that Julie doesn't find out."

"He really doesn't say anything about me?"

"Julie sees you like he sees everything else," Bailey said.

"And how's that?"

"You represent a number. But I think you're worth every cent," Bailey continued, "and that's all that really matters, right?" She stepped up to give me a little kiss on the cheek.

"What was that for?" I asked.

Bailey winked. "I can't very well French you right here in the middle of the street, can I?"

I didn't have a response for that.

"You get rattled so easily," she laughed. "Now I know that if you go inside to scrape goo you're just gonna get all crabby again, so I'm sending you on a special mission. You up for it?"

"Depends what it is."

"For thirty-five an hour it shouldn't matter what the mission is."

"Bailey, for you, anything."

"That's more like it."

The salesman at the BMW showroom saw me walk through the door, but didn't make a move for a couple minutes as I checked out the floor models. Even though I was wearing shorts and a t-shirt, I knew the guy couldn't resist for long; it was a grave mistake to judge a person's net worth by his outfit in those days. I suppose that equality was one of the more redeeming aspects of the Internet boom as the money hadn't cared what color, gender, or race you were. Sure, there were plenty of jerk-offs driving around in Lamborghinis as if they had the divine touch, but most of the newly minted millionaires were just Average Joes trying to come to terms with their wealth. But these tech wildcatters were already a dying breed in 2000 as many young entrepreneurs suddenly found themselves holding bags of stock options that were no longer worth the paper they were printed on.

300-point daily losses on Wall Street had become the norm over the spring and summer. Even as the stock market continued its nosedive into the fall, the general feeling was that it was simply a "correction." Silicon Alley bars that had previously kept their TVs tuned to CNBC during happy hour so the clientele could gloat every time their company's stock scrolled by on the ticker, switched over to re-runs of "The World's Strongest Man." The Turks nursed their bottles of Asahi at Mas Sake, assuring each other that the market had hit bottom only to see it break through to new depths the following day. A hush settled over the city and people walked through downtown's Media Gulch looking lost. For many young businessmen, the crash of 2000 represented their first flameout. The Young Turks had finally tasted their own blood… and they were scared.

I could even see the pullback in the Pac Heights. Although there weren't too many dot.commers up there on Old Money

Mountain, there were plenty of private equity guys like Julie in the neighborhood who had made bad bets on the start-up boom. I'm not suggesting that a bunch of For Sale signs and garage sales suddenly appeared along Pacific, but construction projects started to slow down; I had to range farther afield to find Dumpsters to throw the Phelan's surplus garbage into. Boutiques along the Sacramento Street promenade had signs offering 40%-off sales. I even saw some of the gentry park their Jaguars at metered spots and fish quarters out of their Coach handbags to avoid parking tickets. The fact that Bailey had agreed to grant me a raise was yet another indication that Julie's fortunes weren't reversing as quickly as the rest of the field's. I had mixed feelings about that. Although I would've been quite happy to see the bastard go broke, Julie was, after all, still signing my checks.

"Hot enough for you today?" the BMW salesman commented.

"What's the most expensive SUV you've got in stock?" I said, cutting the pleasantries short.

The salesman blinked. "We've got a fully loaded X-5 in the garage."

"Does it have air conditioning?"

"Of course."

"How about a test drive?"

"Right away, sir."

Bailey and Julie had decided to buy a new nanny wagon, and they wanted an SUV. The Volvo had effectively been trashed, and as the kids got bigger, Julie figured they needed something with more room that would allow them to take two nannies along on their very occasional family drives. Bailey was supposed to have already test-driven various models. Naturally, she had neglected this task, and now she was passing it along to me. It was a hell of a lot better than scraping goo off the office cabinets. As a matter of fact, on a hot S.F. day I couldn't think of anything better than toying with salesmen, testing high-priced SUVs, and getting paid thirty-five bucks an hour to do it.

The salesman brought the SUV around and I hopped in the driver's seat. As I started down Van Ness, he took a look at my scuffed Adidas and asked why I wanted an X-5.

"It's not for me, per se. It's for our nannies. You know, for the kids?"

"Really?" At every dealership this comment had raised the salesmen's eyebrows.

"Yeah, we've got twins and the car we've been letting the nannies use is getting kinda small."

"What line of work are you in?" the salesman asked.

"Investment banking. How's business for you?"

"I won't lie to you, it's slow. But this can't last much longer."

I got to the end of Van Ness and took a left into the Marina district.

"I'm gonna go over here and try it on some hills, okay?"

"Sure."

"So, does this thing come in a V-6?"

"Yes, and I'm thinking that if it's just a car for your nannies that might be the way to go. They're not driving out of the city, are they?"

"They're not supposed to be."

"Well, the three liter V-6 has still got plenty of pop on the hills. No problem there. And if you're not using it out of town then you probably don't need the GPS system either. I could get you in a nice V-6 model for about forty grand."

"What's this go for?"

"This one is top of the line with all the bells. Say, sixty-eight."

I gunned the vehicle up Divisadero.

"I live right here," I said. "How about you drop me off and save me the cab fare home?"

"No problem." The salesman looked at all the big houses on the block and I could see him calculating his commission. I stopped in front of the Phelans and he handed me his card. I told him I'd give him a call.

He watched me use my key to let myself in the front gate. I waved as the door closed behind me.

I caught up with Bailey as I was about to leave for the day. I told her about my visit to BMW, and that they had a nice V-6 that would work for the nannies.

"Is that the top of the line?" she asked.

"No, but what do the nannies need a V-8, sport package and GPS for? You get the V-6 and save fifteen thousand."

Bailey said she wanted the V-8.

"I'm telling you, the V-6—"

"Tony, don't start nickel and diming me."

Two weeks later the new V-8 BMW X-5 was parked outside the house. One more car for me to valet park.

Twenty-Six: Combat Promotion

I RECEIVED THE DREADED CALL the following week as I was loading up the cart with toilet bowl cleaner for Junko at Safeway. It was Bailey. She sounded excited when she told me to get back to the house immediately.

I asked where the fire was.

"You're the new house manager," she said.

"You're kidding."

"I'm not."

"Does it matter that I don't want the job?"

"No."

I caught Linda walking out of the house as I unloaded the groceries. She stopped to light a cigarette and scowl at me. She had a UPS box of personal things resting on the roof of her car.

"I guess you got what you wanted," she said, exhaling smoke.

"Linda, you've got to believe me when I tell you that I did not—and still do not— want your job. What happened?"

Linda eyed me for a moment before deciding I might be on the level. She took another deep drag of her cigarette, and when she blew the smoke out her whole frame seemed to sag.

"The truth of it is that I don't even like this job anymore," she said. "You know what I'm saying? Every since I got back from Spain, I've been unhappy."

"You didn't seem like you were having much fun."

"You know how Bailey gets, running around all the time, never making any decisions. You spend every moment trying to tell her things she doesn't want to hear. Maybe it'll be easier for you."

"I'm serious. I'm not taking the job."

"We'll see about that. My advice to you is…" she took a drag and then tossed her butt in the gutter. "Shit, I don't have any advice. How about I just say good luck?"

"I'm gonna need it, huh?"

She laughed. "Maybe not. Maybe you're cute enough to pull it off."

"Thanks."

"Let me ask you a question."

"Shoot."

Linda eyed me for a moment. "Are you sleeping with her?"

"Bailey?"

"Yeah."

"What would make you think that?"

"I don't know. It just seems like you two have something going."

She opened the back door of her car, and I grabbed the box off the roof and put it in the backseat. "Not that it makes any difference," I said, "but we're not having sex."

"Just thought I'd ask," Linda said. "At least she gave me a full month's pay. That was nice of her. Remember one thing: Don't ever quit. Get fired." We shook hands. "It's all yours."

"You make it sound like you're handing over an aircraft carrier."

"Close enough. *Adios.*"

I took the grocery haul to Junko before proceeding to the office where Gladys and Bailey were huddled. It was unusual to see Gladys in on a Wednesday, but no firings went down without Gladys there to write the severance check and mop up the payroll details. The skinny Taiwanese chick was the Angel of Unemployment. They looked up and smiled. Before they could start talking I told them that I didn't want the combat promotion.

"What a combat promotion?" Gladys asked.

"It happens when you're in a war. The sergeant gets his head blown off and you're put in charge because you happen to be standing there. I don't want to be house manager just because Linda got fired. I don't want to be the house manager. Period."

"It's not even going to be that way anymore," Bailey said. "I decided that I need to spend more time at home. With the studio closing there's no reason for me not to be able to handle most of what Linda did. I'll deal with my schedule and the nannies and all I need from you is to keep on doing what you have been and pick up a little slack."

"What about the phones when I go out to run drills? Linda always acted like the world was going to explode if the phone rang more than twice."

"Don't worry about that. If someone calls, they can leave a message or Frank or Junko can pick up. The phones are no big deal. Julie is going to be ecstatic. I'm cutting out the highest paid household position and I'm shutting down the studio. If the ATM is happy, we'll all be happy. Trust me."

"Julie's okay with this?"

"Yes."

"I mean as a personnel move as opposed to a number."

"Promise."

"This is cool with you, Gladys?"

"Way cool groovy, man."

"What did you just say?"

And so it was settled. I was the house manager. The head jerk. The man with the plan. To seal the deal, Bailey gave me a $2,000 signing bonus. In a wintery economic climate it's hard to argue with cold hard cash.

———

During the course of that first week, everyone went out of their way to say how happy they were that I was now in charge. I did my damndest to let them know that I was not. Still, I suppose I was sort of pleased with myself because the bottom line was that the Phelans felt that I was competent enough to administrate their multi-million dollar operation. I decided that I could get the house running a hell of a lot more smoothly than it had under Linda's direction. But any illusions I held about not having to take on more responsibility were shattered that first weekend. The first after-hours call came from Bailey Friday night when she couldn't find the spare key to her car. She was apologetic as I directed her to the file in the office where we kept two extras for each of the vehicles. The Phelans didn't care that spare keys for each of the BMWs cost $75 apiece.

The shit really hit the fan Saturday morning when Julie tripped the security system. Bailey hadn't told him that she'd reset the burglar alarm after Linda had been fired. I'd written the new codes down (every full-time employee had their own) on a laminated sheet and given it to Bailey. She activated the system Friday night and then dropped the sheet somewhere and promptly forgot her code. Julie woke up the next morning and went to get the paper only to find the alarm system flashing "Invalid Code" at him for sixty seconds before all hell broke loose. First the klaxon on the roof started blaring, waking up the kids and starting them screaming, then the alarm company called both the house and my apartment to see what was going on. As new House Manager Bailey had listed me as the secondary notification in case of an activation. So I was awakened at 7:15 Saturday morning by both phones—my landline and the houseboy cell—ringing off the hook. Bailey was on the mobile with the alarm tolling in the background. The security company was on the landline asking for the codes and the password. I was a bunch of jangled nerves by the time we got it all sorted out. I'm sure the Phelan's neighbors were pleased as well. I tried to go back to sleep but knew that Julie had to be as pissed as a wet cat with a can tied to its tail, and I was sure that Bailey was claiming I'd never given her the new information. Yeah, the principle job description Bailey had failed to mention with the promotion was Number One Scapegoat.

Twenty-Seven: Fucking Nannies

THE FOLLOWING WEEK BAILEY GAVE up trying to organize the nanny schedule. Without discussion, the task was handed over to me.

There were still four serious full-timers: Jen, Sally, Astrid and Patty. Counting the night shifts, that equaled twenty-eight slots to fill each week. Since the full-timers needed forty hours, they had to work five shifts a week and then they could pick up extras if they wanted to make more money, which they usually did. The part-timers split the blanks and overnights. It should have been easy, but Sally and Jen needed their weekends off for socializing and man-hunting, and the part-timers were college girls who had to schedule around exams and beer pong tournaments. That left Astrid and Patty working the weekends, but they wanted that time off, too. The only way to have made it work would've been to make strict assignments and then let them swap amongst themselves if there were conflicts. But Patty couldn't switch her shift because it got in the way of her church's annual BBQ, and Jen and Sally *already had tickets* to fly out to Vegas on the third weekend of the month and Astrid's nephew had a soccer tournament.

Okay, go through this same logic eight times and try to make it work. I could understand why "Fucking nannies!" had been Linda and Wanda's battle cry. It was a mess.

I tried lottery drafts, I tried being a hard-ass, I tried letting them hash it out amongst themselves. Nothing worked. I went into these nanny meetings—which my buddies assumed were chick buffets where all I did was score free sex with 20-year-olds—with the intention of getting a solid schedule for the next two months. An hour of pissing and moaning and *that's-not-fairs* later we'd maybe have the next two weeks covered. If something fell through, God forbid, Bailey was going to have to cover a shift. If kids, mom and single nanny made it through eight hours in one piece, it was nothing less than miraculous. It had gotten to the point when I stared in amazement anytime I saw a mom in the park taking care of her kids by herself.

Bailey and the kids. Even the financial security aspect of it (*her pension* as Frank had put it) didn't make sense. It seemed like the only function Emma and Edward served were to get her out of doing things she didn't want to do. If one of her friends was throwing a party she didn't want to attend, I'd hear Bailey tell them that she would love to come... but Emma was sick and so she had to stay home and take care of her. If Julie wanted her to come along with him on a trip she didn't want to make, all she had to say was, "Great, we can bring the kids!" Julie knew that "bring the kids" meant bringing the kids and four nannies. How romantic.

The only thing Bailey was fanatical about concerning the children was their appearance, or rather, their future appearance. Edward was in the developmental stage where he had just learned to run and it seemed like every week he crashed into a door at full tilt and cut himself. The nannies were instructed to take him to the emergency room for even the smallest nick so he could get stitched up and avoid scars. I suppose any mother feels the same way, but Bailey's level of scar panic seemed completely out of hand.

Physical appearance was also the reason why I had to make a trip to the gas station to fuel up the nanny SUV every day. Bailey was afraid that if the kids kept sucking on their pacifiers they were going to end up with buckteeth. The problem with this directive was that the kids wouldn't go to sleep without them. Sally and Jen came up with the solution to the nap problem, which was to take the kids on long drives. The kids slept like college freshmen in the car. Although effective, that tactic got out of hand quickly. I'd call the girls and find out they were seventy-five miles down the coast in Santa Cruz just so the kids could sleep.

At any rate, the whole nanny system was a disaster within a week of me taking over Linda's job. I started to get nervous on the weekends, just waiting for the cell phone to buzz with Bailey on the other end saying that one of the nannies hadn't showed and that I needed to round up a replacement. Finding a 23-year-old girl on a Saturday morning to cover on short notice was virtually impossible. The best solution I came up with—and Bailey and I looked into it—was to hire a pair of foreign nannies who would work all goddamn week if we asked them to and take a pay cut to boot. But the only way that could happen would be if they could live on the premises. Since that was out of the question, I made some calls to see about finding a cheap apartment nearby. In the end, it seemed like it would be more of a headache that the current situation. Until Bailey decided otherwise, we were stuck with the nannies we had.

Astrid and Patty were in their forties and definitely filled the maternal vacuum Bailey left. They tried their best to teach the kids manners only to be undermined by the younger girls, especially Sally and Jen. Those two were more like older sisters than nannies, and when I found myself in the same room with the children, I was shocked at how they'd picked up mannerisms from the girls. Emma had this way of putting her hand on her hip and saying "No way!" that was an exact copy of the way Sally did it. The staff rotation made it so the kids would be denied candy one day and then be allowed to gorge themselves on it the next, depending who was working. There was zero consistency.

But it wasn't a completely bum deal. The majority of the childcare staff was, after all, of the young female variety. My office started to become their preferred break area, and they'd sprawl out on the thick carpet to tell me about their love lives or how drunk they'd been at the Up-n'-Down club the previous night. They also loved to ask me for the man's perspective on their relationship situations. I'd try to sound as authoritative as possible, sort of like a guidance counselor in a sorority house. And I must say that I had a pretty cool office. I had a mini fridge filled with choice refreshments, and I always had the tunes going on the big stereo. The view was partly obscured by the houses on the street below, but you could still see slices of the Bay.

It was easy to swat away the flirts of all the nannies except for Sally. She could keep the most angelic expression on her pixie face when telling me about giving some guy a blow job in the backseat of his car, and that really turned me on. Plus she had an ass like a soccer ball. She kept dropping hints that she was sick of dating "boys" and wanted to get herself a "man."

"And what qualifies as a 'man' in your book?" I asked.

"Some guy who's at least, I don't know…" she looked me in the eye as she sat Indian-style on the floor and smiled. "Well, your age I suppose."

This went on for a few weeks before Frank pulled me outside to smoke a cigarette with him.

"Dude, that Sally wants to fuck your brains out."

"How would you know this, Frank?"

"I can sense it."

"You're gay."

"And that means I can't tell when a human being wants to ball another human being? C'mon. I bet that little one could suck a golf ball through a garden hose. If I was straight I'd be all over that like white on rice."

"I still don't know how you're so sure about this."

"Maybe she told me. You know how these girls like to gab in the kitchen."

"Even so, I'm her boss. It wouldn't be right. Ever heard about fishing off the company pier?"

"Dude, both the pier *and* the fish wanna get fucked. What about Wanda?"

"What about her?"

"Oh come off it, she's a Chatty Cathy. She told me all about you two. I'm never using that office bathroom again."

"Great. But that was different. I was fucking *up* the chain of command, not *down*."

He tossed his cigarette over the wall and shook his head. "You breeders are so uptight. I'd still nail her. She's begging for it."

Twenty-Eight: Dot.Bomb

IN THE END, THE NEW Economy folded faster than a Beta-only video shop. It was almost like once people realized it was okay to fail, everyone gave up. Warehouses went back to being warehouses instead of corporate headquarters; dot.commer restaurants with names like "Silicon Bali" were forced to auction kitchen equipment off to pay their bank loans; bars in the Marina had to start offering drink specials. Nobody boasted about stock options anymore.

My college friend Rumi's spa finding company went under like a battleship broadsided by torpedoes. The previous spring, a large media conglomerate had offered her $5 million for the site. By spring 2000, it was worthless. Rumi couldn't even pay her parents back the seed money they'd invested. It was like Altamont in '69. Rock n' roll was dead. Put the Stones on a helicopter and go home to wait for disco.

Collins and Riley—aka the "Locs," short for "Locals"—were delighted to have their city back. In fact, we started playing a drinking game called "dot.com alley" where we'd take 40-ounce beers and post up in the doorways of abandoned Internet companies, pretending to be down n' out E-commerce wizards.

"Remember back in them good ole days when we drank champagne at that club Butter?" we'd say to each other in our best wino voices.

"I had me a Ferrari *and* a Porsche back then."

"Used to sleep on my yacht when I got sick of my mansion."

"Flew my helicopter to San Jose to meet up with my skeezer."

"Oh, man, I miss them good ole dot.com days."

We were carrying on like this one night when a bum approached to hit us up for a dollar.

"C'mon, homes," Collins slurred. "Can't you see we's broke?"

"Had all that start-up monies," Riley picked up. "Livin' with Grandma now."

I took a long pull off my 40 of Mickey's malt liquor. "Sheeet, man. How 'bout you give *us* a dollar?"

The bum shook his head as he pulled a wad of bills from the front pocket of his ratty trousers. He peeled off a fiver and handed it to me. "Hard times," he said, shuffling away. "Hard motherfuckin' times."

———

I, of course, felt like a genius taking home what were now $1,200 paychecks each week. Twelve-hundred bucks a week for a guy with no mortgage, no credit card debt, no car payments and no family to support; it seemed like a fortune. I bought two Armani suits to go along with my recently purchased Zegna and became a regular at Harris's. I booked three nights at the Hotel Nikko downtown at $300 a night when my brother Stevie's girlfriend came into town, just because I didn't want to deal with the sexual shenanigans in his room. I started drinking Heineken instead of Budweiser. There was nothing in the city that I wanted to do that I couldn't do because of lack of funds. I guess that meant I was rich.

My brother and my roommate Chase were not so well off. Chase was back with the Perfect Fit temp agency after his company did a final round of layoffs, and Stevie's prospects of ever getting Sharkattack.com off the ground grew slimmer every day. I tried to coax them out by saying I'd buy the drinks at the Balboa Café or Mas Sake.

"Why the hell would we want to go down there?" Stevie asked.

"Hold on a second. You guys just said that you wanted to go out and get some beers. What difference does it make where we get them? The beer at Balboa tastes just the same as it does at the Blarney or the Trad'r. There might actually be a couple chicks in there with a full set of teeth."

"All the dicks in there give it a bitter taste," Stevie said.

Chase laughed.

"What?" I asked.

"We don't like the crowd," Stevie explained.

"Fine," I said, pulling on my leather jacket. "You guys can go back to the Trad'r and sit in the dark with your scorpion bowls."

"Why go to Mas Sake and pay $6 for a beer, when I can go to Trad'r and pay $2?" Chase asked.

"I told you I'd pay."

"Marina Tony," Chase muttered.

"What's that?"

"Marina Tony," my brother said.

"I can't believe you guys!" I stepped back into the living room. "Just because I'm making money, you guys get to make fun of me? If you idiots would get off your asses for a minute and find decent jobs, maybe you'd stop acting so stupid. There's a whole world out there. You can leave the goddamn Richmond District for a minute and see that. They'll let you back in if it's too scary."

"So what?" my brother asked. "You want us to go out and get jobs as houseboys so we afford to drink with you in the Marina? Where do we sign up? At the dry cleaners?"

"Forget it," I said and walked out the door. I called Larry while I was trying to flag down a cab. He was already two drinks in at Mas Sake. I told him I was on the way.

Twenty-Nine: The Last Record

Considering the economic climate, it seemed like an appropriate time for the last webcast over at 24-7djs.com. Besides, Bailey wanted to set up a new party pad and Julie wouldn't let her until the studio was completely off the books.

The trick was going to be pulling the plug on the operation without Clive causing a scandal or shooting me in the groin.

"Treats me like a bloody servant, she does," Bailey's British ex-boyfriend told me over the phone. He'd started calling the house several times a day trying to get a word with the boss. "We 'ad some good times, you know?"

Bailey wouldn't talk to him, and the more she refused, the more petulant he became. She claimed that the last time she agreed to meet him they were sitting in his dirty Cadillac (which was about to be repossessed) and he got so agitated that he punched the windshield and spiderwebbed the glass. His lieutenant Jerome had gone back to wherever out of work DJs went, so now it was just Clive by himself with a couple hundred thousand dollars of stereo gear and a stack of bills a foot high.

"What about that thing you said?" Bailey asked as we brainstormed exit strategies in the office the day after the windshield incident. "You and your buddies going over there and clearing the place out?"

"The guys are down for it," I said, "but if Clive is as unstable as he seems to be, then, well, I don't know if it's such a good idea."

"You could go early in the morning," Bailey said. "Believe me, if you went in before ten he wouldn't even know you were there. If there's one thing Clive does better than sulk, it's sleep."

"I still think you could talk him into leaving if you put your mind to it."

"You don't understand. He says the only way he'll leave is if I agree to marry him. That's hardly leaving, is it?" Bailey put her head down on the desk. "I guess I'll just pay him."

"How much?" I asked.

"He gave me a figure," she said, not looking up. "I'm embarrassed to say how much."

"C'mon, how much is enough to leave Bailey Phelan?"

"Enough to make Gladys's nose start bleeding."

I asked Gladys when she came in that Friday. "Huh!" she said. "Enough for you or me to live on like king and queen."

I figured fifty grand.

Gladys asked me to take the envelope containing the check to the post office and get it sent certified mail.

"Wait," Bailey said, taking the envelope from me. "He's coming over to pick it up."

"You crazy!" exclaimed Gladys. "Psycho Clive gonna kill us all! I got husband and kids to worry about!"

"You sure this is a good idea?" I asked.

"The only way he'd agree to this was if I'd hand it over to him personally. Trust me, he won't try anything with people around. The British are like that. They always preserve dignity in public."

I went upstairs and suggested to Jen and Sally that they take the kids out for the afternoon and not come home until I called them with the all clear.

We decided the exchange should happen in the basement to prevent any unpleasantness from spreading upstairs. I'd answer the intercom when Clive hit the buzzer on the front door and tell him the remote opener wasn't working. He'd come in through the service entrance and talk to Bailey in the main office. Just to be safe, I placed weapons in easily accessible spots; a crowbar behind the office door, a sharp screwdriver next to the fax machine, and a can of pepper spray in my desk drawer. I also brought both panic buttons downstairs. These were little devices that looked like garage door openers. When you hit the button, the alarm system went nuts. I knew these worked because Miss Tang had accidentally activated one a few weeks back, sending the house into chaos and summoning the fire department, which Frank was happy about. He had a wicked crush on one of the firefighters. Bailey had managed to sleep through the whole episode.

I placed one of the devices in the laundry room and the other in my shirtfront pocket.

"What's that?" Bailey asked.

I told her it was the panic box.

"For what?"

"Well, you know, in case Clive freaks out."

Bailey laughed until she saw I was serious. The she turned back to her computer and continued working on a new scheduling program. Lots of family time.

Gladys ran upstairs when the front gate buzzed. I wanted to follow her, but Bailey gave me a look that was almost pleading. I picked up the phone and asked Clive to come around the side.

"Getting the servants treatment now, am I?" he said when I met him at the service entrance. He had several days of stubble on his chin and reeked of marijuana. His sneakers were untied and he'd shaved his head. I looked for a bulge in his waistline, but he was wearing a baggy shirt and I couldn't tell if he was packing heat. I explained that the buzzer was broken.

"Whatever the princess sez, right? Watch yourself with 'er, mate. She in the office?"

I followed Clive with the crowbar held behind my leg. I heard Bailey chirp hello like everything was normal. Clive grunted a reply. I set the crowbar behind the shredder and went into my office, not closing the door. Clive and Bailey were standing like high school kids breaking up in the lunchroom.

"Can we go somewhere private and talk?" he asked pitifully.

"I've got an appointment in ten minutes. I'm sorry. Tony forgot to tell me about it. Here's what we talked about."

"Right. Pay me and I'll piss off back to the U.K. Can I close this door?" I reached into the drawer for the pepper spray.

"Clive, we've gone through this already. Can't we just part friends?"

"How do you mean?"

"Please don't do this."

"Okay then."

Neither of them said anything for a minute. I punched up Line Two and dialed Line One. I picked up on the first ring and asked myself to hold.

"Bailey," I called from my office, "it's for you. Your mom. You want me to take a message?"

"No, I'll get it."

"Right. Okay, then." Clive spit the words out. "It's cheers then, innit it?"

She picked up the phone and didn't pause when she found the line dead. "Hi, mom! Is everything okay?"

I followed Clive out of the office. Bailey mouthed "Thank you" as I passed her desk. I caught up to him at the base of the driveway and he turned around. He had a film of tears in his eyes. I wondered if he was really that broken up about Bailey or if it was just the money he was considering.

"Don't panic, mate. I'm leaving." He scrubbed his eyes with the back of his hand.

"For what it's worth, I don't think this hasn't been handled well on her part."

"Thanks. I appreciate that. You know, you've been cool about the whole thing and I... Really."

Before I had time to react, Clive had me in a bear hug. He squeezed me so hard that the panic button in my shirtfront activated. He backed away from me as the bell on the roof started clanging. He looked at the bulge in my shirt and gave me a sorrowful look that seemed to say, *et tu Brute?* I shrugged my shoulders and closed the door on Clive.

Bailey was standing in the laundry room with the can of pepper spray at the ready.

"What happened?" she asked over the din.

"Nothing. False alarm."

"He's gone?"

"Yes."

Frank opened the door to the kitchen to ask if everything was okay. The phone started ringing as I yelled back that it was a false alarm.

"Don't cancel it!" Frank called down the stairs. "I want the firemen to show up!"

Such is love.

———

A few days after the final meeting with Clive, I drove Bailey and my brother—who, despite his bad attitude, had become my on-call assistant—over to the studio in a 25-foot U-haul. We could've managed with a shoebox. The place had been cleaned out except for some broken records scattered on the living room floor. There was also a note taped to the front door from the landlord saying that he was keeping the damage deposit because of "the multiple holes in the doors and walls." We'd be hearing from his attorney after he'd done a full assessment of the mess.

"Oh well," Bailey said brightly. "Time to find a new boyfriend!"

Thirty: Cutbacks

Although initially Bailey had blown off the catastrophe with Clive like it was nothing more than a fling, she spent the following two weeks in bed. Rather, she tried to stay in bed. Anyone who's ever had a housekeeper can attest to how difficult it is to stay under the covers when there's someone (or in Bailey's case, ten people) monitoring your closed bedroom door. Since Max the cat slept with Bailey, Robby couldn't brush his teeth until she got up; Junko couldn't rotate the sheets in the master bedroom; Bailey's personal trainer had to wait fifteen minutes before rolling up his yoga mats and declaring the workout cancelled.

Bailey's shrink had also put her on anti-depressants (which Bailey called "forget pills"), so when she did emerge from her room she was completely wacked. The new pharmacopeia also had a bad interaction with chardonnay, which Bailey got blasted on several times a week. Bailey was now able to use the new meds as an excuse for why she couldn't recall any of the things anyone told her. It wasn't like she had much going on those days, anyway. After a fortnight of sulking, she emerged filled with manic energy and bounced around the house starting new projects. One afternoon she began to chronologically sort all the photos of Emma and Edward, only to leave them scattered on the basement floor before the operation was a quarter completed. She tried to catalogue all her handbags, but got bored at "F" for Fendi. The Barney sing-alongs with the kids gave her a headache. Going to the gym made her feel fat.

I kept waiting for her friends to show up and take care of her, but the female posse never appeared. In fact, since I'd been working for Bailey I'd only met two of her buddies, despite the fact that her computer database had almost a hundred names in the "Personal Friends" file. One of them had an uncanny knack for stopping by the house at the end of her supposed "jog" right when Frank was putting the finishing touches on that day's food. She liked to take samples home with her. The other one always needed a loan. The rest of the names were purely phone relationships. But it was no surprise that Bailey didn't have anyone knocking at her door. For every five invites to play dates with the kids or shopping excursions she got, Bailey accepted one—then it was fifty-fifty that she'd blow it off at the last minute.

Instead of dialing some of those numbers in the Friend file, Bailey hung out with her staff. On nights when Sally and Jen were off, the boss would roust them for a drink and dancing escapade. The nannies would creep into work the following day and have to deal with the kids while Bailey slept it off. One Tuesday night Bailey got so bored that she showed up unannounced at my apartment and took Chase, Stevie and me out for sake and sushi, in that order. We came back to the flat for more drinks after dinner. My roommates and I watched in awe as Bailey pillaged our liquor cabinet, scattered our CDs, and danced around the living room knocking over plants. I finally had to drive her back to the Pacific Heights at 1 a.m.

"Let's park," she said.

"Yeah, right in your garage," I replied.

"No, silly. I want to *park, park*. C'mon, pull over."

I found a spot of curb without any streetlights four or five blocks from the house and killed the engine. Bailey was in my lap as soon as the key was out of the ignition. She started to French kiss me, tasting like a handful of chewed up Altoids. At first, I held up my hands like someone was pointing a pistol at me, but slowly I let them drop to Bailey's hips and helped her grind her crotch into me. She'd just started working the fly of my jeans, when I turned my head to the side to break our lip-lock.

"Wassa matter?" she slurred into my ear.

"Not here," I said.

"We'll get in the backseat." Bailey started to crawl over the center console.

I grabbed her by the waist. "That's not what I mean."

Bailey gave me a pouty look over her shoulder. "Then where?"

"We should get you home."

"Why the hell can't I get anything I want?" she complained as she plopped back into the passenger seat.

"Because we work together. You're my boss."

"Wanda was your boss, too, wasn't she?"

"I don't think that's the same thing. I'm talking about us working together without—"

"Oh, shut the fuck up, Tony!" The sudden vehemence of Bailey's words hit me like a slap.

"Hey, I didn't mean to—"

"You scared? Afraid Julie's gonna find out and fire you?"

"Bailey—"

"Or is it Sally? Don't want to ruin your chances with the nanny by fooling around with me, huh? Now that

Wanda's gone, you've got find someone new in the house to fuck?"

"That's not it at all," I said, trying to keep my voice under control. I gripped the steering wheel hard.

"So where are we going?" Bailey asked, crossing her arms.

I turned on the ignition and flipped a u-turn. "I'm taking you home."

"Then hurry the fuck up."

I got the car into the garage and Bailey stumbled out without saying good night. She tripped on the way into the laundry room, but slammed the door in my face when I tried to check on her. I listened to her stumble up the stairs before I ducked under the closing garage door. I walked down the block far enough so that I could no longer see the house and called a cab.

———

Bailey decided to fire a couple people the next day, and surprisingly, my head wasn't one of those on the chopping block. True to form, Bailey hadn't said anything about our ride home, but she did tell me to summon Gladys when she slipped past me on her way to the closet. When we sat down with the house accountant an hour later, I got the distinct impression that Bailey was avoiding eye contact with me. I wondered if I should have just fucked her; if the situation at hand was already this uncomfortable, sex couldn't have made it much worse.

Bailey told us that Julie was of the opinion that since the kids were now two-and-a-half they didn't need a tag-team of nannies working each shift. Bailey had decided to get rid of Patty and Astrid. She said we could justify the cuts by saying it was to insure Emma and Edward's safety; she didn't feel like either of the older nannies were in the physical condition to keep up with the little terrors. There was some logic to this. The heavyset and asthmatic Patty was too damn slow to catch them when they ran away, and she'd sealed her fate when she'd asked for a couple of those kid leashes. Astrid, on the other hand, was too small; Bailey argued there was no way she could pick both kids up in case of, say, a tsunami. More than the children's safety, Bailey was uncomfortable with how the older nannies had been hinting that the kids were becoming even more emotionally unstable due to the fact Bailey didn't spend any time with them. Bailey knew this, of course, but that didn't mean she wanted to hear it verbalized.

As for Sally and Jen, they were quitting after the next trip to Jackson Hole in January and moving to L.A. to try and find jobs keeping books for movie stars. They had, after all, spent two years studying accounting at junior college.

But first, we had to break the news to Patty and Astrid. It was going to be Bailey and me in my office and Gladys outside to distribute the final paychecks and severance packages. Patty was to be the first dismissal, but right before she was to report to the office, Bailey bolted for an appointment that I hadn't seen on her schedule.

I'd never fired anyone before, and Patty sat there looking at me with a faint smile as I stuttered my way around the subject before finally blurting out that we had decided to "go in another direction." I think I'd picked that line up from a TV show. Patty didn't say a word as I continued to hack my way through the execution. Finally she put her hand on mine.

"I was planning to get upset when this day came, but I can see you're upset enough for the both of us. The thing is that

I'm really gonna miss those kids. Maybe I can come back and visit them?" We looked at each other for a brief moment, both of us knowing that wasn't going to happen.

"Okay," she hefted herself out of the chair, "I suppose Gladys out there has my last check?"

She turned back to look at me with her hand on the door-knob. "Don't take offense, sweetie, but I don't think you're cut out for this kind of thing."

"You mean firing people?" I asked.

"I mean the whole thing."

Astrid was next, and Bailey still wasn't back from Mystery Appointment.

"It's about time," Astrid cut in before I had time to explain about her being too small to carry both kids out of a wildfire. "*Esperando este momento para dos meses*. My key is here. Gladys has my check, yes? You're a sweet boy," she got on her tip-toes to give me a kiss on both cheeks. "I will miss you and the little monsters and Frankie, but that is all. You should find a better job than this."

And that was that. It was probably good that Bailey hadn't been there because then I'm sure the nannies would've felt like they needed to make a big show of dismay. Like Linda said: never quit, get fired.

Hiring new nannies proved to be more problematic than I'd expected despite the glut of childcare workers on the market now that so many young women who had previously worked for the dot.coms had been reduced to babysitting. I signed contracts with two agencies and also put an ad in the paper. As a result, I was deluged with applicants over the course of the next month. After I'd sifted through stacks of résumés, I did phone interviews. If those went well, I made appointments to meet the prospects at the house. It all felt very much like a dating service—or calling an escort. I'd lead the girls into the library after offering them something to drink, taking a seat in Julie's leather wingback chair while the prospective nannies perched on the edge of the sofa.

In my mind, a good nanny was someone who wasn't going to be a pain in my ass, who'd put up with Bailey's inconsistency, and stay out of Julie's way. And if they were good-looking, all the better. But when it came to questions about what they would bring to the kids' lives, I drew a blank.

The girls didn't know what to make of me, either. I always told them I was the house manager, but they didn't seem to buy that. They'd interviewed with other people in my position, and none of them wore Guided by Voices t-shirts and cargo shorts. One of them even went so far as to ask if there were really any kids involved, which was a legit question because they were never present during the interviews. Neither was Bailey for that matter. I ended up interviewing twenty nannies. Some had worked for movie stars, others had babysat for middle class mom and dad's. There were European professionals, and college kids who did it just to pay tuition. I decided that I liked the ones who had worked for wealthy people before (so they wouldn't be shocked by the excess,and also because Bailey seemed to like a certain pedigree) but who didn't want to make a career out of it. In short, I didn't want a nanny who acted like a nanny. But again, this was all me and had nothing to do with the kids. I complained about this to Bailey. But she didn't want to hear me.

I only found one that I thought would fit. Her name was Meredith and she was 24-years-old, had just graduated from college, and had worked for a very rich family all through school. Meredith got me when she told a story about how she used to take the kids to the batting cages. Edward needed a couple fastballs to the ribs to toughen him up. Meredith also happened to be a hottie. 5'10", short blonde hair and a way of rolling her words around her tongue stud when she spoke.

I set up a final meeting between her and Bailey the following day, and within three minutes Bailey said, "You're hired." I told Meredith to come in Friday to fill out her tax paperwork with Gladys.

"You sly old dog," Frank said when Meredith left.

"What?"

"Dude, you're stocking the house with breeders. Like your own little bordello, isn't it?"

"Give me a break, Frank"

"Hey, I don't blame you. Trade out those two old bags for fresh chicken. You're a lot smarter than I thought. Try this meatball." He spooned one out of the sauce for me.

"Very good," I said about the meatball. "But I'm not quite sure if I know what the hell I'm doing."

"I don't know, dude, I think you've got a pretty nice set up. If I was Julie I'd give you a raise for improving the scenery."

Thirty-One: What Recession?

With the nanny situation under temporary control, the remainder of the year settled into an easy routine. I still came in around 8 a.m., more for the $35 worth of peace and quiet than due to any pressing need to take care of business. After checking the garage for Julie's car and the voicemail for any urgent messages, I'd go upstairs for breakfast. Then I'd return to my office with a bagel, some of Julie's fresh-squeezed OJ, an espresso and the paper. Reading through the *Chronicle* and checking my E-mail would take me to around nine, when the rest of the staff showed up. From nine to ten I'd make phone calls and cancel appointments for Bailey. The mail came around 10 a.m. and I'd sort through all that. The biggest problem with the post was cornering Bailey for the five minutes it took for her to look over everything she needed to approve or reject— parties, donations, reunions, magazine renewals, personal mail. Putting correspondence on her desk was folly. And since she was still wacked out on those forget pills, it was a good bet that she'd fail to show up for half of the engagements she'd agreed upon. The anti-depressants, I was coming to understand, were becoming just another line of defense for my boss, one more excuse for her to pretend not to know what the hell was going on.

Bailey started moving around 11:30, but now that I was house manager—and thus bearer of bothersome tidings—I usually didn't even get to speak to her until she had fled the premises. I'd hear her clip-clop from her closet to the garage and start her Beamer. Then she would call me on her cell phone. Most of the time, the phone rang before she was even out of the driveway. Not only was this necessary because she was always running late, but she also knew that if she stuck around the house, someone—Junko, the nanny, a contractor—would force her to make a decision.

I made my rounds of the city after lunch. I checked with Junko and Frank for things they needed from the grocery store, picked up the nannies' list from the nursery, asked Robby the Cat Lady about pet supplies, and called Gladys to see if any checks needed to go to the bank. Then I switched from house manager to houseboy and took off in the Volvo for two hours. I had started using the Phelan's discarded Volvo because somebody had stolen the stereo out of my Nissan while it was parked outside my apartment.

I'd get back to the house from my errands around 2 p.m. and spend the next few hours looking for stuff to do. I'd save the magazine filing on the top floor for nice days, and then do it as slowly as possible so I could soak up the view. Junko always had little jobs for me: pulling items from high shelves, fixing broken cleaning implements, moving furniture around so she could vacuum. The housekeeper also maintained a chart of all the light bulbs in the house. Despite the new financial directives which had included paring down the fleet of nannies, Julie still insisted that no bulb ever burn out. I tried to take the used bulbs home as they still had many hours left on them, but I quickly ran out of places to store them. All these tasks had previously been farmed out to a local handyman who charged $50 an hour. Seriously, the guy billed $50 to change light bulbs. It made me feel better about the Speed Sticks I had started to sneak in with groceries on the company credit card.

And then, for the last two hours of the day, I'd read magazines, speed dial the college radio station using all five of the Phelan's phone lines to try and score free concert tickets, and occasionally jerk off to pixelated Internet porn when I was sure I was the only one in the basement. A quick rub out was better than taking advantage of Sally when she skipped into my office during those slow hours to demonstrate new yoga poses. Internet skin was my way of avoiding sexual-harassment violations.

Once or twice a week Bailey would have a late afternoon freak-out and call the house to have me scramble the fighters. But usually she only needed me to drive downtown and meet her at a store to help carry home her fresh kill. These calls came without fail at 4:55 in the afternoon.

If I was feeling industrious, I'd pick up where I'd left off on the filing. In my office there were three monstrous cabinets chock-full of old documents. I'd started looking through them out of boredom only to realize how ancient and absolutely useless the majority of the files were. Linda had kept every receipt and a copy of every memo from the past three years. Now that I had experienced the boredom that came along with the job, I started to understand why she'd churned out so many documents, but this was ludicrous. She'd printed each in *triplicate*.

Going through the files and throwing stuff out was actually pretty enjoyable. In the process of sifting through everything I found all kinds of useless, but interesting, information about life in the house before I'd arrived. There were old trip itineraries, insurance filings from car wrecks and ski injuries, personnel files of former staffers complete with copies of driver's licenses and old pay sheets, menus from the former chef (which I showed to Frank, causing him much concern about his current dish selection), receipts and records from things so long gone that they may as well have never existed. One file was dedicated to the search for Emma and Edward's sperm and egg donors. It included rejection letters to candidates explaining why their chromosomes had been deemed unworthy.

The files were also useful. When Bailey or Julie came home unexpectedly I could stick my head in the cabinet with the files strewn around my feet and look exceedingly industrious. With that in mind, I limited myself to just a few sections each week so I could stretch the job out as long as possible. It took me almost three months to separate the wheat from the chaff.

It was during one of these file cabinet afternoons that I came across the memo Linda had sent to The Perfect Fit before I was hired. It read, in typical Linda fashion, like this:

We're looking for a full time handsome "gay" gentleman (polished) who will do: 1) errands, retail shopping, day-to-day organization, purchasing fresh flowers, some decorating, answer front door to receive guests, drop Bailey downtown when needed, check all household supplies (certain food/drink items, propane gas for barbecue, paper goods supplies etc.) and any other house related items that come up. Kind of like a "major-domo"—additional household assistant that can think on their feet and most importantly "anticipate other people's needs" (all staff members, not just Bailey or Julie)!!! A very nurturing, caring type of individual who loves great people, good food (our chef spoils us) and especially someone who loves babies as there is always one to help hold, feed or keep occupied from time to time.

Can we specify gay?

The memo was dated two days after I'd first gone into the temp agency. Damn, did I laugh my ass off after reading that. They'd been looking for Rupert Everett and they got Vince Vaughn. I tucked the memo into my wallet. Maybe if Bailey ever got really mad at me I could whip it out and use it as my *mea culpa*. It wasn't my fault they hired a straight guy.

I was so amused by the job description that I asked for another five-dollar raise, my justification being that I had essentially allowed them to combine two, $73,000-a-year, jobs into one position. I was surprised when Bailey said yes. A couple more months and I'd be making six-digits.

Thirty-Two: Sex Education

"First of all," Sally explained, "I'm moving to L.A. and need the experience. Second, I've still only slept with two guys."

"Your high school boyfriend and that guy whose name you don't remember from La Barca?"

"Right," the nanny said.

"I'm sure you could fix that problem without my help." I turned back to my computer and pretended to organize Bailey's schedule.

"But I don't want to hook up with just *anyone*," Sally protested. "I want someone I can trust."

"What makes me so trustworthy?"

"I don't know." Sally rolled onto her back and stretched out on the floor of my office. Her shirt rode up to reveal her flat stomach. "You just *are*."

"I'm your boss."

"Not for loooong," she sang. She and Jen were both counting the days until their last Phelan family trip the first week of January. "Technically, I've already quit."

"Ah, I'd like to, but…"

Sally sat up and smiled. "But what?"

"It's just not right."

"Not right?" she was pulling a face now and I felt my dick start to get hard. I scooted my chair further under my desk.

Sally crawled over to me and put her arms around my neck. "Just think," she whispered into my ear, "we could have sex all over the house when there no was no one else home."

"Ever heard of video cameras?"

"You and your video cameras," she said, running her hand over my chest. "I think it's hooey. Besides, I bet Julie would totally get off watching that video. I was thinking we could do it in the nursery closet. For some reason I always get horny in there."

"Sally. Stop." I unwrapped her arms from my neck. "You're putting me in a very unprofessional state of mind."

"Good."

Young Sally had been putting the full court press on me for over a month at that point. The more I protested, the more adamantly she insisted that we had to make it happen, especially since she was quitting. This talk about her needing sexual experience was her latest tactic, and I was having a very hard time resisting. And it wasn't just Sally who had me in a knot. Meredith, the new nanny with the tongue stud, was also proving to be a terrible flirt. I realized that the idea of finding a gay guy to fill my position from the start might not have been an entirely aesthetic thing. The dude who decided to have eunuchs guard his harem knew what he was doing.

"Can I just see it?" Sally asked.

"See what?"

"Your…" she giggled. "Your penis."

"Sally, go upstairs."

"C'mon," she protested. "I've only seen a couple."

"Go!"

"Wanda said you had a big one."

"Sally, I swear to God, you better get the hell out of here right now."

Sally did a gymnastic handspring off the floor and gave me a good look at that ass of hers as she sashayed out of the office.

"If you change your mind," she called over her shoulder, "Jen and I are going to the Black Cat Club tonight."

As soon as she was gone I ducked into the bathroom and jerked off. The relief was temporary. I went upstairs to bum a smoke from Frank.

"Dude," he said, lighting my cigarette by the barbeque, "you've got that Sally going every which way but loose."

"Tell me about it," I said.

"You need to tell me your secret. I haven't gotten laid in four months."

"It's really simple, Frank. You've just got to put up a fight."

He gaped. "You mean you haven't fucked her yet?"

"No."

"My God, that's genius! No wonder Bailey put you in charge."

My genius and I went to the Black Cat Club on Market Street that night. I was already half-drunk when I got there and totally unprepared to defend myself from myself. An hour after arriving, I suggested to Sally that she take me home and do with me what she would. Sally grabbed my wrist and pulled me out of the bar. She drove us back to her flat—running over a garbage can in front of her building in the process—and we went up to her room. She made me sit down on the edge of the bed while she undressed, and then made me do the same for her.

"Am I doing this right?" she asked, looking up in the middle of giving me a blow job.

I pushed myself back into her mouth, but made her stop before I came.

"What do we do now?" she asked, laying back on the bed and gently stroking her pussy. "I've only done it missionary style."

I told her I had several things in mind.

"Good," she said as she pulled me into bed. "I want to do *everything*."

———

Sally, obviously feeling that she needed more practice, stopped by my apartment two days later. Considering the terribly exposed position of my room and not wanting Stevie or Chase to interfere with Sally's education, I sent them down the street to the Blarney Stone with forty bucks and instructions to stay there until I called with the All-Clear.

Now that young Sally had given me a taste, I was hungry for more. The next time she came into my office, I tried to pull her into the bathroom for a quickie.

Sally made a face. "You had sex with Wanda in there, didn't you?"

"Who told you that?" I asked, unbuckling her belt.

Sally backed away. "Look, I think you were right," she said.

"About what?" I asked.

"About us. You know, about us hooking up. I think we should just stay friends."

"You're kidding."

"It's just that I really, really respect you and I want us to be friends," Sally said as she refastened her belt. "I'm afraid that if we keep having sex then we won't be."

"Who the hell gave you that idea?" I asked.

"I don't know," she said, checking her hair. "I went out with Bailey the other night."

"And Bailey told you to stop hooking up with me?"

Sally laughed. "Nothing like that. We were just talking about…things. Besides," she added brightly, "I met this guy last night who's from L.A. I think I'm in love."

"After one night?"

"Yes! Isn't that crazy?"

"What about all these weeks you've been telling me how much you wanted to sleep with me?"

"We did, didn't we? It was fun, right?"

"So why do we have to stop now?"

Sally cocked her head and smiled. "Well, you're my boss, right?"

I threw my hands up. "Okay, Sally, you got me."

The nanny gave me a hug. "Oh, I'm so glad you're taking this well! I knew there was a reason why I wanted to have sex with you."

Bailey came into the office a few minutes later to ask how everything was going. It was unusual for her to start a conversation with an inquiry. I told her things were fine.

"No problems with the nannies?" she asked as she collected her purse and sunglasses.

Fucking nannies.

Thirty-Three: Tow Away Zone

The holiday season finally pulled Bailey out of her post-DJ doldrums. Bailey loved to spend money, give gifts, and, probably more importantly, she thrived on the holiday chaos around Union Square. Since parking downtown was such a bitch in those frenzied days before Christmas, I spent a lot of time ferrying her back and forth between the house and the stores. The traffic didn't bother me so long as I was on the clock. It might seem extravagant to pay a guy $40 an hour to sit in the car and read magazines while you shop until you considered the fact that when Bailey drove herself it was guaranteed that she'd pick up at least one ticket. She had a complete and utter disregard for parking regulations and would park her sedan in red zones, bus zones, loading zones, on sidewalks, and in spots reserved for police cars. It got so bad that she instructed me to collect a month's worth of tickets and take them over to the Department of Parking and Traffic in order to pay them off with petty cash so Julie wouldn't get wise. I'd drop over $500 each time I went to the DPT.

Therefore it was no shock when Bailey finally got towed a few days before Christmas. The surprise was that she had been driving Julie's coupe.

"I don't know what happened," she told me when I picked her up outside of Nordstrom's. "I parked in front of Gump's, and when I got back the car was gone."

"Did you see any signs?"

"There weren't ANY. There was just some stupid fire hydrant."

"The fire hydrant might have had something to do with it," I said.

"But not that fast! I was only in the store for half an hour."

Thankfully, Julie was out of town for a couple days, so we could have his car back in the garage by the time he got home. And since we'd pay cash for the fine, he'd never find out. Bailey and I drove across town to the yard at the end of the day, and had the car out by 5:30. It was cold, but the city hummed with pre-holiday energy, surprisingly vibrant considering the economic situation. While the dot.commers had seemed omnipresent to me when I'd been out of work, the resilient buzz of Christmas activity made me realize that they'd been a relatively small percentage of the population. Now that so many of them had packed up, the city fell back into the hands of the old guard. Natives like my buddies Collins and Riley slugged eggnog in the raucous bars around Union Square while wealthy women glided through the golden glow of Neiman Marcus in their ankle-length furs.

Since Julie's car had managed the impound without any damage, Bailey figured we should pop into Luna for a celebratory drink. We valet parked the cars at the restaurant and pressed through the crush of people to get seats at the busy bar.

"Remember," I said, "We've got to wash the tow truck driver's wax marks off the windshield when we get back to the house."

"You're so cute when you get bossy," Bailey said. Things between us had improved since I'd stopped sleeping with Sally.

So much of my relationship with Bailey was based upon flirting and the possibility of sex, and the subtle back and forth had made my job bearable. Perhaps it was just a way of keeping my self-respect intact; so long as Bailey wanted to hook up with me, I still had some measure of control.

I introduced Bailey to bourbon. One Old Fashioned turned into two and then three and then dinner at the bar. Bailey and I were scrunched up against each other as patrons reached over us for their drinks. We talked about Clive and the staff and the holidays. I felt so fuzzy that I insisted on getting the check.

"Wow," Bailey said. "I can't remember the last time anyone besides ATM picked up my tab." She didn't have to lean over far to plant a smooch on the side of my mouth.

The problem was that after four bourbons Bailey was in no condition to drive. We didn't want to tarnish our triumph by having her get popped for a DUI on the way home, so we decided to leave her car with the valets and I'd drive Julie's coupe. Bailey insisted that I detour through downtown and up over Telegraph Hill so we could see the Christmas lights. The little white bulbs strung up in the trees along the undulating street made it look like a giant nighttime toboggan run.

"The Tonga Room!" Bailey cried. "One drink! I insist upon one drink in the Tonga!"

The Tonga Room used to be the Fairmont Hotel's indoor swimming pool area. The pool remains, but it's been filled in with artificial reefs. Out in the middle there's a floating pagoda where a Chinese band plays Sheena Easton covers for the mixed crowd of tourists, hotel guests, hookers, and wealthy drunks on the slum. That night they were working through Bing Crosby's holiday songbook. The lighting was provided by flickering tiki torches, which resulted in an ambiance similar to being inside an enormous cave where they serve $20 drinks. Bailey and I sat at one end of the bar and ordered a scorpion bowl. Bailey lamented that she hadn't found a new boyfriend as we sipped the high-octane concoction through neon straws. The scorpion bowls at the Tonga weren't quite as poisonous as the ones at the Trad'r, but they still got right on top of you.

"There's this really cute guy at work," she said. "But I don't know. Last time I hooked up with him he got all grouchy."

"Office romances are tough," I agreed. "I try to avoid them."

"Yeah, I heard all about *that*," she said sarcastically.

I tried to look innocent. "What are you talking about?"

"You've slept with everyone on the staff aside from me and Frank."

"I never touched Junko!"

Bailey laughed. "So what can a little innocent mashing do?"

She shook her hair out of her face and I slid my hand down the back of her stretch pants as we kissed. It was so dark in our corner of the bar that I didn't have any worry about being recognized. Just a couple tourists feeling the scorpion's sting. We broke the clutch and Bailey smiled devilishly.

"I forgot what a good kisser the guy at the office is," she said. "Maybe I should get a room and invite him on up?"

"I think we need to find you a new boyfriend. Someone you don't work with."

"You're a spoilsport," she pouted. "One more kiss for Christmas, then."

"You're the boss."

My cell buzzed and I pulled away from Bailey's embrace to answer it. She snapped her fingers at the bartender to order another scorpion.

It was Stevie on the phone and I got a bright idea that would solve our transport problems as well as prevent me from taking Bailey up on her offer of a room for the night. It's one thing to sleep with co-workers and quite another to shack up with the check signer. I told my brother to catch a cab to the Tonga so we could swing back by Luna and get Bailey's car on our way home. When Stevie balked, Bailey took the phone and suggested that as an on-call employee it might reflect badly on his Christmas bonus if he didn't get his ass down to the Fairmont, pronto. The lady had a way with words. Once that had been decided, Bailey and I resumed our make-out session.

Stevie tapped me on the shoulder thirty minutes later. He didn't seem surprised to find me in a lip lock with my boss. The general consensus amongst the fellas was that I spent most of my days in just that type of clutch. Of course we couldn't leave the Tonga until we'd shared another scorpion.

By the time we staggered out of the hotel lobby—Stevie and I flanking Bailey like bodyguards, which she loved—we were drunk as loons. Since Stevie was the most sober, he drove back to Luna while Bailey sat on my lap.

It was decided that I'd drive Bailey's sedan and she and Stevie would stay in Julie's coupe. It was past midnight, and since it was a weekday, the streets were almost empty. At the base of Franklin—a three-lane, one way boulevard running from downtown, up over the Pac Heights and all the way down to the Marina—I pulled alongside Julie's car to see how my boss and Stevie were fairing. Bailey looked over at me, smiled, then turned back to say something to Stevie. The light turned green and my brother put his foot down so hard the tires smoked. I hit it right after him.

The lights on Franklin are timed, so when we took off from the first green on Market, all I saw ahead of us was open road. After four blocks I was going 75 mph and Stevie, in the sports car, was pulling away. I put the pedal to the floor. At Van Ness we caught up with a Porsche in the middle lane and blew past him on both sides like he was in a Yugo. He got on it after us but there was no way he could catch up. I knew Stevie, like myself, was thinking Steve McQueen and *Bullitt*. I could see Bailey urging him on like a jockey whipping a racehorse. I was up to 85 now (in a 40 zone) and Stevie must've been going 90 when he slammed on the brakes, cursing I'm sure that he wasn't driving a stick so he could heel-toe, and power slid around the corner of Sacramento, the back end of the coupe missing a parked car by a foot. I kept on up Franklin, took a hard left on Pacific and hauled ass straight to the house. I got there ahead of them and killed the engine, assuming a casual, what-took-you-so-long pose. Thirty seconds passed and they still hadn't showed. The only sound was the ticking of the Beamer's engine.

When I heard a siren coming from the direction of Sacramento Street, my buzz leaked out of me like a plug had been pulled. My concern was not if my brother was okay or if Bailey was hurt, the thought was *how the hell am I going to explain this to Julie?*

I was just about to drive down to investigate what had happened when Stevie slid Julie's coupe past me and headed into the garage.

"We beat you!" Bailey screamed as she tumbled out of the passenger seat. "We had you fucking beat!" A couple neighborhood dogs started barking at the ruckus.

"She told me to stop for gas," Stevie grumbled. "I had you clean."

"Whoo, what a rush!" Bailey gushed. "I say that kind of race calls for champagne. Champagne for the winners. Champagne for me and Stevie. No bubbly for Tony."

Bailey broke out the Dom and I drank deep in relief. One cop car, one truck pulling away from the curb, one alley cat wandering into the street and we would have been truly and completely toast.

Driving home in my Nissan—which felt like a golf cart compared to the Phelan's heavy German machines—I asked Stevie if he understood how stupid we'd just been.

"I don't know about you," he said, still pissed that Bailey had prevented him from winning outright, "but I was in control the whole time. What would've been really stupid is if you'd kept going at it like you were at the bar. If I hadn't shown up, you'd be in *really* deep shit."

My hangover the next day was blinding, as if the Gods were punishing me for the previous night's foolishness. I still made it into work before nine and sat there in the office trying to figure how many lives I'd squandered. Julie had already come home from the airport and left for the office.

Bailey crawled downstairs around noon to find me lying on the floor under my desk with a cold wash towel over my eyes. Bailey laid down on the floor next to me and groaned.

"We forgot to erase the wax marks," she said.

Thirty-Four: Reaganomics

Bailey wasn't kidding when she'd convinced Stevie to meet us at the Tonga Room by invoking his part-time status as a Phelan employee. The only income Stevie had at the end of 2000 came from the Julie Phelan fountainhead. His company, Sharkattack.com, was as dead as a can of tuna fish, so I called him whenever I needed an extra pair of hands. You would have thought that muscle-bound Frank would have been helpful when it came to moving furniture, but he couldn't even hold up his end of a short sofa.

"Dude," he'd gasp after carrying a chair up one flight of stairs, "My body, it's a Hollywood set. All definition, no strength."

Stevie's going rate as Special Assistant to the Houseboy was $25, about the same as the temp agency charged to send someone over and half of what the movers billed. Stevie wasn't my only associate on the gravy train that season. I had a regular patronage deal going as plenty of unemployed friends needed dough for Hanukkah shopping. The Phelans paid well—and in cash. All Bailey said was "get some help" and I don't think she knew or cared that these folks weren't coming from the temp agency. During the weeks leading up to Christmas, I had Collins maximizing his winter break by hanging holiday lights in the courtyard, and my roommate Chase decorating the living room tree in between eating all the leftovers in the fridge. ("Dude, I love this guy!" Frank gushed.) My brother was secretly assembling Emma and Edward's pile of X-mas toys in the basement, and I hired an old colleague from Denver to address the Christmas cards and care packages. The sole employment condition for these temps was a multi-drink kickback to me after they got paid. I think Reagan had this in mind when he introduced the term "trickle down economics."

Heather, the girl I used to work with in Denver, had always been a left-wing radical type. Since moving out to Berkeley, her anti-corporate feelings had taken on an almost militant bent. She'd been laid off from the non-profit Free Mumia organization a month previous (Mumia Abu Jamal was on death row for shooting two cops) so when Bailey suggested that my penmanship wasn't appropriate for the Christmas cards, I called Heather to see if she'd be interested in spending a few days at the house as a handwriting expert. Heather had been giving me loads of grief the whole time I'd been working for Julie, e-mailing me factoids about how the companies on whose boards of directors he served were enslaving third world children and clear-cutting the Amazon. She finally agreed to come in only so as to "get a look inside the dragon's lair." She showed up wearing Birkenstocks, a Ralph Nader for President T-shirt, and a very Grinch-like scowl. I set her up with a box of two hundred Christmas cards and fifty tags that would later be affixed to the cookie care packages Frank was preparing for Julie's especially influential friends.

While Heather's politics were so far left of the Phelans's that she was almost back around to the right, her handwriting was perfect. Heather even went the extra mile and drew little mistletoes (which looked remarkably like marijuana leaves) and holly berries arranged in quasi-Soviet hammers and scythes around the edges of the cards.

"Look at this shit," she said when she came across the greeting going out to the chairman of Dow Chemical. "This asshole is a mass murderer and he's getting Christmas cards. Hey, here's Dick Cheney!" And, like she did with all the cards going out to notorious corporate scum, she sealed the card, stamped it, and rubbed it on her butt.

Despite her ranting, Heather was sort of confused by her foray behind enemy lines. Everyone was so damn nice to her; Frank delighted in cooking special vegan meals in her honor, she could drink all the organic Earl Gray tea she wanted, and there were no ritual killings in the garage. Bailey even took her on a tour of the house one afternoon. I could tell that she had been hoping for…I don't know, more *evil*, I guess. When the week was over and all the cards had been mailed, Bailey gave her two extra C-notes on top of the $20 an hour she'd been making.

"That's blood money you know," I told her as she tucked the cash into her hand-woven hemp purse.

"The Devil is the most beautiful creature God ever created," Heather said sadly.

Still, she took the train back to Berkeley with the unique satisfaction of knowing that she'd rubbed Dick Cheney's Christmas card on her ass. Anarchy, indeed.

Thirty-Five: Bailey's New Business

THE BOSS FINALLY FOUND HERSELF a new boyfriend at one of the many Christmas parties she attended that season, and the affair caught fire quickly. He was a Belgian guy my age from L.A. who claimed to be a movie producer. His name, naturally, was Luc. By the time Bailey and the rest of the Phelan circus left for Jackson Hole in January, their romance was such that he was going to quit L.A. for S.F. This changed the parameters of the new office search as Bailey now needed to find a workspace that Luc could also live in. Since she was skiing in Wyoming, I spent that first week of 2001 looking for suitable digs. This was my chance to exact revenge on all those bastard landlords who had jacked me around when I'd first moved to the city.

With the majority of start-ups residing in the trash bin, the Bay Area was full of vacancies, and landlords were anxious to get cash flow working again. Bailey agreed that in order for us to find just the right spot, I needed to show the landlords that I was representing serious money. Therefore, I rolled Bailey's BMW to all the showings and displayed a very Bailey-like disdain for money. $5,000 a month? Yeah, but does it have a Viking gas range?

The only hitch was that before Bailey could lease a place Julie said she had to consolidate the loot in storage. This was accomplished with Staff Giveaway Day.

To facilitate this event, I put all the crap that Bailey said she didn't want into one room and then set up a lottery system so my co-workers could choose their items—after I'd taken my pick of the litter, of course. What a mess that was, another illustration of how one man's garbage was another man's treasure. Frank now had a mismatched set of J.P. monogrammed luggage and Junko owned a bag of crooked men's golf clubs. Miss Tang scored three baskets of fake fruit and Robbie the Cat Lady picked out a rolling wardrobe. I came away with a drinks cart and a pair of strange crystal figurines that I thought I might be able to re-gift. Julie considered this rummage sale the staff's holiday bonus, but Bailey went ahead and cut everyone checks anyway. Mine was for $2,000.

One other condition for Bailey's new digs was that the office could be no more than a ten-minute drive from the house. Julie insisted on this proximity to the Pac Heights for safety reasons—what if one of the kids got hurt? It sounded reasonable to me, but I'm sure it had more to do with keeping his wife in sight. He had to know that she needed an office not because of her insistence that she couldn't "get any work done" at the house, but because the domestic crowd interfered with her ability to get laid. I always figured rich guys would do everything in their power to ferret out infidelities, and I kept dreading the day Julie when would take me aside to demand to know what was *really* going on.

Word around the service entrance was that all Julie required of his wife sexually was one night a week. The nannies, who slept across the hall from the master bedroom, insisted that every Wednesday night Bailey would stay at home and get blasted on Cakebread chardonnay before submitting herself to Julie's Priapus for a half-hour of crazed sex. Frank said that he'd been instructed to keep a jar of bacon grease in the refrigerator for these conjugal evenings. It was hard to know if this was bullshit or not (the Wednesday nights, I mean. The bacon grease I dismissed as a chef's fantasy). The fact that Julie was prepared to let his wife move into a new love nest so long as it didn't interfere with his regularly-scheduled demands made me marvel at how something so arbitrary as money could keep a husband and wife together. But when Bailey really put her mind—and body—to getting something like a new office, she usually scored.

I enjoyed running landlords and real estate agents around as I searched for that perfect place in the ten-minute radius. When I found something I thought was good, I'd whip out my cell phone and call Bailey in Jackson Hole. She liked to talk on the chair lifts. I could imagine her ski instructor sitting beside her on the gondola as she asked me questions about the office I was standing in, mouthing an apologetic *real estate deal* to him. Meanwhile, I relayed information while mouthing *skiing* to the real estate broker. I'd then hang up and say that my boss didn't think the place was expensive enough.

Luc finally arrived to help me winnow down the finalists while Bailey was still in Jackson Hole. I played along when he introduced himself to the landlords as Bailey's business partner. The idea was that they were going to open up a production company away from all the L.A. bullshit.

"Up here in Frisco we can actually get movies made," Luc said earnestly. Whatever, *homme*.

Luc was a decent-looking guy who wore khakis with white tennis shoes, but he seemed to have an eating problem as there was usually a dab of mustard or salsa on the collar of his

Izod shirt. He had grown a little Van Dyke beard to complete the look. Luc played the producer role convincingly, framing walls in potential offices for movie screens and screaming at production assistants over the phone who were not pleasing him back in L.A. Once, when he was on a tirade about how audition tapes for his new project hadn't been FedExed properly, I noticed that his mobile was actually turned off. It reminded me of the little cell phone games Stevie and Chase had played when we'd been hunting apartments. I think the whole L.A. charade was due to the fact that Luc was fairly embarrassed about his situation; I'm sure there was no doubt in his mind that I knew what "business partner" really meant. On several occasions when Luc started sharing his vision for the production company, I wanted to sit him down and tell him the story of Clive and the DJ studio and how well that "vision" had worked out. In the end, I figured that a man has to make his own mistakes, and Luc deserved to find this out for himself.

By the time Bailey got back from Jackson Hole, Luc and I had found an office in the Marina (a block away from Mas Sake, no less) that had only three major drawbacks: It was on the fourth floor of a building with no elevator, there was no heat, and no parking. Other than that, it was perfect—$6,500 a month.

"Are you sure you want to do this?" I asked Bailey while we waited for the real estate agent.

"The location is perfect!" she said, her cheeks still rosy from a week of skiing.

"I mean…" I struggled to find the words. "Are you sure you want to do this…with Luc?"

Bailey narrowed her eyes. "What are you talking about?"

"You know, all the stuff that went down with the studio before...I just think—"

"I'll tell you when I want you to start thinking," she interrupted. "I don't need you going all Julie on me, okay?" She got out of the car to greet the agent.

Aside from the tinges of jealously I felt seeing Bailey getting so excited about her new boyfriend, I had a more practical reason why I tried to talk her out of the new office; I knew that I was going to be spending a considerable amount of time lugging stuff up those narrow stairs. It didn't matter. Bailey was going crazy without a clubhouse. She took one look at it and said yes. She then spent several thousand dollars renovating the place with new paint, new carpets, new bathroom fixtures—on a rental, no less—and racked up two or three parking tickets every day. They bought a $20,000 projection system—which Luc used to play FIFA Soccer—and enough computer equipment to run NORAD. I longed for the old studio where you could actually park. Now I not only had to carry stuff up four flights of stairs, but I had to *run* because my Nissan was always in a red zone. Luc had an uncanny knack for being on the phone whenever I made a delivery, and would only hang up when I had finally carried everything up the stairs. Sometimes I brought Stevie along just so that he could sit in the car and move it when the meter maids rolled up. By the end of January, I was longing to be fired.

Luc was obviously a chump (really, what Belgian filmmaker of any merit couldn't name three Jean Claude Van Damme movies?), but there was something else about him that annoyed me more. In some strange way I had become accustomed to having Bailey all to myself. In the wake of Clive I had become her confidant. And although I'd seen her on the way out with a lover, I'd never witnessed the way in. I was no longer rescuing her from Clive; instead I was actively participating in handing her over to Luc. The dynamic of Bailey wanting to fuck me and telling me her secrets had made me feel that I was something more than just an errand boy. It had also given me some form of control. Since she now had Luc, I was once again only needed to do the heavy lifting. With Bailey's attention focused elsewhere, I could no longer pretend that I was anything more than a line item on the Phelan's quarterly budget.

And each time I carried a TV set or a CD player up those stairs, I promised myself I would not be around to help her move out. I promised myself that on every single step.

Thirty-Six: Union Trouble

WITH SALLY, JEN, ASTRID, AND Patty gone, the childcare staff was nothing like the one that had been in place when I showed up for my first day of work. We still had some part-time holdovers, but they were around so infrequently that I hardly noticed them unless my recent hires called in sick. The nanny schedule was still in a state of flux and it had come to the point where it was so fucked up that I got used to it being fucked up. I'd stopped getting friendly with the new hires, because like fresh recruits in Vietnam, they had a tendency to get washed out after just a couple weeks. Three au-pair agencies had open files on the Phelans and would call me up whenever they found a good fit, regardless if we had a vacancy or not.

The biggest problem for me in regards to the nannies wasn't the hodge-podge schedule or all the new recruits, it was Meredith, who—tongue stud or not—had quickly become a serious pain in the ass. Gone was the fun blonde with the let's-go-to-the-batting-cage enthusiasm, and in its place was a Norma Rae union activist. Meredith wanted a new contract not just for herself, but for the entire household staff.

I guess this was partly due to something I'd told her during our first interview when she'd asked about vacation and sick days and overtime.

"You have employee contracts, right?" she'd asked.

"Sure, sure," I'd said, anxious to be finished with the nanny-hiring nonsense.

"So there's a pay structure and insurance and all that?"

"Insurance?"

"Yeah."

"Well, we're working on it." At the time that had satisfied her, and nothing more was said about it until she came into my office to report that she had a gyno appointment coming up and needed her insurance card. She was displeased to find that I hadn't even brought the subject up with Bailey and Gladys yet. In fact, I'd say Meredith was pissed off.

Up until that point, insurance had been handled in a rather haphazard fashion. Say Frank got sick and had to see the doctor: He'd mention it to Bailey and if she'd had her coffee and was alert she'd tell him to bring the bill in and give to Gladys. Taken care of! When I threw out my back pushing Gladys's Buick three blocks to the garage because she didn't want to pay for a tow truck, Bailey sent me to her physical therapist and picked up the tab for six, $150 sessions. But once Meredith mentioned it, it seemed odd that an operation with as many folks on the payroll as the Phelans's didn't provide formal insurance. Meredith was out to change that.

The nanny also wanted a document that laid out all the other employee benefits like vacation and sick days. Again, this was something that had never come up before. When I left for week in Hawaii, Bailey had slipped me a thousand-dollar "vacation bonus," which was basically a week's pay. I assumed she did the same thing for the rest of the staff. If I got sick and didn't show for work, I marked it on my timesheet and Gladys went ahead and billed for eight hours. It was an informal system, and up until Meredith started squawking nobody had any problems with it.

"Oh, that little girl," Gladys grumbled. "I gonna kill her. What she think this is? Xerox?"

Part of the problem was that having an employee contract put a lot of things in writing that we as a staff didn't really need Julie seeing. Vacation bonuses and sick days and insurance bills were all the sudden going to become line items on the quarterly budget. While Julie didn't necessarily pay much attention to actual cash-money flow through the house (river that it was), he did pay attention to the quarterly write up. In short, Meredith was going to louse everything up.

The first idea was to fire her, but since we'd found her through a childcare agency, we'd already paid them a five grand fee. That was a hell of a bath to take. Meredith also struck me as the litigious type who might sue for unjustifiable termination of employment. She'd already threatened to post anti-Phelan pamphlets around the neighborhood if she didn't get her contract by February.

"You wouldn't do that," I said as she paced the floor of my office.

"Why not? You said I was going to have insurance, vacation, sick days and a pay scale and I've got nothing. Maybe a few fliers would get this thing going."

"You're crazy." I wanted to add that you couldn't distribute fliers in Pac Heights, but that might've just gotten her more excited.

"I want my benefits."

"Why can't you just trust me when I say you'll get everything you want without it being in writing?"

"I know who Julie Phelan is," she sneered. "You think he wouldn't screw me over if I gave him an inch?"

"We're working on the damn thing, but you know how hard it is to get Bailey to make a decision. It could take months." I left out the part about how I hardly ever saw Bailey now that she had her new office. I still talked to her several times a day on the phone, but there were two and three day stretches when I didn't have any actual face time. "If you're so damn unhappy why don't you just quit?"

"Ha!" Meredith laughed. "Quit! And get nothing? You're crazy."

"What if I could promise you a severance?"

"Sorry, Tony. I don't think you can do that."

The truth was that we could ill afford to lose Meredith. She might have been a union-agitator, but she was a good nanny. By good I mean that she always showed up for work and didn't try to monkey with the schedule. The kids seemed to like her as well, but I could only judge that by the rare occasions when I was called upon to help watch them for a second. The kids might have been emotionally neglected, but they were never left alone without adult supervision unless they were sound asleep. In extreme circumstances I would even sit down on the nursery floor and play trucks with Ed or admire Emma's new dolly while the nannies moved their cars to avoid parking tickets.

The Phelans went through nannies like bottled water, and the kids had a tendency to look like baby birds fallen from their nest. I wasn't there in any child protective capacity, but I could see those kids becoming very unhappy adults. I wanted to do what little I could to keep things a bit consistent for them.

Regardless of all that emotional stuff, logistically the only way we could fire Meredith was if Bailey decided to take over some shifts, which she'd been musing about for some time now on the advice of her psychiatrist. God only knew that would create more problems than it would solve. So while Gladys worked on the contracts, pounding her calculator like a Worldcom accountant to bury as many line items as possible, I finagled $500 shush money for Meredith so she could pay for her pap smear. She was not impressed, but at least she gave up on the pamphlet idea for a week.

Thirty-Seven: Suitable Digs

THE LEASE ON OUR RICHMOND District apartment came up that April, so I suggested that we take a look at other neighborhoods before we signed on for another year. In the course of searching for Bailey's new production facility, I'd seen quite a few places that I thought would be suitable. Rent in neighborhoods like Noe Valley and the Marina hadn't necessarily come down, but with all the dot.commers running home to momma, there were a lot more spots available. My brother and Chase weren't as enthusiastic as I was about a domestic upgrade.

"You've got to put down another deposit, first and last month's rent," Chase said. "It would be a grand each just to get into another place." He looked around the living room, which this Sunday morning was strewn with pizza boxes and empty beer cans. "That's assuming we could get our deposit back on this."

"Aren't you getting sick of me having to walk through your room to take a piss?" I asked my brother. The arrangement we'd started off with had been getting on my nerves for quite some time, and I felt that at the very least we should switch rooms so I wasn't stuck in the back. Then again, I didn't especially want my brother coming and going through my room, either. But even without the awkward room set-up, our place was getting to be an embarrassment. The dank winter months had bred a resilient, dark green mold that was eating away at the drywall, and no amount of Mr. Clean could rid the lone bathroom of its faint urine scent. New tenants had moved in upstairs and I could hear every move they made through the thin ceiling. I was starting to spend as much time at the Phelan's as possible, not just for the hourly wage, but for the relative peace and quiet. It's a hell of a thing when your office is about thirty times more comfortable than your home.

But as Chase had pointed out, moving would cost money, and neither of them were in great financial shakes. Chase had scored another entry-level job, but my brother was making ends meet through his continued employment as a Phelan temp.

"If you guys are so set on staying, then what do you think about getting someone else to move in?"

"And where are we going to put them?" Stevie asked.

"My room," I said.

"I don't know anybody looking for a spot," Chase said.

I kicked a beer can across the room. "Have you asked?"

My brother sat up. "I don't know if this news has hit you up there in the Pac Heights, but people are *leaving* town these days, not the other way around."

"So that means I've got to stay in this hellhole?"

"It's not all bad," Chase said. "Besides, it would be kind of unfair to leave us hanging."

"What if I paid two months rent?" I suggested. "That would give you plenty of time to find a roommate."

"So let me get this straight," Stevie said. "You want to move out?"

"I'm just saying this place is getting old."

"Dude, that's going to make it awfully tough," Chase said. "I mean, there's bills and all that."

"So you noticed? I thought we just had some unspoken deal where I was paying for cable, electricity, and the telephone." I had, in fact, been footing those bills since the start of the year. It had come up in January that both Stevie and Chase were light, and I'd agreed to cover them. Somehow, my roommates hadn't resumed paying their portions. I hadn't said anything about it, not only because I had enough money to pay the bills, but also perhaps because I'd been anticipating this moment. It would be a lot easier to justify moving out if it was confirmed that my roommates were deadbeats.

"Hold on a second," my brother said. "You told us that you'd take care of those bills. As a matter of fact, you suggested it."

"Why would I do that?"

"You did say something…" Chase offered. "You said it wasn't a big deal."

"Yeah sure, for one month, but now you expect me to keep on paying for the cable and the phone when I'm not even here to use them most of the time? I haven't made a long distance call in six months!" I pulled the last statement out of a drawer and threw it at my brother. "Look at this! There's like forty dollars worth of calls to that crazy girl of yours in Chicago."

"I guess it's too bad we don't have bosses who pay for our cell phones," my brother said.

"Excuse me?"

"What about when we moved out here and *you* didn't have a cell phone?" my brother asked. "You didn't ever think about reimbursing us for our bills."

"So that means I've got to pay for everything now?"

Chase put on his jacket and headed for the door. "I'm really not in the mood for this kind of hassle."

"Where are you going?" I asked.

"I can't handle this, man." Chase walked out.

"There goes your roommate," I told my brother. "You two are going to be sitting in here watching network TV with rabbit ears."

"And where are you going to be, big shot? Sharing an apartment in the Marina with Larry? That sounds great."

"Why is it that every time something like this comes up, you've got to bring up the Marina? What is so scary about the Marina that you've got to be giving me grief all the time?"

"Look at yourself, Tony."

"Look at what?"

"You've got the slicked back hair, the leather jacket, the fucking pink shirt. You should move down there and make it official. Slumming out here is bad for your image." Stevie walked past me to his room.

"And that's it?" I yelled after him. "It's my fault that I want to get out of this shithole and you two guys can't afford to? I've got to stick around and carry you?"

My brother came down the hallway with his backpack.

"And where are you going now?" I asked him as he went to the door. "You gonna set up camp in the park like Charlie-fucking-Brown?" I followed him down the steps to the street. "I'm not signing that lease!" I called after him.

My brother looked back at me sadly.

"What?" I asked. "What's that look supposed to mean?"

He shook his head and walked away.

I had no desire to be in the apartment when my roommates got back, so I called Larry to see if he wanted to grab a drink. Larry said he had something even better lined up.

Thirty-Eight: Kid Koala

An hour later security was escorting Larry and me through the crimson velvet lobby of the Clift Hotel to a private elevator. Plasma screens on the lounge walls morphed colors and psychedelic designs to the beat of house music, and the guard wore a gray cashmere sweater that made him look like he should've been selling expensive sofas. He called upstairs to confirm that Larry and I were expected in the Presidential Suite. Our host, a 24-year-old Australian, was in the midst of a week-long bender after selling his Internet company for $300 million dollars. The Clift security team was helping him keep his wallet open until he headed back to Melbourne.

Larry had run into the Australian earlier that week in the Ruby Skye VIP area, and, in true biz dev fashion, had attached himself to the party as a social liaison. It had become increasingly hard to locate millionaires that spring amid the tanking economy, and Larry was holding onto this whale as long as he could. If he couldn't land him as a client for his company, he could at least enjoy his generosity for the week.

"This guy just bought a fucking Falcon 50," Larry exclaimed once we were in the elevator. My friend was sporting a shimmering blue silk shirt and had his hair spiked dangerously. "I'm talking brand new. Not some used piece of junk with 3,000 hours on it. I'm flying out to Vegas with him on

Tuesday. Play your cards right and I might be able to get you a seat."

The Australian met us at the door. He was thirty pounds overweight and hadn't shaved for a week. His PaRappa the Rapper tee shirt had serious armpit sweat stains, and I could see the big toe of his left foot through a hole in his white tube sock. We shook hands after he wiped a gloss of sweat from his upper lip. The kid's pupils were the size of marbles. There was a molehill of cocaine on the glass table in the suite's living room and every sink—and one of the bathtubs—was filled with iced bottles of Cristal, Grey Goose, and Heineken. Four young girls in mini skirts and tank-tops made room for us on the leather sofas. The backs of their skinny thighs made sticking sounds as they detached from the couches. The Australian plopped down between two of the girls and handed me a rolled up hundred-dollar bill that was crusted with snoot on both ends.

After I'd taken a turn, our host told me to call down to room service.

"Ask for this bloke named Russ," he said. "He'll go good on ya. Order anything you like."

"Thanks," I said. "But I just ate."

"No worries, mate. Anyone else?"

The brown-haired girl (the other three were bleached blonde) picked up the nearest phone. Keeping her eyes on the Australian, she ordered a $55 steak, a $30 salad and another bottle of $200 champagne, despite the several bubs already on ice. The girl hung up and giggled maniacally. Her food arrived a half-hour later and she took one bite of the bloody porterhouse and picked a single tomato off the top of the salad. The new bottle of Cristal went into the sink with the rest. We passed the rolled hundred around the table, trying to make a dent in the mound.

An hour later, the Australian decided we should go to a bar. Despite the fact that it was only five blocks from the hotel to the club, Larry called for a limo. One of the girls started making little folded bindles out of pages torn from *Interview* magazine so we could take rations of coke with us on the journey. We hung the Do Not Disturb placard on the door of the suite and blitzed through the lobby to our waiting stretch. The Australian gave Larry six hundred dollars—two hundred of which Larry used to get us in the side door of Backflip even though the line out front was only a half dozen deep. Once seated at a reserved table by the indoor swimming pool, the Australian asked me if I wanted a hit of ecstasy.

"How much?" I asked, reaching for my wallet.

"Put that away, mate," he said. "The E's on me." He shook a pill out of a dime bag. The blue tablet was stamped with the image of an ice cream cone.

"Then how about I use this twenty to buy us some drinks?" I asked.

He waved my money away. "Tell the bartender to put whatever you want on my tab." I shrugged, popped the tab into my mouth, and sauntered towards the crowded bar.

45 minutes later I was back in our reserved area and the brown-haired girl who'd ordered the room service scooted close to me on the banquette—sniffling and grinding her jaw like a bunny going at a big carrot. She asked how I knew the Australian. I told her I was his gardener. She excused herself for the bathroom and I watched as she wove her way towards the back. Thanks to the strobe lights and E, it looked as though I was watching a film with every fifth frame missing. I resisted

the urge to projectile vomit across our table, and instead un-wrapped one of the little bindles and tipped the contents out. Not even bothering to cut it into lines, I leaned forward to snort the lot of it. I settled back into the leather booth seat and listened to Larry brag about the ZR rating of the tires on his buddy's Ferrari.

Eventually we made it back to the hotel along with two Persian guys in tracksuits who assured the Australian they could score GHB. The ladies resumed their huddle over the coke like Girl Scouts around a campfire. By this point Larry had gone completely demented, stripping to his huggy Calvin Klein underwear and dashing around the living room with a Bic disposable razor, hollering, "Which one of you hotties is gonna let me shave your pussy?!" One of the blondes followed him into the master bathroom to investigate. She emerged a few minutes later to report that Larry had passed out on the tile between the bidet and the bathtub.

Despite a serious buzz from the ecstasy, champagne, and coke, I took my leave not long after our return from the night-club. My brain synapses were sizzling and the girls had started to look like gargoyles. I feared Larry was going to wake up and fuck a light socket, and the Persians had continued to order room service even though they weren't eating anything. Sitting in the middle of all these leeches was the Australian kid, who seemed strangely ambivalent about the damage being exacted upon his suite. I had a picture in my head of Mark Antony and Cleopatra having their final orgy while the Romans battered down the walls of their fortress. And somebody must've cut the ecstasy with a couple milligrams of hallucinogen, because I kept on thinking I could see Julie's reflection in the plate glass window overlooking Union Square.

The Australian walked me to the door.

I thanked him for the hospitality while groping for the deadbolt.

"No worries," he said. "I appreciate you trying to pay for that E back at the club. So far you're the only bloke who's said thanks for anything all week. If you don't mind me asking, what do you do?"

"I'm a houseboy."

He looked puzzled. "What the hell is that, mate?"

"It's kind of hard to explain," I said. "But you should think about getting yourself one."

Thirty-Nine: Diamonds

Bailey had a habit of losing jewelry. She'd come home tipsy, take off her wedding ring and forget where she'd left it. The next day she would announce a "ring bonus" for whoever came up with the merchandise. The reward was usually a hundred-dollar bill, so you can imagine the Easter egg hunts after those announcements. I had half a mind to deliberately misplace her jewelry when I knew she was going out to party so I could collect my finder's fee when she realized it was missing.

Despite the bounty, some of the baubles were never found, most significantly a five-carat diamond pendant hung on a white gold chain. Bailey and the rest of the staff gave up looking for it after two weeks, and I was instructed to file a claim with the insurance company. Bailey couldn't be bothered with the details, so it was pretty much my show. I dug up the original appraisal ($45,000), talked with the insurance company and they put me in touch with a local jeweler who would make a replacement. Bailey got involved only to talk to the jeweler about minor design changes.

Something seemed hinky in that the original necklace had only been insured for $32,000. I brought this up with Bailey and she concluded that someone—Linda probably—had screwed up the paperwork when the original details had been filed. No problem, Bailey told me, the insurance company would send the

$32,000 to the jeweler and the Julie would make up the $13,000 difference. A month after filing the claim, the jeweler called to say all was in order. He faxed over his invoice and I told him we'd get a check in the mail when Gladys came in at the end of the week. The insurance company would pay the jeweler when we took delivery of the rock. Bailey signed the check and I gave it to Gladys.

The policy for Friday afternoons was that I'd take the invoices for any big ticket items—jewels, cars, art, big contractor bills—and put them on the dresser in the master bedroom for Julie to review over the weekend. At 4 p.m. the house was empty and I was getting ready to split. I took the invoices upstairs, and passed Julie as I headed back down. I gave him my usual, "Hey, Mr. Phelan" (the "hey" thrown in for casualness) and got out of his way. I was just about to leave the office when I heard him thundering down the stairs. I figured he was late for a tee time, but when I ran into him in the laundry room he was sweating.

"Who approved this!" he screamed, waving the necklace invoice. I could see the pulse of a big vein bisecting his forehead.

I started to say that Bailey had, but for some reason—most likely the instinct I'd developed for covering her ass all the time—I heard myself say, "I did."

"YOU have no authority to make thirteen-thousand-dollar decisions in MY house!" he bellowed. "What the hell did you think you were doing? You IDIOT! I want this money back!"

I managed to say, "Yessir." My right leg was trembling in a way it hadn't since I almost got the shit kicked out of me in high school by five football players.

"And if you don't get my money back, you're going to PAY FOR IT!"

"Yessir."

"Do you understand me?"

"Yessir."

"Fucking IDIOT!"

He stormed into the garage, got into his coupe, and peeled out of the driveway. I must have stood there in the laundry room for a full minute before I walked back into my office. When I picked up the phone my hand was still shaking. I called the jeweler and told him that we would no longer be buying the necklace. He started screaming at me, but I told him that I'd just been fired and was sorry for any inconvenience. I hung up while he was still cursing. Then I called Gladys.

"What the matter with you?" she asked. "Drunk already on Friday?"

"I just got fired. I need you to cancel that necklace check."

"Oh my God, what happened? I send that check this afternoon!"

"Whatever you have to do. Cancel it. Do you understand?"

"Yes."

"Goodbye, Gladys."

"Wha—" I hung up on her.

The next call went to the insurance company. I told them not to under any circumstance send the check to the jeweler. I said that from now on they'd be dealing with Mrs. Phelan. I was no longer an employee.

Bailey called next.

"What the hell happened?" she asked, sounding freaked. "Julie's going crazy." I told her the story and said that I supposed I was fired.

"I wish I could say that you weren't, but I don't know. I'll talk to Julie, and if we can get the money back I think everything will be okay. He gets like this, trust me. He loses his mind, but he'll calm down. I've seen it. Really, I think we're okay if Gladys and the insurance company are canceling the checks. You go home and I'll deal with it."

"Okay, thanks Bailey."

"Now you know," she said.

"Not to buy jewelry for you?"

"How Julie got so rich."

"How?"

"By being an asshole."

Despite Bailey's assurance that she'd set things right, I still cleared out my desk. I didn't have much—some pens, my address book, a little clock. I put it all in a paper lunch sack. I left my company credit card in the drawer but kept the cell phone in case Bailey or Gladys called.

On the way out I met Miss Tang in the laundry room. I thought she had already gone home. She reached up to straighten my shirt collar.

"Is not your fault," she said. It was the first time she'd said anything more than hello to me.

"I'm afraid it is," I said, feeling like I was about to cry.

Miss Tang smiled. "You go now. No problem." And then she gave me a quick hug.

I don't remember the drive home, but I was happy to see that Stevie was on the sofa watching TV. I'd been avoiding him and Chase since our argument about the lease, which wasn't easy considering I had to walk through his room to get to my bed. I had in fact talked to Larry about getting a place in the Marina. He was anxious to finally get out of his grandmother's basement and, since he had managed to keep his job, had the money for the move. But after Julie's tirade, I was suddenly relieved that my roommates and I hadn't finished our argument about not renewing the Richmond lease.

Stevie ignored me as I drained a beer, but when I popped open another right away, he asked me what was wrong. I told him what had happened.

"*That's* what you're so freaked out about? You said all the checks were cancelled, so no harm, no foul."

"But," I started to say, pausing to take a sip of beer, "It's just the way Julie yelled at me."

"Yeah, getting chewed out is never fun," Stevie replied, reaching over to grab another beer for himself. I kicked off my shoes and sighed,

"Nah, it's really not the getting yelled at part—it's the fact that I just stood there like a moron while he did it. I mean, who is the guy, really? Why am I afraid of him? Is it the fact that he's so fucking rich? Is it because everyone around me is afraid of him?"

"Heat generates heat, and fear generates fear," Stevie commented.

"But why do I care? I should be pissed that I got fired for such a bullshit reason—for something that isn't even my fault," I drained my beer and chucked the empty across the living room, "Instead I stood there, terrified, and then stumbled all over myself trying to make it right. For what reason? Who gives a shit? And the worst thing is that I was covering for Bailey. Why did I even do that?" I closed my eyes and let myself deflate, leaning back into the couch.

I knew why I had laid down in front of Julie, and it wasn't because of the money they were paying me. It was the *idea* of money. The fact that this guy was so rich had somehow created a force field around him. His millions meant that he was always right. So instead of this coming down to a confrontation between an angry old man and a young physically-superior man, Julie's wealth had spun the situation on its axis. Never for a moment had I thought of speaking up and defending myself, or even just explaining the situation to him. Instead, the power of his money had frozen me to the spot. Had I wanted something from Julie—if I'd needed an investment or a political favor—my fear might have made sense. But I didn't want any of those things, and the psychology of the whole situation made me feel like an absolute weakling. Julie paying me to haul his laundry around was one thing, but letting him humiliate me was something else. And as I ran my mind back over the brief incident in the laundry room, I hated myself for how I had let the job rob me of my backbone.

I remembered something I had read about one of the recently minted dot.com millionaires. The guy had said that in the end, the money didn't really matter. The money, he said, was just a way of keeping score. If that was the case, then mark it down Julie: 1000. Me: Zilch.

"Well," Stevie said after a few minutes of silence, "you've been wanting the guy to notice you. I'd say he just did."

Forty: Cost Overuns

I CALMED DOWN OVER THE weekend, but told myself that I was quitting on Monday no matter what happened. That is, if I hadn't already been fired. Mostly this determination sprang from the fact that I was still ashamed at how I'd let Julie lambaste me. And the way I'd instinctively taken a bullet for Bailey had also been weighing heavily on my mind. The more I thought about it, the more I realized that I couldn't let Julie break me off like that. But I was also suddenly more than a little bit concerned about my financial situation.

I'd squandered so much money over the previous six months that it made me sick. It certainly wasn't on par with the Australian and his open tab at the Clift, but it was pretty hideous by my standards. Covering utility bills for Stevie and Chase was one thing, but renting Lincoln Town Cars for weekend drives to Santa Cruz, $400 steak dinners, Italian suits, shoes, more $400 steak dinners, CD shopping sprees at Amoeba Records, concert tickets, $500-a-night hotels suites rented just so I didn't have to walk through my brother's room…so much wasted money. I went to the bank that Saturday and confirmed that I had $4,408 in my checking account. A little more than $4,400 wouldn't last long in S.F., economic downturn or not. After the visit to the bank, I realized that despite my wounded pride, I had to keep my job for another month or two if I could. Then, with the four paychecks a month, I'd have close to ten grand. I figured that would get me out of town or onto another job in style.

I was not completely surprised to go into work Monday and find the situation normal. Julie had left me a note in the kitchen instructing me to stock up on firewood, but there was no mention of the diamond necklace and certainly no apology. When Bailey woke up she told me that she'd smoothed everything over with Julie by spending Friday, Saturday and Sunday nights at home. She didn't, however, assume any responsibility for the incident. She made it sound like she was just covering my ass, which didn't make me feel any better.

It turned out that the discrepancy between the appraisal of the necklace and what it was insured for came from the fact that Julie, true to form, had haggled the price of the rock down thirteen grand with the Hassidic Jew he bought diamonds from in New York. Julie was mostly pissed, Bailey explained, because he couldn't stand the thought of paying retail for anything.

Bailey didn't have any such restraint, and she continued to outfit her party pad with custom sofas and carpet. Gladys complained that if she kept going at this rate, the movie biz was going to end up being more expensive than the music industry. Luc stayed in character though, hamming it up on the phone and scattering *Variety* magazines around as if he was really trying to close film deals. It got to the point where Bailey was hanging out at the office so much that she had me set up a play area for the kids in a far corner. Bailey took the precaution of having Emma and Edward, who were too old to be trusted not to blab about Mommy's special friend, call Luc "Betty", the name of one of the part-time nannies. This way when Julie asked them what they'd done that day they could say, "We went to the zoo with Betty," and he'd be none the wiser.

With Bailey, the kids and the nannies down the hill most days, the house became increasingly quiet. Frank, the house-keepers and I started joking that we were running a hotel with no guests. I was lucky if I saw Bailey twice a week, and that was usually when I was called upon to deliver something to her at the new office. After hauling a mini-fridge up the stairs one after-noon, I found Luc, as usual, talking on the phone. I was about to leave when he waved me over and handed me a note. It was a grocery list. When I looked up wondering what the list meant, he gave me a dismissive wave. I called Bailey from the sidewalk.

"Luc just gave me a shopping list," I reported.

"He's getting quite demanding, isn't he?" Bailey said.

"Yeah, you could say that. Do I really have to buy this stuff for him?"

There was a long pause on the line. "Bailey?" I asked.

"What do you mean, Tony?"

"I'm asking if I have to do it. For him, I mean."

"I'm not sure if I like your tone," Bailey said.

A few choice responses ran through my mind, but in the end I just said okay and went to the store. I added a case of beer to the list for my effort.

When I'd finished lugging the bags upstairs, Luc cradled the phone to inspect my work.

"Everything there, Betty?"

"What did you just say?" Luc demanded.

"Nothing," I said as I headed for the stairs. "Have a nice day."

The employee contracts finally materialized on the brink of summer and Meredith became less adamant about her worker's rights and more concerned about the kids' emotional well-being. Well, that was the kiss of death in the childcare division, and the week after Meredith spoke to Bailey about how she needed to spend more time with the kids to avoid "abandonment issues," Bailey told me to get rid of her.

"We need to get another nanny before we do that," I explained.

"I'll pick up a couple shifts during the week," Bailey said as she gathered her purse and headed for the garage. "Just lose her in a way that she won't try and fucking sue us, okay? Who hired her anyway? Was it you or Linda?"

I admitted that it had been my call.

"Well you really should have asked me to sit down and interview her first. I'm the one who should be making childcare decisions." I didn't think Bailey would appreciate me bringing up that she had, in fact, interviewed Meredith… for three minutes.

"You're right," I said, following Bailey into the garage. "I'm sorry."

"I want Meredith gone this week. I'll pick up her shifts."

"Bailey."

She held her car door open, looking extremely put-out. "What?"

"I'm afraid we haven't been seeing eye to eye on some things recently."

"Such as?"

"Such as…shit, I don't know. It's just like we never talk anymore."

Bailey rolled her eyes. "What? You need more attention?"

"No," I said quickly. "It's just that it's really hard to run your house without ever being able to check things out with you."

"You're running the house now, are you? Well how about demonstrating it by getting rid of Meredith? I'm late."

I stood there as Bailey drove away. Out of habit, or to properly end our conversation, she punched the remote to shut the garage door on me.

———

I'd suggested to Meredith a couple weeks before that she might want to start considering other work options. So when I called her into my office to tell her she was going to be let go because Julie wanted to cut back on nannies and she was the one with the least seniority, she didn't make much of a fuss. She was sick of dealing with Bailey, anyway. Gladys came in to hand her the envelope and bye, bye Meredith.

We were now operating with a skeleton crew of five nannies, four of whom were technically part timers. Somehow we kept the schedule patched together, and before the next nanny meeting I let Bailey chose two shifts a week for herself so the other girls could fill in around her. I posted the schedule in the nursery, the kitchen, and over both of our desks in the basement office. When I left work that Friday, I made a point of calling Bailey and telling her that she was "on" as of 9 a.m. Sunday morning and would be relieved at 6 p.m. that night. She said okay.

The phone started ringing at 7:30 Sunday morning and did not stop for fifteen minutes until Stevie finally succumbed and picked it up. Against protocol, my cell phone was turned off. I knew it was Bailey on the other end, but hoped she might think I was dead and simply take care of whatever it was that was so pressing on the Sabbath. Stevie threw the cordless into my room and collapsed back into bed.

"Hello?" I croaked.

"Where the hell have you been?" she demanded. I could hear the kids bawling in the background. "What happened to your cell phone?"

"Out of batteries."

"You know you're supposed to have it charged at all times."

"I know."

"We have a *major* problem," Bailey reported. "I didn't realize I was working this morning and Julie has us going to brunch. There's no way I can take the kids. Absolutely no way. If you had told me about this beforehand I could've found somebody to cover."

"Sorry," I said.

"Well you need to find someone—I don't care who it is—in the next hour or there's going to be a major, major problem."

"What about Luc?" I asked.

"What?!" Bailey barked.

"Right. I'll have someone there in forty-five minutes."

"This is serious," she warned.

I considered staying in bed and taking my firing and to hell with the severance. I'd managed to save a couple paychecks since the necklace incident, but I still wanted a couple more before I showed myself the gate. But it really didn't matter, because the odds of finding one of our nannies at this time on a Sunday were miniscule. I dragged myself out of bed and called all the names on the childcare roster, not surprised to get 100% answering machines. I opened the phone book and, sitting there in my boxer shorts, called every babysitter agency in the Yellow Pages. None of them were open. I had T-minus thirty minutes before Bailey freak-out and there was a certain martyr-like consolation in knowing that all of this was going to come down on my head.

Then I remembered Muriel. The upstairs neighbor. She was perfect. I mean if you designed a prototype of an au-pair, she was what you would've come up with. She even had a French accent and milk chocolate skin, kind of like Sade. She and her husband Robert (pronounced "Raw-bear") were from the French West Indies or the Ivory Coast or something and they were my last best hope. I threw on a T-shirt and knocked on their door. By God, Muriel was already dressed. She didn't seem surprised to see that I was not.

"What are you doing today?" I asked.

"Well, I was going shopping…"

"I mean are you free?" I asked. "To work as a nanny."

"For that crazy family of yours? You're kidding."

"Totally serious. I'll pay you…" I searched for a number, "…five hundred bucks—cash—to work from right now until six tonight."

"Five hundred dollars is a lot of money," Robert called from the living room. He added something in French. She responded, sounding angry. They had a little tête-à-tête.

"Okay," she said. "Give me a moment to get ready."

"You're already dressed, you look perfect."

"I'm not going out like this," she said. I could tell this was not negotiable. "Ten minutes."

I took the opportunity to jump in the shower. When I got back out to the landing Robert was leaning against the wall enjoying his morning cigarette.

"Where's Muriel?" I asked.

"Still getting ready."

"Jesus, I've got to have her there in five minutes."

"My friend," Robert said, "I have known Muriel for eight years. Four of those years have been spent waiting for her to get ready."

Ten minutes later Muriel emerged in pretty much the same outfit she'd been wearing and I rushed her into my car, which was idling at the curb. I briefed her as I sped to the house.

"Okay, number one," I instructed. "You don't know me. I found you in the Yellow Pages and your boss said the fee was five-hundred dollars because of the short notice. Okay?"

"Okay."

"We've never seen each other before, right?"

"*Oui.*"

"Perfect. God bless you, Muriel."

"I get paid in cash, yes?"

"I'll pay you personally. Tell that to the wife, okay. Tell her I took care of the payment on my credit card."

"But you'll pay me cash."

"Yes."

We arrived at the house four minutes after nine and I could hear the kids screaming from the courtyard. When we got into the kitchen Bailey was holding Emma in her arms and Edward was thrashing on the floor. Bailey's hair was all over the place and she only had half her make-up on. I introduced Muriel, who was so perfectly calm that I thought she must've been on tranquilizers, and we gathered the screaming kids. I took Edward into the kitchen nook and held him forcibly in my lap. He kept screaming, "No hunch! Mommy, no hunch!" with no indication that he was going to stop anytime soon. He nearly disintegrated my eardrum when Bailey went upstairs. I felt like I was trying to hold a rabid muskrat. Emma, on the other hand, quieted right down in Muriel's arms, and within five minutes the child was sitting calmly on the kitchen counter while my upstairs neighbor made French toast.

Bailey and Julie came downstairs a few minutes later and the kids went bonkers again. Julie strode up to each of them purposefully and gave them a dry kiss on the forehead. Julie didn't even bother to say good morning to me despite the fact that Edward was sitting in my lap.

Bailey made the mistake of lingering, and Edward completely lost control and started fighting so hard that I feared I was going hurt him if I kept restraining him. I let him go and he scrambled across the kitchen to attach himself to Bailey's leg, screaming "No hunch!" in between gasping sobs. I pried him off her leg and she disappeared downstairs. I kept trying to rationally explain to him that Mommy would be back, but all he could babble was, "Mommy goes basement and never comes back."

Five minutes after Bailey and Julie departed, the kids were quiet and in their high chairs, spooning Muriels's French toast into their mouths and watching Powerpuff Girls. My head throbbed so intensely that I thought my eyeballs were going to pop out of their sockets. Before going home I took Muriel on a tour of the house to show her where the diapers and such were. I ducked downstairs and grabbed five hundred dollars from the petty cash box.

"Are you sure you're going to be okay?" I asked.

"Fine," Muriel said. "It is no problem. They're just kids."

I went back to my apartment, but was unable to relax until later that evening when I heard Robert come back from retrieving Muriel. I met her on the landing and handed over the money. She looked haggard.

"Would you be interested in doing this again?" I asked.

"Never," Muriel said.

"That bad?"

"It's not the kids," she explained. "It's the parents."

"You're gonna love this," Chase told me the following afternoon when I got back from another lonely day at the office. "My company is having a party tonight."

"Cash bar?" I asked.

"Open bar AND luge!" Chase exclaimed.

Stevie came into the living room to investigate. "I haven't heard about a party with an open bar all year."

Stevie was right about that. San Francisco once had so many lavish launch parties that it was possible to stay drunk on free booze and full on appetizers all week. The big thing when we'd arrived in 1999 was to have ice sculpture centerpieces that doubled as shot luges. I hadn't seen one of those frozen alcohol delivery devices since the great market blow-out the previous spring.

"Yeah, I think I heard about this," I said, getting into it. "Something about a keg and a warehouse. Bring your own cups."

"I'm serious," Chase insisted. "My company just got bought out by Microsoft."

"Microsoft," Steve whistled. "Not bad."

"My boss rented out a bar to celebrate."

"Now all you need is a date," I said.

"Well, I figured we haven't had a roommates' night out in a while, so I put you two down as my guests. But here's the best part. The party is at Mas Sake."

I didn't say anything.

"What's the matter, Tone? I thought you'd be pumped."

"I don't think I can make it," I said.

"You're kidding?" Chase laughed. "Marina Tony?"

"You know that office I told you I set Bailey up in?" I asked.

"Yeah, so what?"

"It's a block away from Mas Sake."

"So?"

"So I don't want to run into her, okay?"

"You've got to be kidding," Chase said. "I've got an open bar at Mas Sake—the place you've been trying to drag me and Stevie to for a year—and now you don't want to go because your boss's office is close by? We're talking free frozen booze! Dude, there's probably a one percent chance of seeing her."

"That's one percent too much. Me, personally, I'm heading to the Trad'r."

Forty-One: Acceptable Loss

At the end of July I intercepted Bailey between her closet and the garage to tender my resignation. The laundry room seemed to be an appropriate location for the meeting. I'd been considering giving just two weeks, but despite all the bullshit, I still felt some weird sense of loyalty to Bailey and the rest of the staff. I didn't want to abandon ship without fair warning. Bailey was not used to getting dumped—I was, after all, the only person aside from Jen and Sally who had ever announced their intention to quit—and she went extra frosty on me. She put her hand on her cocked hip to regard me for a moment before she got into her BMW and pulled out of the garage without saying goodbye.

She returned to the house an hour later to announce that she expected me to find my own replacement.

"You want to discuss this?" I asked.

We sat in office chairs five feet apart, facing each other.

"No offense Tony," she said, "but I think we really need someone who's a little more, how can I say…"

"Warped?" I offered.

Bailey didn't think that was funny. "How about sophisticated?" she countered.

"Okay, I can see that."

"Actually, it's a good thing that you're leaving. I think the house needs to be shaken up."

I ignored her last comment. "That's all I've got to go on? Sophisticated?"

Bailey gathered her purse and left without expatiating. I didn't see her for a couple days.

The staff didn't take the news calmly. They all had their routines and were comfortable with how things ran, despite the constant threat of impending collapse. As demonstrated by that Sunday with Muriel, the whole operation was really just a few minutes from implosion at any time depending upon Bailey's mood. Like the former Louisiana senator Huey "Kingfisher" Long, she created—and thrived on—the chaos. I still had not figured out if she, like the Kingfisher, had set things up that way to intentionally keep everyone off kilter, or if it was just a byproduct of her nature. Still, Frank, Gladys, Miss Tang, and Junko worried that a new house manager might disrupt things. Even Robby the Cat Lady was distressed. There was talk of promoting Gladys, but Bailey decided she was too high strung.

I put the word out to the staffing agencies and posted the opening on the Internet. We did the web advertisement to placate Julie, who was sick of paying thousands of dollars to employment agencies for finding him overpaid staffers who were just going to get fired in a few months. Folks on the 'net saw the starting pay of $30 an hour and flooded me with résumés. Every laid off dot.com supply closet manager thought they had the stuff to run a "Large Pac Heights Home" and within the week I had a backlog of over two hundred applications, none of which piqued Bailey's interest.

I went to speak with Clarissa at the Perfect Fit about the job opening. I was not surprised to see the waiting room packed with people looking for work. When I'd last been to the temp agency, there'd only been one other candidate in for an appointment. The Perfect Fit sent over the cream of S.F.'s domestic crop. I met with people who had served in the homes of movie stars, magnates, politicians, and heiresses. These candidates—the men universally homosexual and women high level administrative types—tried to wow me with their pedigree ("I worked for Larry Ellison/Sharon Stone/The Haas Foundation") and their plans to get her house running smoothly. The future looked organized, but Bailey was dragging her heels.

I would have liked to think that her reluctance to hire a new house manager was that she didn't want to see me go. Instead, I think that she, like the rest of the staff, knew a new person at the helm would cause drastic changes. As fucked up as the place was, it worked on some basic levels. With a new house manager Bailey might also feel compelled to wake up at a decent hour so rumors didn't start that she was out partying every night. (One benefit of having me running the show was that I didn't socialize with other estate managers in the neighborhood. Like in every rarefied society, there was plenty of service entrance gossip going around Pac Heights. That alone might have been reason enough to not make a decision right away.) The search dragged on through August.

Even though I was on my way out, my last months were not very fun. As a lame duck, Bailey started to use me shamelessly. I was the reason she forgot about a party or a play date for the kids. She showed up late for a big dinner with Julie and some of his Washington D.C. cronies because I'd failed to remind her about it that morning. We ran out of cottage cheese because of me. It was like she was determined to get as much mileage out of me as possible before I left, and that obliterated any nostalgic feelings I might have otherwise entertained about my stint at the house.

———

Bailey and Julie were scheduled to take a trip to Mexico at the end of September, so that became the deadline for hiring a new manager. As usual, I ended up making the decision. I choose a plucky (but not too plucky) 37-year-old woman from Scotland to take my spot. I felt that a Scot might be hearty enough to handle some of the heavy stuff without calling in the movers, and I hoped that her countrymen's famous what-the-hell attitude would cushion the chaos for her. Previously, she had worked for an internationally known media mogul, taking care of his various California operations. The Phelan's big money didn't seem to faze her. I forced Bailey to meet with her for twenty minutes, and after the meeting she told me to call the agency and get a contract.

Bailey had been intending to take me out for a farewell drink and to give me my goodbye "present," which Gladys assured me was still a couple grand despite the fact that I'd gone against the Cardinal rule and quit instead of waiting to get fired. Regardless of the pay-off, it wasn't a date I was particularly looking forward to. Things had been notably different between Bailey and me since she'd started shacking up with Luc; I suppose that in some ways I was just another affair she was trying to get away from with the minimum entanglement. I'd realized that one of the best things about being rich is that when something starts going bad, you can just write a check and walk away. All the rest of us poor plebes have to stick around and sort through the debris. Bailey and I made and broke several dates until finally deciding to go out the night before she left town.

As for my own future, I had no idea aside from the fact that I was leaving San Francisco. My roommates and I talked the landlord into letting us break our lease by showing him the layers of fungus that had infiltrated the walls. We also hinted that we'd been having respiratory troubles. He even agreed to give us half our deposit back. My brother, like so many former dot.commers, was looking for a straight gig and had come up with a real estate job that would probably force him to leave the city as well. "Straight" in this case meant a job that he had to show up for every morning and a boss he had to answer to. Chase, on the other hand, was looking like a survivor after his company's deal with Microsoft. He even had a cubicle with a window. So what if the window looked out onto an alley?

Perhaps the fact that I had made plans to pull up stakes influenced my perception, but when I went out at night there was no longer that air of excitement or that sense of collective consciousness that had made everyone feel like an integral part of the city's success in 1999. Oh, there would always be guys like Riley and Collins to keep the city anchored, but the dilettantes had had enough. I guess I was part of that latter group. The boom was over. And like the 49'ers and hippies before us, we were limping home from the coast spitting sand, wherever home might be.

Stevie and I borrowed a friend's truck and started clearing out our flat. Our first task was to take our ratty furniture to Goodwill. On the way down Van Ness my brother asked me how I was going to cope without my surf and turf lunches, the $1,400 weekly checks, my carpeted office with a view of the Bay and the rotating rack of nannies.

"The rich are a sorry bunch of bastards," I told him, recalling Steinbeck's line. "I'm not going to miss any of that stuff."

"C'mon," he said skeptically.

"I'm serious."

We pulled up at a stoplight, the furniture in the truck bed groaning under its own weight. A bum stood on the median with his shopping cart and a cardboard sign that read: *Dreaming of a Cheeseburger*. I pulled a five-dollar bill out of my wallet and passed it to Stevie. He looked at the money and shook his head. He rolled down the window and put the bill in the man's grubby hand as the light went green. The bum looked at the fiver and called out his happy thanks as we drove away.

"Easy come," Stevie said, "Easy go."

———

The phone woke me up on Tuesday morning. It was my brother calling from Chicago where he was interviewing for his real estate job. He told me to turn on the TV. I stood in the bare living room and watched the World Trade Centers collapse. I don't remember getting dressed or driving to the Phelan's, and didn't really come to my senses until I was seated at my desk in the basement trying to get on CNN.com for updates. The house was completely silent.

I'd been downstairs for half an hour when Bailey pulled a chair into the office so she could look at the computer over my shoulder. Neither of us spoke. The whole country was shut down.

The intercom buzzed, and Julie told Bailey to come upstairs.

For some reason, I wanted to see Julie. I wanted to find out if he had anything wise to say about what had happened. I followed Bailey into the kitchen, where the nighttime nanny was holding the kids in her lap, watching the news on the TV. The kids were dressed and ready to go, but there was none of their usual fussing even though Bailey was around.

"What are you doing?" I asked.

"Julie wants to take them to the park," Bailey said.

We were still huddled around the television when Julie came into the kitchen wearing jeans and a dress shirt. He did not break stride as he walked across the room and turned off the TV.

"Let's go," he said.

"But honey," Bailey said, "Shouldn't we stay inside in case something else happens?"

We looked at him expectantly. If there was anyone in San Francisco who knew what was going on, it had to be him. Surely he could explain this to us.

"It's over," he said. "Let's go."

"But—" Bailey started to protest.

"Acceptable loss," Julie said. He headed for the front door. His wife and kids followed.

FORTY-TWO: SEVERANCE

THE LAST TIME I SAW Julie was in a hobby shop a couple days before he left for Mexico. Despite the turmoil around the world caused by the 9-11 attacks, Julie would not cancel his vacation. In the week since the catastrophe, several high ranking White House officials had called to speak with him, and I suppose I was a little assuaged by the fact that Julie was not altering his schedule. I figured that if he was going about his business as usual then there was nothing more to fear. He was, after all, solidly in the loop. Or, as Stevie suggested, maybe he was heading for Mexico because the *real* shit was about to go down.

At any rate, Julie had gone to the hobby shop with his daughter Madeline to buy supplies for an art project. Bailey had tagged along. I don't know if it had to do with the staff transition taking place, but she'd been hanging around the house a lot more. Then again, September 11th was still on everybody's mind, and lots of people were behaving oddly. In fact, she'd been so scarce at the film production office that Luc had started making very Clive-like phone calls to the Phelan's, demanding to be put in touch with her. She'd apparently been screening him on her cell phone. Luc's calls to the house provided me with plenty of opportunities to page Bailey over the intercom, saying that "Betty" was on hold. I even figured out a way to do this so Luc could hear the pages on his end.

Bailey was having me meet her at the hobby shop so that she could trade her BMW for the SUV and then pick up the kids from a play date. I walked into the cluttered shop and saw Julie trying to get the attention of the dwarf who worked behind the counter. The dwarf could have cared less that it was The Great Julie Phelan demanding that he find a spool of blue yarn in the storeroom. The more Julie snapped his fingers and barked at him, the more determined the dwarf was to attend to other customers. Young Madeline, who turned out to have the same unfortunate lemon-sucking mouth as her father, was whining that she was missing her favorite television program. Bailey was yapping away on her cell phone over by the jigsaw puzzles.

I traded keys with Bailey, pointing down the street to let her know where the SUV was parked. On my way out, the diminutive clerk walked right past Julie to ask me if I needed something.

"Yeah," I said. "Could I have some blue yarn?"

The clerk smiled and headed back to the storeroom. Julie, as usual, didn't acknowledge me.

A few months after I left San Francisco, Chase sent me a long piece about Julie that had appeared in the *Chronicle*. He looked like his sour old self in the accompanying picture. I imagine that he remains plugged into what's left of the sputtering Republican war machine, waiting wolfishly on the sideline to step back into power when the Democratic dream turns back to reality. I still think about him every time I see the name of that prominent think tank in a magazine. But when I consider him I don't picture him screaming at me about diamonds or being ignored by the dwarf in the hobby shop or sauntering down the hall of his high-rise office with that toothpick in his mouth. I think of him standing up on the top floor of his house as the daylight fades, looking out at the Bay. And right smack in the middle of his view is Alcatraz.

As the man would say, *Acceptable loss.*

———

Bailey and I never had that farewell drink as she got tied up with the kids prior to her departure. In this case, it was actually the truth and not just an excuse to get her off the hook. At least I think it was. E & E, like her husband, had been getting a lot more of Bailey's time since the fall of the World Trade Centers.

I would not be at the house when she returned from her trip to Mexico. My replacement had already taken over the day-to-day operation of the Phelans's lives and I was basically hanging around, getting my last lunches from Frank and clocking my final houseboy hours.

"Dude," Frank said, "Gladys told me you're gonna get four thousand bucks! For quitting! I swear to God, you roll off a log and fall right into a pot of gold every time. This new British chick's got nothing on you."

"She's Scottish," I reminded the chef. "And a professional."

Frank put his arm around my shoulder and gave me a squeeze. "That's the problem, dude."

Junko passed by with her mop. "In a way, I cannot understand what the new lady saying." The housekeeper shook her head. "And I finally teach you the right things to buy…"

The opportunity for any maudlin farewell with Bailey at the house was thankfully lost because she was in a massive rush to pack on the day of the trip. I tried to explain to the new house manager that this was par for the course, but she was still rushing around in Bailey's wake trying to herd her into her closet and the still empty suitcases. At the last moment, Bailey realized she didn't have a suitable bikini. She asked me to drop her off downtown so she could pick one up. She'd catch a ride home with Luc, who after a couple weeks of being ignored, was willing to take any audience he could get with his girlfriend.

As we headed down Pacific in her BMW, Bailey said that I should call her the following week so we could re-schedule our date.

"I still need to give you your good-bye present," she explained.

Bailey was on the phone with Luc for the rest of the drive downtown, trying to explain to him that there was no way she could fly him to Cabo San Lucas and put him up in a condo near her beach house. I stopped in a red zone in front of Neiman's and she got out of the car, assuring her boyfriend that she'd be back in a week and that everything would return to normal. I started to pull away, but she knocked on the window. I rolled it down. She held the cell phone against her chest.

"You'll call me next week, right?"

"Of course. Have fun in Mexico."

"Okay," she said. She paused as if there was something else she wanted to add. After a moment, she gave me a brief smile and resumed her phone conversation.

I watched her walk to the corner and wait for the light to change. Pedestrians gathered around her, and they moved across the street en masse when the signal turned green. The people from the opposite sidewalk met Bailey's group in the middle of the intersection, and I lost her as they merged into a blur of bodies. I waited for a moment to see if she would reappear on the other side, but Bailey was gone.

I pulled away from the curb and, for the last time, took the long way back to the Pacific Heights.

For Jonathan Burke Betzold and William McNutt Martin. I miss you both.

Made in the USA
Lexington, KY
24 May 2014